My Wife's
Last Lover

My Wife's Last Lover

Martin Golan

CREATIVE ARTS BOOK COMPANY
Berkeley, CA 2000

For Marian, of course

My Wife's
Last Lover

— 1 —

The night I walked out Melissa and I had a fight over who used up the milk. It was not a serious fight, but the kind between couples who've been together years and stifle smiles as they trade nasty, go-for-the-jugular attacks. Long-term relationships teach you the game element in an argument, its wicked, irrepressible sense of play.

"Soup was a nice idea," she said about the cream of mushroom soup I had made. From scratch, I might add. "So now we're out of milk." She prodded the container with her flute. "Barely one, tiny, little sip. Count on it, pal."

This was a congenial, though shrewdly aimed, stab at me for using up the milk. Not for herself, mind you, but for the children. It gave her the moral authority to work into a froth of righteous indignation.

"Like you always *have* to use so much? And leave a teeny, teeny drop? You don't know what breakfast's like, here, in *this* house?"

"We have two children sleeping upstairs, you know," I said, feigning distress at her rising voice but really incensed at the reminder that I always served breakfast. "So I made a lot of soup. Well *excuuuuuuse* me!"

"I'm afraid we can always use food to eat," she said, yielding a smidgen of credit, but mostly scolding herself for not doing more.

"I thought what I left was enough. You used some too, you know."

She slapped the flute on her palm and rocked, as if to music. She began shaking her head, half in disgust, half in time to a melody I knew she had secretly started humming. She was next to the stove in my flannel shirt. I loved her in my shirts; if I hugged her all hostility would dissolve, but I just couldn't.

She surveyed the kitchen and spied a shred of sautéed onion from my soup pot that had fused to the burner. She scraped it off with the register key. It drove me crazy when she used her flute like this.

"No big deal," she said, scraping viciously.

"But *you* think it is."

"We do have two children. As you just *had* to remind me. I get back and find this waiting for me. After *that*, I come home to *this!*"

With the flute she carved out a section above the stove, to hold the horrors she had come home to. The mouthpiece paused over the milk. She tugged the refrigerator open, grabbed the milk, and slid it in. Her hand turned a graceful arc before the door slammed shut. The gesture, as glorious as swinging the flute, revealed how light the container was, and how negligent I had been. Both accusations were far too subtle for me to nail her on them.

"By that you mean Boston?"

"By that I definitely mean Boston."

She tucked the mouthpiece under her lower lip and blew a whistling toot. It irked me, it seemed intended to, but it was nothing next to her mood. Even when I picked her up at the airport she was in her zombie state. (If I said this to her face it would blow the argument into the stratosphere, as would any suggestion that, heaven forbid, a mood might be related to menstruation.) In her zombie state Melissa's dark eyes take on a haunted look. She moons about, dead to everyone, tormenting my life with only the energy to criticize. Even her annoyance at petty slights (like using up the milk) becomes part of a vast solar system of grief, where a thousand troubled planets revolve around my inability to take proper care of her, of the children, of myself. I found this mood most devastating, with its hellish absence of emotion.

"Don't think you can just *forget* and I'll run out," she said, emphasizing the word "forget" to mean I might pretend to forget, something she insisted I did. But her mood was softening when she said, once again, "Count on it, pal."

We had joked with this expression for years. Even the children used it, like a Weil family language. Melissa was signaling she wanted to rouse herself from her zombie state. The flute became a magic wand, to lure dust off the toaster, then a back-scratcher, to dig under the flannel shirt. She guided it down between her shoulder blades, twirled it so the keys would scrape her skin. She thrust out her chest and squinted her eyes; she gave off an icy eroticism that took my breath away.

"Bos-ston was one big bum-mer."

She spoke in clipped syllables, which she often did in this mood.

"My pro-gram? From hell. Tru-ly. From. Hell."

In Boston she coordinated a gala dinner concert, the culmination of an elaborate fund-raising campaign. My wife, star flutist, Juilliard graduate, gifted soloist and wind ensemble performer, had in adulthood become a virtuoso fund-raiser for symphony orchestras.

"The dishwasher has to be emptied," she said in her drained and lifeless zombie voice. "And someone has to load the dishes in the sink."

I had learned over the years to understand simple instructions like these, and hauled open the door. A bubble of heat burst in my face and dampness soaked my eyelids. Few actions better express the Sisyphean nature of family life than emptying a dishwasher and then immediately reloading it. Once, back in the Village, I awoke to find Melissa sitting on the bed in my flannel shirt, practicing silently. Her fingers were whirling so fast they blurred, making airy, hollow pops on springing metal keys. Her eyes were closed. Her head was bent. It was the first time she ever wore any clothing of mine.

"Was Barry Alter there?" I asked. "In Boston?"

She clenched the flute in two fists, like a baseball bat, and stroked the air above the stove. She had no idea how to swing a bat.

"He's in Europe, I told you. Left this humongous mess in my lap!"

She was suddenly incandescent with rage, lips quivering, cheeks on fire, throat blood-red and throbbing.

Another piece of goddamn evidence.

"You're getting one percent fat-free milk," she said, voice still shaking. "Half gallon, no plastic. They won't let us recycle it yet. You want cardboard. It'll be there. If you look you'll find it."

If you look you'll find it!

It was the moment I had been waiting for. So much was on my mind that night. I was feeling overwhelmed, exhausted, at the end of my rope, and I desperately needed to talk about it. But I was in a modern marriage, with a modern woman, meaning my wife was also feeling overwhelmed, exhausted, at the end of her rope, and desperately needed to talk about it. The real subject of all our spats was always who needed attention more.

At first I had taken it for a typical mid-life crisis. I was, by external standards, a great success, an editor at the *New York Times*, an author of best-selling books. Yet I flirted with suicide, even planned faking my death. Finally it came to me that it was my identity, not my life, that I wished to obliterate. Whenever I got into a long-term relationship with a woman I felt myself take on a new identity, at least in my own eyes. I wanted to cast off that new identity and revert to what I once was, before marriage, children, and my comfortable suburban life (we had moved from Greenwich Village to a merrily misshapen Victorian with a wrap-around porch in Montclair, New Jersey) which was impossible to complain about.

"I'm perfectly willing to go," I said.

I would be reasonable and accommodating to the end. I had, after all, crafted a plan. It called for me to slip out and take the number 66 bus to Manhattan, as I did every day to the *Times*. I had learned that buses leave the Port Authority terminal for invisible cities in New England and upstate New York. I'd hide out and begin a new life, if that's not too grandiose a way to put it. In time, on walks through town with the kids, I'd worked out the fine points, like my letter. It was only fair to let Melissa know I had not been murdered or anything. It was crucial she understand I had *chosen* to go.

Dearest Melissa,

I am physically all right. I just need to be alone for a while. I am truly sorry.

Love,
Daniel

"Sooner's better," Melissa said, scratching her back with the flute again. She shoved out her chest, too. There was definitely a swagger in how she did it, flinging back her shoulders and drawing a breath, eyes narrowed.

"Don't forget money, like you did that last time."

Don't forget money!

But I was in control. The letter was in my coat, stuffed there in our last argument, which had been over whether to cut down a tree in the yard. It was surprisingly bitter, as our arguments often were on the practical matters neither of us cared much about.

"I'll get my coat and go," I said. "Right now."

My heart was pounding. I was scared to death, but I had to do it.

I took a last look at her. She was lovely, with her dark, haunted eyes inspecting the flute and her body in the edgy posture of a woman who has always known she's attractive but has never been sure how to handle it. Her beauty allowed me to throw on my coat, open the door, and walk outside.

In the chill of the car I eased down the driveway. Gears bit evenly as I shifted (our Volvo station wagon had stick shift; *she* had wanted automatic, but I'd insisted on manual). When I hit the street the engine yanked me forward like a locomotive with so much power it was beyond my control to stop it. I was being hauled along not only through space but also through time. Yes, I wanted to break through time, to stop time, because so much had happened. I was forty-four years old and it was the last month of 1990. That was impossible: my age, the year. I couldn't really gripe about my life, but I kept thinking, *This* is my life. I hadn't felt on the brink like this in years. I was filled with panic, a sweet, giddy, terrifying panic. It was one of the most exciting moments of my life.

The car of course belonged to her, and it would be wrong to take it. My life was mine, and I had the freedom to go; my possessions were hers. The equation was elegant and I welcomed it. I backed the Volvo up the driveway (near the street, how she liked it) and walked to Valley Road. I had left everything in its proper place. My soup was divided into containers, dated, stashed in the freezer. A luscious whole-wheat onion bread I baked the day before lay frozen beside it. I debated picking up milk (one percent fat-free, half-gallon, no plastic) to leave in the refrigerator. I toyed with getting the wrong kind, on purpose, a childish impulse, I admit. I stopped dead in my tracks, furious at Melissa all over again. *Her damn zombie mood! Her scratching her back with the flute! That swagger in how she moves!*

With anger now goading me on, I strode down the street, not worrying about right or wrong, just what *I* wanted, which was to do something (this I thought with the gushy intonation of women's magazines) for *me!*

I met Melissa the second time she was crazy.

Her therapist, Dr. Fine, was on vacation, so she found a new therapist named Dr. Feld, without telling him she was already in treatment. When Dr. Fine returned she couldn't get up the nerve to tell him about Dr. Feld. She kept seeing both, Dr. Fine on Tuesday, Dr. Feld on Friday, which massaged out the psychological kinks in her week rather well.

Seeing two therapists was fascinating. She'd present the same problem and compare their responses. Their solution was often the same but their way of guiding her to it was different. Dr. Feld coaxed and cajoled, with smirks and frowns and smiles, while Dr. Fine stared, poker faced, and asked what she thought she should do. If she knew the right answer he would nod once.

The bill for two therapists wiped out Melissa's graduate student income. Her roommate, a dancer she knew from Juilliard named Shula, persuaded her to earn money performing in Washington Square Park. Shula, thin and as flexible as a strand of spaghetti, would sit in the lotus position with her hands folded over her head. Melissa would play a snake-charmer melody on her flute as Shula twitched her neck, gyrated her hips, and undulated higher and higher. The act was hokey, even for Greenwich Village, but coins dropped on the blue felt of Melissa's flute case. Back then I wandered the city day and night. Melissa looked so tense, so out on a limb, that the nicest thing I could do was *not* toss any change. She swayed, elbows tilting, breasts lifting. I watched the sleeve of her white T-shirt skid down to a bare shoulder. Her eyes refused to focus on mine.

Afterward, I walked her to her studio apartment. She swung the flute case as we strolled through the Village (already then, in the seventies, it felt fraudulent and out-of-date) and she told me of her dilemma with the two therapists. Only once before, in college, had she felt as crazy as she did now. I began the Chronicle of Daniel the Younger. The first installment in the saga was on my early sorrows, how as a teenager I was too dreamy, too loving, too gentle for this harsh world. She listened devoutly, hugging the flute case to her chest. I elaborated inside. I described the later years, when I roamed the city in a quixotic quest for the perfect woman. The guy I described was so romantic he just broke her heart. Suddenly Shula was at the door. She had gone to meet a juggler, poet, and high school science teacher named Luigi, at a Bleecker Street cafe. She ducked into the bathroom, came out in a leotard, and started twisting and stretching on a little Mexican rug. Melissa and I sat on the sofa bed and analyzed our relationship. Soon she was teaching me about women.

Melissa was devoted to this. She believed that to have a relationship a man had to be taught what a woman wants, the way you teach children what the world expects, to share, say thank you, not whine. I loved being taught because it cracked the mystery of what women want. And she loved teaching, I think because it was her chance to create a perfect man.

An essential trait of the perfect man is to be "sensitive," namely to take the other person's feelings into account. The problem is I had no idea the kind of tacit, intuitive understanding Melissa expected, but she quickly clued me in. I was taught to understand simple commands. For example, I'm in a restaurant and she says, "I'm thirsty." It doesn't mean I should say, "I'm thirsty, too. Where's that waitress?" It means I should remind the waitress to bring water, get up and tap her shoulder if necessary. And *never* ask if I should.

Melissa's lessons opened up a whole new world. I got a sense of how it feels to be a woman today, to prize your independence yet yearn to be taken care of. Society teaches you that your ability to attract a man determines your worth, and is your only real power. Few accept this, Melissa explained, but no woman is indifferent to it. I learned something men have no notion of, how physically vulnerable women feel, and how it shapes their feelings about men.

The next night Melissa and I were on the sofa bed as Shula leaped and stomped. She kept turning cartwheels on the Mexican rug, which squeaked another inch across the floor each time her pink ballet slippers slammed down. Melissa had seen Dr. Feld that day, and it had been an unusual session.

"Stephano," Shula shouted, on her feet, upside down, then on her feet again. "Stephano says it's like un*real.*"

Shula was always meeting men, in the subway, at a newsstand, on line at the deli, and they always had names like Luigi or Jean-Paul or Stephano.

"The name thing," Melissa said.

"He knows Marcia?" Shula asked.

She was on her back, feet pedaling. She rolled on the rug and hugged her ankles in a brutal yoga stretch.

"She told me," I said.

Marcia was Melissa's real name, and she hated it. She had crossed over from Marcia using Marcie, then Melanie, as stepping stones. With Dr. Feld, the new one, she had introduced herself as Melissa. With Dr. Fine, however, she was Marcia, and he was suspicious of her wanting to be someone else.

"So today I'm seeing Felderman, the one you call Feld, and I tell him this really intense dream. It was about you. Meeting you."

"Monster?" Shula said. She was rolling sideways.

"Marsh. Practicing."

Shula and Melissa talked in a kind of code. Shula would know to get water if Melissa said, "I'm thirsty."

Melissa turned to me and explained.

"I live in this marshland, this swamp, loaded with beasts and snakes and monsters. I said it was about us? So it's this sizzling-hot little Freudian swamp. And I get this very jazzy insight doing scales this morning: Like, marsh, that the marsh, means Marcia. I am *really* impressed with myself. So I say to old Feld, 'I see! Marsh–A! Like, marsh land, land of Marcia!' I mean this *has* to wow him. But instead he goes—he's the one always making faces—'Marcia? Who's this Marcia?' I forgot the names! I was *stunned.*"

"So ooh wha," Shula said. "Yake wi wup?"

Her voice was distorted because her throat was against her ankles.

"Make it up? Count on it, pal! Told him Marcia's this old friend, since childhood. He starts grimacing. So I go into my feelings about Marcia, she's half tease, half uptight goody-goody. I get him to smile. We discuss my fear of sinking into a marsh. Of letting go. Of surrender. Surrende*ring!*"

Her eyes came to mine. Her fear of surrender had dominated our talks.

"But the funny thing about talking about Marcia? It was the *best* session in history, far and away, with either one of them. And old Feld never knew what he was talking about. *Literally.* He never knew."

Shula, meanwhile, had finished exercising and joined us on the sofa bed. Melissa launched into a story about a disastrous date. She was with a guy she was crazy about in his West Village loft; I think she met him through Shula. She uses the bathroom (years later I'd learn she was putting in her diaphragm) while he waits on this very chic Persian rug. But the toilet overflows under the door and into the room where this clown Reynaldo or something is waiting. He's barefoot. His living room is flooding. Water drips down and shorts out one of those pretentiously antiquated manual elevators lofts have. There are sparks and thick black smoke. Fire trucks roll up, sirens shrieking.

"And I was afraid to flush," Melissa said. "'Cause it might make noise."

By this time Shula had stretched out and fallen asleep between us, her pink ballet slippers pointing at the ceiling. She began to snore quietly, then with more and more vigor until a snore got caught in her nose and exploded, throwing her head at a slant. It was hard to believe so slender a frame could produce such a massive jolt. I reached over her contorted neck to stroke Melissa's shoulder. Melissa kissed my hand with uncommon tenderness. It was inviting, irresistibly inviting, the way she did it, staring at my palm and kissing, then staring again. We proceeded to make love over Shula's sleeping body. I'm not sure how we pulled off this gymnastic feat, but we did, even as Shula erupted with a fresh explosion of snorts that landed her head in my naked crotch.

Melissa told me later my hands could soothe the suffering of the world, that my lovemaking had healed her. I asked of what. She said, "of everything."

Dr. Feld and Dr. Fine found it significant. They got her to see that because she feared surrender, of sinking in a swamp, she liked being intimate with a man while circumstances kept him at arm's length. Dr. Feld widened his eyes to remind her of the marsh-Marcia dream. Dr. Fine nodded once when she said I made her feel healed. Both agreed it allowed us to begin.

And begin we did, discussing every step. No researcher ever studied a virus, no scholar ever scrutinized a poem, no detective ever pored over a crime scene as painstakingly as we dissected our feelings. We even dissected our need to analyze. When I moved in, I think it was to discuss the relationship with fewer interruptions.

In our talks, the way we first made love got particular attention. Melissa argued that Shula was "passive-aggressive" for conking out between us. It had to do with my being a man who was there for Melissa. This would never have occurred to me before Melissa's lessons. I had never viewed my maleness as carrying special value; in fact, I saw myself as the underdog in relationships with women. But Melissa insisted Shula was jealous because she had a man there and Shula didn't. She made much of the symbolism of Shula's climbing onto the bed in a leotard and falling asleep beside me. She really blew a bolt when I said Shula did it innocently, that there was no other place she could sleep, and it wasn't her fault if she snored like Mount Vesuvius.

The quarrel over Shula resurfaced one night a decade later, after three-month-old Ramona had been nursed to sleep between us. "Don't think I'm pulling a Shula, being passive-aggressive," Melissa said, and instantly fell into her stone-dead new-mother sleep. I stroked her shoulder, as I had over Shula, in the long-shot chance it would wake her. It didn't. The woman who had said my hands could heal didn't even know she was being touched.

I held Ramona the first minute she was alive. She smiled, dazed from the rigors of being born, yet pleasantly weary, as if life were a peaceful bath in which she was now immersed, the reward at the end of a bone-rattling journey. She found the world fascinating, judging by her level-headed gaze of bemused attention. She was (imagine it!) thirty seconds old.

Her birth had not been easy. I don't mean Melissa's experience of childbirth, or Ramona's experience of coming into the outside world, but my experience of becoming a father. I heard a joke about this once, from Melissa. This woman goes through two days of labor, one of those Promethean labors featured in stories beloved by pregnant women, and when the baby is finally born her husband says, "Boy, that was rough! I didn't think I'd make it. I'm totally exhausted!"

Melissa and I had been living together for years, but I still could not adjust to her moods. She could be affectionate to the point of maudlin, then snap graveyard cold in her zombie state. She'd be the dedicated artist and practice for hours, then gather up her music and nose-dive into the woman of mysterious sorrows. During labor the shifts were compressed. She made heroic efforts to stay in control. She charted the physiology of hormonal changes, calculated in centimeters the dilation of never-seen parts of her body, cited statistics on drug-free births, and explicated on the hospital's bureaucracy with a droll digression into its complex funding involving third-party reimbursement. As her labor intensified and her pain increased, she weighed the pros and cons of a contraction-inducing drug she knew by name. She vacillated between treating me as an obtuse servant scarcely capable of fetching her flute to the single human alive whose presence she required to survive a moment of titanic need. As the birth of Ramona approached and our ascent into parenthood neared, she crashed into a state I had never seen: she was helpless. All I could do was watch as she clung to my shoulder and shut her eyes with the legendary pain of labor, which is and has always been an exclusively female experience.

The pain of labor, like the sex that creates it, is rhythmical, a chant so compelling I couldn't help but sing along. There was nothing I could do to protect Melissa from the beating chant of pain reverberating louder and louder inside her, a pounding kettledrum of pain. She closed her eyes as a chorus of pain beat through her skin, eyelids beaded with sweat, seeing me, then not seeing anything at all. This time the man would watch from the sidelines, be unobtrusively helpful, would sit, and would wait.

We went home with Ramona and Melissa went immediately crazy. I know this sounds like a cheap shot, but you have to understand that giving birth gave fresh gusto to her moods. She used the flute a new way, not playing but pointing, to show me what to do. Ramona demanded more than we had ever given, and we had no idea even what her needs were. One of them clearly was nursing, and she and Melissa established an intense and, I admit, private relationship. Ramona was an instant addict. She even looked stoned when she finished, eyes glazed, body slack, as she nodded out on Melissa's swollen, dripping, milk-and-honey breasts.

The first day home I hatched the idea for my second book, *How to Baby A New Mother: Surviving the First Three Years.* I thought up the most controversial chapter, "Odd Man Out," on the abandonment felt by many men of my generation when we become fathers. The book contrasted with my first, *Emotional Terrorism: How Women Control Men in the 1980's.*

That night Melissa sunk into her stone-dead slumber while Ramona slurped up a storm. Peculiarly alone, I stretched my arm around my daughter and my wife. After a while we slept, enclosed in comfort so lush and complete none of us had yet come to terms with it.

We slept two hours, three the most. As if it makes a difference.

Then Ramona awoke, made a pass at nursing, and began what we would later call her nuclear meltdown cry. Melissa felt entitled to sleep, so I scooped up Ramona and pried myself out. It was something I'd never done before: climbing from a warm bed, sleep shattered, to have to get up and stay up. And I did, stumbling as if ill, amid feverish tension between me and her over who should or should not be getting up this time, who heard the cry, who heard and pretended not to, who can best comfort her, a whole universe of new things to create friction between me and that woman in my bed, back in her coma-like sleep, a pillow squashed on her face.

I lugged Ramona's whimpering body across the room, knocking over the music stand, surely placed there on purpose. It was the first time I'd ever taken care of an infant on my own. It was another new experience to stand there like that, an added dimension to my life as a man, rocking a baby on my shoulder with a woman's hip-jiggling motion as I gazed out the window in the middle of the night. Ramona, forty-eight hours old, was sobbing from the mysterious demons of childhood, and I was trying, with my paltry, forty-eight-hour-old father skills, to banish the monsters from her brain.

Ramona shuddered, eyes clamped tight. She clung fast; I was heartsick with love. Before she gave birth, Melissa had also shut her eyes and gripped my shoulder. In the last two days the landscape under me had shifted forever. I was now joined to two females who had clutched my body and shut their eyes with a pain I would never know.

The bus to the city took its time coming. I got into a conversation in my head, a habit of mine to work out ideas. When I read anything, I constructed flawless opinions because I'd have to present them to people who questioned me. I had to know every detail, every angle, every nuance to defend my position. Yet no one ever asked. The conversations in my head, about my books and my life, were practice for events I had been certain would occur. I was taking this bus tonight because I'd finally realized I'd never have to explain anything to anybody, despite how well-prepared I was.

The bus lumbered into sight. The door buckled open before its nervous wheels stopped. The first step is high, so I had to hoist my foot in a quick and perilous leap. But the impatient manner of the bus—that breathless bluster they always have —didn't give me a second to think. I managed the step, and the door was whisked closed, at my back, shivering, shut.

— 2 —

It was easier to get set up in my new city than I'd expected.
Imagine. Here comes this guy out of nowhere, with a story that
doesn't really make sense, if you think about it. I once had a
theory—I had theories about everything at one time—that the
world is so disorganized I could get away with anything. So far
it had proven true. I had chosen the place with care, an obscure
city that still had three small- to medium-size daily newspa-
pers. In a few days I had a copy editing job on the overnight
shift of an afternoon paper called *The Herald-News Journal*.

I selected the job for reasons both practical and spiritual.
The practical reason is the availability of jobs on copy desks,
particularly those on shifts like midnight to eight, because most
people try to switch to more regular hours as soon as they can.
Also, a person's background is never scrutinized. You're hired
after a "tryout," where you do a simulated night's work. The
spiritual reason is the hermetically sealed environment of an
overnight desk. It's usually a corner of an empty newsroom,
and you sit before a computer screen and edit words written
by people you have never met about events you have never
witnessed. As a city dreams, you wrestle with words that describe its reality.

The newspaper that hired me expected me to make stories conform to "style," the way they think words should be spelled and the like, and they always act not like it's their style, arbitrary and idiosyncratic as all styles of usage are, but right in some absolute sense. And you write headlines. Let me explain what this is all about, why I love it so much.

Before I met Melissa, even before I wandered the city, I wrote poetry. I scoured the English language for rhymes. I spent hours studying the way the accents fell. I wrote sonnets and villanelles, tanka and senryu. (Senryu do exist, although few dictionaries define them and no one knows what they are; hence they are splendid things to compose.) I especially liked syllabic poetry, like haiku, where style matters far less than form. I wrote hundreds of haiku. Of course, a haiku is not merely a poem of seventeen syllables, five on the first line, seven on the next, and five on the third, but I tended to get caught up in the discipline of a form and overlook the art it is meant to inspire. Then I started writing headlines for this newspaper, which I was pretty good at. I mean, there's a certain poetry to a good headline, and it's just as disciplined. Most people think the secret lies in short words, which of course is part of it, but that's like saying a haiku is just a poem of seventeen syllables. The secret with headlines is shaping the idea to fit; the charm, as with a diamond, is in how it's cut. And so I was able to make money using language this way. At first I viewed myself as a serious painter who picks up cash drawing caricatures at parties, or a ballerina who feeds her family as a go-go dancer. It let me connect with Melissa when she caught my eye in Washington Square. But soon I forgot what I imagined myself to be and became what I did every day.

The guy who hired me was the type of copy desk chief who'd spent years on overnights engaged in an arcane pursuit no one understood. Charley rarely looked up from his screen. He spoke about seven words, as if his very conversation had to be condensed into a headline. I sat next to a guy wearing Mickey Mouse ears, which I was expected to ignore. Two of the oddest stories I was given in my tryout were from the same reporter, one saved from 1989. I deduced that he or she (the name was only "Simon") was the whipping boy of the desk, an atrocious writer everyone loved to edit because you could gut the work ruthlessly. I rewrote it, with vicious comments that it was so horrendous it would take all night to get everything right. I had a squirt of fear when I realized there was a chance Simon was a star who broke rules and took chances, and no one was allowed to alter a syllable. If I did a job on his copy I'd be out the door in a flash.

An hour later I got a "screentop" from Charley. These flash on the screen and make up most communication at newspaper offices nowadays.

Wan wood ewe stot, iph ewe r awf erred jobberwacky?
(CHARLES)

Sune az ewe wont. Eye at liber T (GUEST)

Perhaps he could only send gag messages? But it was essential to let him know I fit in. I got no response, only another at 5 A.M.:

Y knot cawl id a knight. eye scene ee nuf (CHARLES)

I walked back to the room I had rented, through a frigid dawn in a city where no one knew me. Winters are arctic up here, and I felt colder than I ever had in my life. I was secretly thinking about Barry Alter. This is another habit of mine. I think one thing, but secretly, as if it's not just me inside my head, I'm also thinking about something else.

I found the letter buried in Melissa's Boston Symphony Orchestra bag. I was on a legitimate mission, digging out her paycheck to deposit the next week, when she'd be in Houston. I tried not to play back the phrases. ("For sex, pure and simple, we did it, a quick lay on a hotel bed." "You invaded my life, Barry, and I didn't stop you because I wanted you to." "That kiss was the biggest mistake of my life!!!") The first time I read it every word flashed in my skull for hours, like a blaze of fireworks.

———————————

First we had to dodge the Gleasons.

We were going out for ice cream on a Sunday evening in early October, and we were taking a long way around because the Gleasons were on their lawn. Not only were they always outside, but they were the nicest people we knew. They shouted hello and kneeled to chat with the children. Even at dawn they'd greet us in the cheeriest tones. Melissa and I went to any length to avoid them. We just wanted to strangle them for being so friendly, especially early in the morning.

It was the night Ramona and I had listened to a radio show on what would have been John Lennon's fiftieth birthday. (She had recently become a Beatles fan.) We walked a roundabout route on Norwood Avenue, stretching out on the sidewalk like a series of flags unfurled in the autumn air. We were in front of a hedge, over scraggly leaves, past a hydrant and the middle school and the branch library, me the tall one in the middle, Ramona in front in an orange jacket, Zach taking up the rear with his conductor's cap over his ears. I was bursting with the wholeness of family, the agreeably overloaded feeling I knew to be the surest antidote to loneliness. I've been haunted as far back as I can remember by loneliness. It seems a part of me, as eternal as my name being Daniel Weil.

"Khe! Khe! Gotcha kango butt! Yeah? Khowwwww! Gaoooong."

Zach's last sound was a bullet ricocheting, rendered as I had made the sound thirty years earlier. It was close to forty, actually, which seemed insane when I thought about it, that this is what forty years feel like. I hate how all those big things, love and death, birth and time, trust and hope, in the end feel pretty much like what right now feels like.

"They didn't see us," Ramona said, meaning the Gleasons. "I feel bad 'cause they're so nice."

"There are some people everyone loves," I said, "but no one can stand."

"It's sad about John," Ramona said, suddenly about to cry. "He what?"

I knew what she meant.

"He said he was only killing an image, an album cover."

The despair on her face magnified, her lips curling. The existence of the universe hung on whether she would cry. Instead she gave me a smile, pleasantly weary, like the one she gave after she was born.

"When you die, you stop getting older?"

"Yes."

"So John won't ever get older because he's dead?"

"Yes," I said. "He won't get older anymore."

"And neither will Grandpa? He'll stay seventy-seven forever?"

"Not so fast, bing brain. Khe! Khe! Khow! Khow! Gaoooong!"

"Yes. Forever."

"Since you're forty-four you're halfway dead," Ramona said.

"Yeah, kango brain-butt. Khe! Khe! Gaoooong! Oh yeah? Khe! Khe!"

"And if you were John you'd be dead four years already."

"It's weird, Monie, but people die. It makes no sense to me either. I just read in the *Times* that F. Scott Fitzgerald—he was a famous writer—died exactly fifty years ago. And he died at forty-four, my age now. And so did these other famous guys, D. H. Lawrence, and someone called Chekhov. He was Russian. He wrote plays."

I had been thinking, as I got well-ensconced in my forties, of famous men who had died at my age. I looked over at my daughter. She had slowed to walk closer, as secure as she would be next to anyone. Golden autumn light shined through her hair (October light in Montclair is quite beautiful, silvery and sharp) as she stooped to study an enormous leaf. She slid it into her pocket, bending the stem so it wouldn't break. I have not mentioned how beautiful my daughter is. She's really fetching, how she glances at you with the winsome eagerness that lurks under the skin of certain eight-year-old girls. Even strangers comment on her.

"I don't want to kill that tree, even if it's sick," my foxy daughter said. "Mommy said someone in Boston told her big trees can fall any time. Without yawning, she said."

"Who told her? It's without *warning*."

"What?"

"Who in Boston told her I said."

"I don't know."

"She didn't say who? Did he play anything? Or raise money with her."

"I don't know, Dad. Dad, you ever meet the Beatles? Ringo even?"

"I thought you liked Ringo."

"He's my favorite. And it's no fair they don't let him sing."

I was learning about the Beatles daily from the multitude of books Ramona had accumulated. I felt sad for Ringo. I heard a line once, that every man is a failure in his own eyes. John was dead, and the surviving Beatles seemed to feel betrayed. They felt they had not been appreciated for what they did to make the Beatles what they were. It was bewildering, when you got down to it. Poor Ringo. I was overcome with sadness. Kids bring out these crazy thoughts. I mean, the Beatles! How much success could you dream about? Of course, my whole generation was betrayed when time wouldn't stop in 1969.

"They let him sing sometimes. I thought you liked 'Yellow Submarine.'"

She stroked her hair. She was too innocent for it to be a pose, despite how she looked, coy and earthy and vulnerable. She smiled her weary smile, and said, "And 'Octopus's Garden,' Dad, which they let him write."

Ramona was perhaps the first person in history who viewed Ringo Starr as the creative genius behind the Beatles. She intuitively understood Ringo's pain, what I imagined Ringo's pain to be, a sense perhaps he had about how hollow life had become. Poor Ringo. No wonder he had problems with alcohol and drugs and identified with an octopus and a submarine. I was aching for the guy. This was crazy.

"You know who my favorite Beatle is, Monie?"

"John?"

"Not John. This guy named Pete Best."

"No Beatle was named Pete Best."

"Everybody always says that, but listen. There *almost* was one. He was the drummer before Ringo, but he left before they made it big."

"Why'd he leave? John kick him out? He was sort of the boss."

"I think he was asked to go. It's true, Monie. I used to be obsessed with Pete Best. When everyone was loving the Beatles in the sixties, I kept thinking about him, how he missed it by this much, by just *this* much!"

"I bet Ringo gave him lots of money."

"I certainly hope so. How many mornings did Pete Best wake up and say to himself, I'm a complete nobody, I could've been a Beatle, a *Beatle*. He *must* have seen them on TV, he *must* have picked up their albums in stores? Think of him holding *Rubber Soul!* How in the world did that feel? He's my favorite Beatle, by a long shot he is. I feel horrible for him, even now."

Behind us Zachary was shouting, "Don't go for it, lingo brain. Khe! Khe! Gaoong! You a dead man. Count on it pal! Khe! Khe!"

"Why, Dad? Why should you care about *him?*"

I stared at my beautiful Ramona. But we were father and daughter, and there were limits to what we were allowed to share.

When I called Charley, he didn't mention whether I got the job, but told me to come in at midnight. Like many men, he wasn't comfortable on the phone and expressed it by being curt.

As in many American cities there used to be a dozen dailies up here, which merged as they lost their readers' eyes to television. Consequently, they ended up with hyphenated names: the *Times-Journal-Press*, the *Daily-Record-Post-Tribune*, and *The Herald-News Journal*, the one that hired me. Note, by the way, the capital "t" in *The Journal*. With the unparalleled self-centeredness of publications everywhere, *The Journal* printed its name that way but left the "t" in the *the* down for others, the competing dailies, the *New York Times*, the far less influential *Journal* on Wall Street. I knew it would dazzle them if I got this trivia right on my tryout, and it did.

When I arrived at the newsroom at midnight Charley handed me some papers and told me to fill them out. His voice was baritone, almost theatrical, and I realized it was because he was speaking aloud; I had hardly ever heard his voice. He had a headline cut out that said "Charles in Charge" taped on his computer. I sat next to the guy in Mickey Mouse ears. I loathe filling out forms. The spaces are always too small, intentionally it seems, but this time I relished scratching in the information. I'd get to test my Theory of General Disorganization. Usually, when someone disappears as I did he has to take a menial job because he needs to get paid off the books. When I first thought about running off I assumed that's what I'd do. Then I figured out how to get a decent job and fulfill a fantasy along the way. I wrote, in the tiny squares that were of course a jot too small: *VEIL WALDO DANIEL*

I put my rented room as my address. I put my Social Security number, but transposed two digits. (In my research I had learned I could use the number of someone my age who had died, but I couldn't imagine the government being organized enough to notice.) For job history I put the *New York Times,* which I knew would floor them. I had dropped it during my talk with Charley, who of course scowled, as everyone in the profession does. I gave for supervisor a guy named Steve Glickstein, and called him "night news editor." I had spoken to him in my planning stage and told him I was trying to freelance at a little newspaper and needed a reference. Journalists are always trying to freelance something somewhere, or planning to. I said I was using "Veil" so the *Times* wouldn't know I was selling pieces to someone else. *The Journal* would probably check with him, and he'd cover for me without knowing what he was doing; my theory was that no one would be thorough enough to find out what was up. If Glickstein forgot about my using "Veil" he'd think *The Journal* misspelled my name; when the reference came back, *The Journal* would think the typo was his. If he forgot he'd write off my new name as the mistakes people make, like letters with your name misspelled. In an inspired moment I threw in "Waldo" to further throw people off. Not only was it a name so outlandish it had to be real, it was also an inside joke with myself based on a popular children's book.

In other squares I wrote Waldo D. Veil, so Social Security numbers and tax records would list me as Waldo D. Veil, but less formal matters like job history checks would use Daniel W. Veil, easily confused with Daniel Weil. If called on any of it I could say I misread last name for first. The idea was that if detectives came looking they would comb the official listings, like income taxes or apartment leases. They would pass over a Waldo D. Veil, not even close to Daniel Weil. On a reference check the name Daniel W. Veil would read as a typo of Daniel Weil, with the W accidentally spaced out before an errant V.

That's the name I used in the short résumé I had to type for Charley. I knew I would get mail addressed to endless variations of my name, but I always had, even when I was only Daniel Weil.

In the middle of everything I talked with a guy who seemed to know the ropes, called Gregory Gregory. Every office has a Gregory Gregory. He's like a patient from a psychiatric hospital who'd been granted a day pass during which he started to work. No one understands what he does. Gregory Gregory kept a pile of newspaper clippings on his desk and yelled at anyone who disturbed it. He came in every night at one, stayed till precisely three-forty-five, when he'd say he was "going to grab a quick bite," and not come back until the next night.

Gregory Gregory helped me find a typewriter (an old IBM Selectric that was bouncy on my fingertips) to do the résumé, and we began to chat. Because I was new I didn't realize he was a borderline psychotic, and we talked about the paper's history, which I used in my brief interview with Charley; I had to pretend every minute of my life had been spent preparing for the opportunity they just happened to have available. I introduced myself to him as "Daniel" so I would be called by my real first name. It isn't unusual for records to list someone with a different first name, especially if it's "Waldo." And I pronounced "Veil" to rhyme with "whale," so it didn't even sound like Weil, which I pronounce like "while."

I said good night to Gregory Gregory when I left, but he just nodded and continued rearranging his files with the fiendish devotion of a child setting one block on top of another. I never found out if anything was checked. I hoped it was, that my theory had been tested, and that it worked. But we never find out things like that. We just don't hear anything. The nightmare we worry about never happens exactly as we imagine. You can take my word for it.

— 3 —

The first taste of a new identity came last October, when I went trick or treating with the kids. They begged me to wear a costume, and that Halloween I tied on a sheet and became a ghost.

I did the same when I was about seven. The memory is vivid. I followed some older boys along my street until they turned a corner. From the distance they seemed to become entangled in the bush that stood there, and their bodies shriveled up right before my eyes. I turned the corner after them into an alien place, though only a block from home. It happened so fast, as if I'd climbed a tree and inched out on a limb that suddenly wasn't there. The darkness was smeary and closer to my skin. The houses were in foreign styles, and they eyed me with a kind of peaceful terror. I glanced inside the bush. I saw a washed-out candy wrapper snagged in the wildness of its branches.

Then I looked down and realized I was a ghost. I ran, through filthy darkness, before I wanted to; my feet just started by themselves. It was the tranquillity of those houses, the sensation that I was seeing the world *as it really was.*

But this Halloween I was forty-four and no longer afraid.

Ramona was a rock star and looked smashing in a little blue skirt with black tights. Zach was a Ninja warrior, with two wooden swords in his belt and a conductor's cap. We knocked on doors, and Ramona and Zach hauled away their loot, gloating, gleeful, pretending to get scared when they looked at the ghost who was their dad. I was surprised to find people in beards and theatrical makeup and playing scary music, the kind with a sinister laugh. Everyone gets into Halloween in Montclair.

We stopped at a house on Park Street, a hulking green Victorian decked out for Halloween, with plastic tombstones on the lawn and a witch made of light bulbs strung across the porch. Dracula's spooky chuckle shivered from an outdoor speaker. I confess to a twinge of fear as we—a Ninja warrior, a rock star, and a ghost—approached the forbidding house. The spooky music was ear-splitting on the porch, rollicking, cackling laughter: Could you ever escape from here? The kids made me ring the bell. I was surprised when the door was opened by a woman as young as I was; I'm always startled when a palatial Montclair home is owned by a person my age. The woman was wearing a witch's outfit and she invited us in. She said her name was Susan Spiser, and she got the kids to announce their names, which they muttered. I could tell she had no idea who I was.

The funny thing was she had managed to make the witch's outfit sexy. The bodice was black gauze, and I could see the edges of her bra, a shinier, blacker black, and her breasts squirming around under a dark film. The heavy makeup made her look more slutty than scary. She held a black shawl over her, angled so the kids couldn't see what I couldn't take my eyes off. As we chatted in the foyer the kids picked treats from a pottery bowl in a marble wash basin. She had an overpowering way of standing, erect yet at ease, so her whole body seemed focused on me. Her gaze was all-embracing and gave the impression she was offering not only her attention but also her body, as part of the bargain.

"Lou's in Texas for a change," she said. "Or New Orleans. Or both."

She was mentioning someone I didn't know by name, forcing me to identify him by context. Like her body, it was presented as something I was already familiar with. I lifted off my sheet; the house was stuffy after the outside chill. I could hear the spooky laughter from the porch rising, falling, scheming to get its creepy hands on us.

"Betcha didn't know it was my dad," Zach shouted, proud for some reason, and assuming as children do that everyone knew who his dad was. Ramona studied us, checking out Susan's outfit.

"Why no, I didn't," Susan said. "I thought it was a ghost coming home to his haunted house and his *oh so witchy* wife. Love your hat, Zach."

Zach clenched his railroad cap. He didn't like anyone mentioning it. He felt his Ninja sticks by twisting his belt.

"I don't know what Jason is yet. I honestly have no idea what he'll be." She used a talking-to-a-kid voice, which wasn't necessary with Ramona. "I have no idea where the little monster is."

She looked at Ramona's short blue skirt and black tights, smiling for some secret reason.

"Believe it," she said. "Those bicycle pants are actually loose on her."

Ramona wasn't sure being told her thighs were thin was a compliment. Her pants weren't really tights, but the black skintight leggings women were wearing, although (Melissa had pointed out) always with a large top or blouse to mask their hips.

Another child came down the stairs, a girl. She was a ballerina, in a pink petticoat over a pink tutu.

"That one's mine, bonko brain!"

"You took it, umpho face!"

"No," Zach whined. "Mine."

"Chincho umph face! Count on it, pal!"

"No!"

"Conko bonko bain-brain!"

Ramona and Zach managed to start fighting over the candy. This was something new, their sniping at each other. Melissa and I had forbidden nasty words, but they got around it by inventing insults. Within a week, they had a private language in which to fight.

"Concho gong brain," Ramona said.

Zach whined again. "No! Miiiiiiiine!"

Your child's whine is the most diabolic sound ever to grate on the human ear, chalk on the blackboard writ large, each screech an eternity of howling direct from the portals of hell.

"Maybe we'd better go," I said. "He's fading."

"I'm not failing," Zach said. "Wanna stay with Monie. And more trick-a-treating. Dad."

"You can leave Ramona here with Jason," Susan said. "If you want to take him home."

The ballerina was her son, dressed as a girl. Ramona never played with boys, but I guess she made exceptions if they dressed as ballerinas.

Zach was tugging my sheet. "Home," he said.

"I thought you wanted to stay with Monie."

"Dad, only before I was joking. Now I'm serious."

This was a new expression. He said it very flat.

I took Zach home and trotted back to Park Street, sheet flying high. Just for the fun of it I kicked a roll of toilet paper a prankster left in the street. It spiraled off a tree, sliced through a hedge, and unwound bouncing down the sidewalk.

"They went out trick or treating," Susan said when she let me in. "The adults can chill. You're off the hook."

We went into the living room, a ghost and a witch, as Dracula cackled on a loudspeaker. Susan sat on the couch with regal composure, a small furry afghan rug crumpled at her feet. She spread the shawl on both sides, so it ran from her neck out along the cushions in a massive salute to her cleavage. She had on a Beatles album—*Sgt. Pepper,* I think. Actually, it was a compact disc, and she snapped the volume up with a remote control that she twirled in her palm like a Spanish dancer clicking castanets.

"Ramona told me you're a Beatles fan," she said, shooting the volume up another notch, her arm looping out from the shawl. She clicked it lower, switched songs, shut it, then started it, as a row of obedient green lights pulsed on and off in annoyance. Her struggle was a joy to watch: not in years had anyone put on music simply because I liked it.

"Your daughter's really into the Beatles. That's *so* great! He showed her his monsters. That's an honor, trust me. She's so beautiful, so slender, her *hair!* She looks like you, I think. Yes, the eyes."

She stepped over the rumpled rug to come up to me, dragging the shawl, and search my eyes. The shawl hung down, suggesting a negligee. The house felt empty, with laughter echoing in every room. I relaxed in my comfortable chair, the Beatles clapping their hands especially for me.

The doorbell rang, spitefully loud. The floor vibrated. The house was exorbitantly electronic, and Susan was connected to the circuits, judging by how her body recoiled. She drew the shawl modestly tight as she became a witch again. Outside were a cheerleader and a rock star. She gave them candy, bringing over the pot. When she sat she didn't take off the shawl or extend it over the cushions, but threw it back to reveal a jolly triangle of black gauze. She adjusted it without looking down, and stretched her legs out to touch the rug. Her calf muscle swelled, then went slack.

"I must say you look quite bewitching," I said.

"Thank you."

"Ramona's very into monsters," I said.

"It's not horribly commercial, at least. I think kids have a fascination with pure, unadulterated evil."

"Speaking of the Beatles," I said. "Can I tell you this idea I had for a great toy? I guarantee it would make us a million bucks."

"Of course, by all means tell me, tell me," she said, leaning forward, happy for an opportunity to please me.

"It's called the Happy Singing Killer Frogs. I guarantee every kid would become obsessed in no time."

This was a pet idea of mine. I had to practically tie Melissa up to get her to listen, only to have her tell me it sounded like the Teenage Mutant Ninja Turtles, which were just becoming popular.

Susan, in contrast, immediately loved it.

"Like what *are* they?" she said. "Frogs?"

"Not frogs exactly."

It was wonderful to tell someone I didn't have to force to listen.

"There're these four brothers, Grongo, Pongo, Rongo and —get this—the long-lost brother, Jongo. The gimmick is that Jongo was kidnapped when he was a tadpole, when they lived in the Home Swamp, by the evil monsters, Wouzy Vibes and his evil cohort Baddie Karma."

She liked it so much she had to gather the shawl in her lap because it kept rocking off her shoulders as she laughed. Each time her head bent down the dress opened and I could see the little black flower at the center of her bra.

"And here's where the big bucks come in. You see, that's why Jongo isn't on sale anywhere, because he was kidnapped, so he wouldn't be in CVS or anything, but we, the company, say they're out there and promise any kid who finds a Jongo an all-expense-paid trip to Disneyland and the whole collection for free, including every Happy Singing Killer Frog character, their walkie-talkie, the Croc-a-Dial, their *Star Wars* villain, Darth Gator, their favorite band, the *Beached* Boys, who play their favorite music, *croak* rock, their favorite snack, French *flies*, and of course their singing psychiatrist, Pink Freud."

"You're *brill*iant. Did you tell anyone? A*bout* this? Anyone at all?"

Her words were crackling, with little sparks shooting off.

"No," I said, knowing Melissa was not included in her question. I had a fear, crazy I admit, that Lou would steal my idea and make a killing. But I imagined Susan always alone, in one costume or another, sailing through endless well-appointed rooms.

"The search for Jongo—and I guarantee kids'll go completely ape over this—becomes wild when we, the company, lets one be found in a Toys R Us in New Hampshire, say, or a drugstore in Southern California. We'd do a lot of publicity about the discovery, fly a kid somewhere. That would keep it from being a scam, I mean a *total* scam. Parents would be told by the kids they have nothing to lose by browsing in the Happy Singing Killer Frog section to look for a Jongo to *rescue*."

"It's *brill*iant," she said again. "It'll make us a *for*tune. We'll advertise on *all* the Saturday cartoons."

"We'll call the craziness Frogomania, like Beatlemania?"

"*Fab*ulous. *Per*fect."

"They'd be called the Frog Four, 'stead of the Fab Four?"

"Fab*uloso!*"

"There'd be bad guys, too, with goofy polysyllabic names —Hopalong Threnody and his sidekick, Skipaloo M. Darling.

Remember, we also have Wouzy Vibes and Baddie Karma, who kidnapped Jongo when he was a little frog. In the Legend of Paradise Swamp."

I hadn't realized how much there was to this idea. It was spilling out, as though I were having a conversation in my head.

There was noise in the kitchen. Susan leaped up. She walked haltingly, waving her arms as if climbing over rocks. In a moment she was back, standing in her off-balance way. She had been thinking over my idea.

"We'll make the stores give us kickbacks to sell a Jongo," she said. "We'll pull in extra cash letting them have a Jongo here, a Jongo there. Not *too* many! They'll have to ante up, pay through the nose, for the publicity."

"Great," I said. "The stores are very important, to get them on our side. There's also a psychological aspect in here. About children."

Her attention immediately flagged. I had lost her by mentioning children.

"Remember, parents buy the stuff. They're our age now, and the crazy names would make it like the manufacturers were from their generation, making secret jokes from the sixties like Baddie Karma, etc. I have another theory, too, that I think is very clever. If I say so myself."

I couldn't stop talking about it. I rarely brag; it's a fault I have, selling myself short all the time.

"I think kids like it when bad people have bad names. They believe they can control the evil in the world, the ghosts and goblins and monsters, that have power over them, make them get lost, feel alone and scared, if they can just say their names, the monsters' names."

I wasn't sure she was picking up the subtlety.

"Boy, you really *have* thought this out," she said. "I'm impressed. A fortune is waiting here. I'm talking big bucks. *Mega*-big bucks!"

"You'd get parents by the frogs being politically correct. They leave the Home Swamp only to search for their lost brother or fight injustice, pollution, or bias against frogs of any faith, color, or swamp origin."

"So our frogs are teaching good family values," she said. "*Excellent.*"

The music stopped. She couldn't figure out how to get the remote to start it again. Gruesome laughter distorted the silence, seeping in through the walls.

"Yes," I said. "We'd end each TV show with choreographed battles, so beneath the progressive values, the respectability, the cuteness, would be enough mindless violence to thrill every four-year-old boy on the planet."

"The girls? We gotta hook *them*, too."

"Oh, there's this girl frog who goes on adventures with them, called Lily Pad. She'd be a kind of Barbie Doll with a long tongue."

"The dream of *every* man," she said.

She struggled up, stepped over the rug, and staggered into the kitchen.

"Trouble with Lily Pad," she called, "is it sounds like a sanitary napkin."

A crash came from upstairs. Jason came down, the pink petticoat on his tutu awhirl. Ramona stood on the stairs. "*Revolver*, I said," she yelled to Jason, who snatched the remote, clicked once, and had John Lennon instantly urging us to relax and float downstream.

"I thought they went out," I said.

Susan didn't seem to have any idea what was happening in her own house. There was something scattered about her; even her sexuality was erratic, like a powerful electronic device with an intermittent malfunction.

"Thought," she said. "They must've come back."

Jason clicked the music off and ran back upstairs with Ramona. Then a crazy thing happened. The afghan rug got off the floor and trotted after them. It was a dog.

"Sarge finally woke. Exhausted after your play date, weren't you?"

The dog jogged back, lay down, and became a crumpled rug again.

"Play date? Like kids have?"

"With this lab we know on Glenwood. A retriever. Lou in*sists* he needs the contact with his own species. So I drive him every Tuesday. Except when Abbey was in heat."

She flipped off her shoe and stroked the dog's neck with a stockinged foot, a lush caress, her toes bent. He yawned and crept over, stretching his head on the couch. Susan nuzzled her chin in the dog's fur.

"Although Sarge really *wanted* her then, to see her, the little rascal, to get his rocks off. You hornyyyyy little dogeeeee!"

She whipped her nose around in the fur and planted a kiss that made Sarge extend an enormously flexible tongue and lick her cheek in long, sloppy strokes. After the third stroke she pushed him away, and he jumped, chain collar jingling, cavorting, thinking it's a game, then realized it wasn't and padded off, shaking, snorting, and thumping up the stairs.

"So," I said, "dogs have play dates now."

"Yes. You know the Wittensteins? He's something at *Esquire* and she's something at *Redbook?* Or vice versa? Abbey's theirs. Short for *Abbey Road*. Which is really weird, 'cause Sarge was named after *Sgt. Pepper*."

"No," I said. "But I might know them. After all, it's a Dickensian universe. Sooner or later every one you know turns up."

"Dickensian universe," she said. "That's cute. Like there are really only *eight* people in the world?"

"And they all turn up. Beats saying small world, doesn't it?"

"For sure," she said. "Dickensian universe. I have to remember that."

Of course, remembering it was exactly what I had done years ago when I first heard the phrase. My brain is filled with lines stolen from witty people.

A knock sounded. Susan put on her shawl and gave out candy, holding out her hand. She didn't let these kids make the selections themselves.

"So it's not just a rip-off of the *Teenage Mutant Ninja Turtles?*" That was what Melissa had said when I got right down to it.

"Well, it's similar, of course. But it would be a smash if we marketed it right. Set up so kids'd *kill* to have it. *Die* to find a Jongo. *Steal* their parents' money. *Every last cent!*"

This always amuses me. People like Susan, or me, in fact, are the first to decry the commercialization of toys, but give us

an inside track on the receipts and we're off like a pack of raving capitalist money-hungry lunatics.

Ramona and Jason returned again, with Sarge prancing beside them. It was time to go. At the door, with spooky laughter clutching our throats, Susan shouted, "Di*cken*sian universe.
I'll remember that. Di*cken*sian universe."

Zach was still awake when we got home.

"He has something to show you," Melissa said. "He's very
proud of it." Her eyes wouldn't let go. Like witchcraft, she had
Susan's erratic sexuality.

Zach demonstrated in his room. He had achieved a life-
long ambition: he'd gotten a tiny plastic gun into the hand of
a Mickey Mouse action figure. It was ingenious, the way he had
done it, with a belt from another toy looped around Mickey's
nose. I took him to the bathroom. He wore nothing but his blue
striped conductor's cap. I carried him over the cold tiles, de-
lighting in how spongy and light he was in my arms, his legs
hanging out and Mickey popping off shots at passing towels.

On the way back Mickey was shooting at anything that
moved. "Khe! Khe! Gotcha, zong head! Count on it, pal.
Gaonnnnng!"

Melissa and Ramona passed in the hall. Melissa, smiling
that eerie smile, whispered, "He's amazing. He's such a *boy*.
By the way, I'm in San Francisco tomorrow? You can't forget,
so tonight has to be hat night."

She meant Zach's conductor's cap, which hadn't been off
his head in months. We kept a duplicate hidden, and every
few days while he slept we switched his hat with a fresh one.
It had inspired Melissa to remark that he'd feel about house-
work like a typical man, that all washing and cleaning is done
magically by gremlins while he slept.

While Zach was standing there waiting Ramona saw an
opening and got off a quick one, hissing, "Shie shie lonk face.
Kisho konko."

Zach screwed up his face and was about to cry. Ramona
scooted off just as Zach regained control and wandered into
his room. We had an instant of quasi-privacy, and Melissa took

my arm and pressed it against the flannel shirt of mine she was wearing. She was blinking tears out of her eyes.

"Tonight," she said, "seeing the three of you go off in those costumes, I thought how they're growing up, how everyone's changing. It was, I don't know, spooky, and I got scared being alone again. Halloween was almost *real*, if you know what I mean. And you were gone so long, I—"

"Dad!" Zach shouted, leaning out his doorway.

"One minute, Zach. Please."

"I'll put Monie to bed, have to shower," Melissa said. "In two seconds I'll be out, two secs at the most? I just sort of just need—"

"Da-ad!" Zach shouted again. "Before I was joking. Now I'm serious."

"My flight's so early," Melissa said. "San Francisco?"

I went into Zach's room and read him a totally inane book about a family of pigs who go on a picnic, get scared, and run home. He stared wide-eyed and caught me skipping pages twice. Finally, after about two or three millennia, I got to the end. Through his wall I heard the shower gush on, then settle into a steady patter.

"Dad. Monsters aren't ever really real, right?"

"Who told you sometimes they were real?"

"Monie."

"Only teasing you."

"She said they live in the haunted tree. The noises I hear when I'm going to sleep, she said. Sellikins. What about sell-ekins?"

I explained what skeletons were, saying the word so he would hear it pronounced correctly. We played with his action figures on the pillow. Soon I could tell by the even way his conductor's cap heaved that he was nearly asleep. I squelched an urge to kiss him; my son hated physical affection. I studied his face, pretending I was admiring Mickey's gun. The shower cut to a sprinkle, then trickled to nothing. Zach was asleep.

I remembered the hat. I was so keen to get my hands on Melissa it had slipped my mind.

I stole as quietly as I could to where the spare hat was hidden under a pile of towels. Without warning the bathroom opened and Melissa breezed out in my robe and flew into the bedroom. She grabbed her flight bag with the Boston Symphony logo and slammed it on the bed. As it rocked in place she unzipped the top and snatched her flute. She played in her whistling way (the kids were asleep) but in a frenzy, head dipping, shoulders rolling, fingers flapping like wings of a bird after it leaps off a branch. With the same intensity she stood and whipped her hair back so it smacked her neck. She tossed the flute down and became absorbed in her hair, squeezing it with her fists. She loosened the robe. It was halfway down her back before she kicked shut the door. The ceiling fan revved up and began to hum. I heard the flight bag being zipped, harsh, fast, and crash to the floor.

I dashed back to Zach's room to swap the hats.

When I got back, I found Melissa indulging in one of her few self-luxuriating habits. She was stretched out naked on the bed, letting the ceiling fan dry her off. She was also using the time to floss her teeth, not being one to luxuriate without getting a chore out of the way, especially before a trip. I took the rocker facing the bed. The fan whispered soothing air into my hair. Melissa flossed vigorously, as was her style, and her breasts shook with every jerk of the floss. As a girl she had been shy; her breasts had been too small, then too large. Now, in adult life, she would sprawl stark naked and chat with a man, bare breasts jiggling as her fingers dragged dental floss through her teeth and a ceiling fan fluttered the hair between her legs. I watched her reach to discard a tangle of floss, left hand, and left breast, dangling over the night table, and uncross her legs for the fan. Twice I had seen a baby thrust out from this flesh. Twice I had seen her breasts swell with milk. I had clung to her body through pleasure and much pain. I contemplated Melissa with the mix of ownership and awe I felt whenever she stood before me naked, and I thought, *This is my wife and this is my life.* I would have swept her up in my arms right then, with the lewd and corny romance she adored, if only she'd *quit that damn flossing!*

"I want to talk about something," she said. "But now's not good."

"How you felt? How you felt before?"

"In another sec. That flight of mine's so idiotically early."

She discarded another tangle, arm out, a breast swinging free. She jammed a leg in my robe to help direct the flow of delicate air between her legs. I was so keyed up I had no patience for these weird marital intimacies, Melissa treating her body with exquisite nonchalance, and two lost souls being kept apart by something as ethereal as dental hygiene.

I had a hundred things to ask but instead snapped my fingers and tapped my head as if I'd forgotten to do Zach's hat. I backed out and went up to work in my study (on a crossword puzzle, to be honest).

I miscalculated the time, and she was fast asleep when I got back. But as I slipped into bed she stirred. She had programmed herself to wake, which she could do at will. Lately she'd been doing it a lot. Her arms swung around my neck, and I was flooded with her skin, raw from the shower. Every inch of her was dry but a spot behind a knee, a notch at the small of her back, and a silky strip inside her thighs. She was crazed with passion, frantic to make love. I knew this mood of Melissa's: she felt alone and lost in the dark, and there was a monster behind every tree, but I could still lead her home with the touch of my hands.

— 4 —

Peter ripped off his Mickey Mouse ears and got down to business. "It's a dirty job," he said, "but somebody's got to do it."

B. WEAR Simon store e sited! Veal in tears own lee.
Know hear ohs pleas (CHARLES)

"This ain't gonna be pretty," Peter said as he called up the story with a savage stroke, as if stamping out a cockroach. He eased off, then whacked again, the cockroach still crawling, *Stamp! Stamp! Stamp!*

"A piece of t-total, worthless crapola."

Peter had a hint of a stutter, so slight only I noticed. I've always had a soft spot for people with speech impediments.

"Total," he said, cleanly.

I was editing obituaries, the normal routine for people new to a copy desk. I did them till 4:00 A.M., the obit page deadline, then got a few "brights" (those short bizarre stories used as filler) as a reward. My shift would start with the sublime and end with the ridiculous.

A message flashed above the paragraph of relatives who had survived the death of Edna Jean Wellins, 87, for whom services were to be held Friday.

u can tell peter is having a good time
when he takes off his ears (SPERLING)

I wasn't certain who Sperling was. It had to be one of the two women working that night, Elaine or Sandy.

I typed: "better that than his pants." Then I backspaced it out because I wasn't sure whom I was communicating with, and I would never write that to a man. It was sloppy, allowing people to choose the name on their computer profiles. I wrote instead:

i like a man who loves his work (VEIL)

No reaction on either face. Edna was mourned and buried, her survivors listed, her volunteer work acknowledged, her eighty-seven years boiled down to three perfectly punctuated paragraphs in fastidious *Journal* obit style.

& may i extend condolences on yr jobberwacky, as
Zee Great Charlu insists on calling it (SPERLING)

i have jobberwacky? i never told i hired (VEIL)

nor i, and i here two years. tis said gregory gregory
never told he hired either (SPERLING)

yr kidding! he hired me! (VEIL)

ha! ha! we do need people desperately now
(SPERLING)

i always like to be needed desperately (VEIL)

Elaine smiled, which tipped me off that she was "Sperling." Her hand also rose to make sure the top button of her sweater was fastened; every time I looked she was adjusting something.

being needed is my weakness too (SPERLING)

"English," Peter was saying. "Doesn't our pretty little Mizzzzzz Simon s-speak English? What kind of warped, drug-crazed, tiny little brain comes up with sentences like this? This is gonna be good."

I examined Elaine, drank her in the way I always drink in a woman who has started a conversation with me. She was striking, long black hair flattering her pale yellow sweater, tight jeans, and high heels, one hanging from a toe. I was struggling for a way to resume our conversation when Sandy, the other woman, stopped at my desk on her way from the big dictionary and announced, "This is really *so* unfair."

What was so unfair was that the wrong woman had stopped by my desk. I don't know why, but that's always the case with me.

"You want the reason?" Sandy went on. "I'll give you the reason. It's because she's female, plain and simple."

In the subdued copy desk atmosphere her speaking out loud was like screaming; compared to Elaine (absorbed in her screen, checking an earring) Sandy appeared brazen and crude.

I said, voice recklessly loud, that I hadn't known Simon was a woman. Sandy, working herself into a congenial tizzy, bent over my desk to fill me in. I had never seen her up close: she had jittery eyes, an impatient mouth, and ponderous breasts that she heaped on my monitor as one might bang a gavel for silence. I had rarely heard her speak, except about her boyfriend, Brian, whom she droned on and on about. He sent her roses at the office. I couldn't miss that.

"Let me tell you the deal with her," she said, two finger-nails doing a little jitterbug on my next dear departed soul. "Let me clue you in."

She was giving the new guy the lowdown.

"A bum rap is what it is. She used to work overnights, a rim rat like us, just slogging away on the old lobster shift. So she and I are the only women here before Elaine, right? Okay, so she sucks as a feature writer, like big deal. She's here maybe a month? Gets off overnights and into features? And has a life that's, like, *normal?* And suddenly she's in *charge* of people. In charge of *men?* She's younger, too, than some of them. And they resent her for it. They hate her, if you want to know what's really going on here."

"I never met the woman," I said, suppressing an urge to say, "I never met the lady," because Sandy was so irritating. I looked over at Elaine, trying to include her, but that was impossible given the communication rules of the copy desk. For the first time I noticed that Elaine had green eyes.

"Sometimes she's a little jerky, okay," Sandy said, with her infuriating affability. She lifted a hand to smooth her hair. "Agreed, she's into astrology. But it shouldn't be her fault that she's a woman, that she's promoted over men. It bothers everyone, it threatens them. We're all real open-minded, but not when gender is concerned. Put a woman in charge and everyone goes totally whole hog nutso. It's fragile male egos. That's what it is."

"Only if they write crap-pola like this," Peter said as he hacked away at Simon's story. "It's not because they're women. That's simply not true."

Under Sandy's nails, where she couldn't see, a message popped up.

ignore everything sandy is saying.
she just getting her period (PETER)

"Prejudice is nothing new," I said. "Even among women themselves."

Elaine didn't look up, but Sandy said, "Too true, too true," leaning toward me more. "Even this desk, to an extent. Women're treated very, very, *very* different, if you haven't picked that up, in a subtle, insidious way."

does she realize she's radiating her tits? (PETER)

"I haven't really seen it much."

"It's not that bad here," Sandy said, "but on dayside it's a goddamn *zoo!* There's more bias than you can shake a stick at. Not here. Here they try. Even Peter here tries. Even Peter even."

Peter did not react, except to say, "Frankly, I think it's p-paranoia."

Sandy's nails stuck out, then clicked a two-step tango across my screen.

Look out! she's starting to hump yr desk! (PETER)

"I think I know the difference between reality and fantasy, my friend," she said. "I'm not paranoid. It's an attitude thing. Not everywhere. Here you do get respect. That I'm willing to admit."

imagine her standing there with no clothes on (PETER)

Elaine was still tuning us out, or pretending to. She had resumed her usual posture, focusing on the story she was editing, chin on her fist, as if the story were a confession of love she could not take at face value, despite how much she was dying to. Her green eyes were striking.

Sandy moved nearer to Peter and said, "And I know everyone says I'm paranoid, Peter, but it's only because they're all against me." She hung over his computer in a mock crazy-lady manner. "And I used to be indecisive, but now I'm not so sure."

When he did not respond to either gambit, leaving her facing him but theoretically in a conversation with me, she arched the upper half of her body back toward me and said, "Welcome Daniel, you're one of Charlie's Angels now. I know no one talks to anybody, but we are friendly. I talked Brian into a party last month, really. He has this huge place near the mountain, which we almost had. We're pretty decent. Except Peter here, of course."

she is built like a brick shit house (PETER)

"He's trying to ignore me," Sandy said.

Wot kind of underwear you see her in? i see pink bra w/ lace, matching bikini panties (PETER)

"That's Peter's way of showing affection," I said.

"Oh, I know that," she said. "I know what a sweet guy he is on the inside. He can't hide that. Not from me."

She took a little step, straightening her back to my side so her body was finally in normal alignment.

When Peter continued to ignore her she said, "I have now said my little piece for the sisterhood, the wonderful wonderful sisterhood, and I can go back to my desk like a good little girl."

She moved off, scratching her nails across my screen as she turned.

imagine her naked breasts bopping
up and down as she walks (PETER)

Because it was Sunday night there was little copy, and Peter and I got an early "good night." As usual, he gave me a ride. He's one of those men who hardly talk. He could go an entire shift and utter three sentences. Even his screentops were terse. I am, frankly, in awe of men like that.

"One thing," he said. "Sandy does have nice t-tits."

This was a classic conversation starter for us. Today he had driven forty miles each way to visit his children, but of course it wasn't mentioned, except for a problem with the car heater he had discovered on the road. In fact, I knew he saw his kids on Sundays only because I overheard Sandy mention it. She was an expert on Peter, in that way some women are experts on certain men they work with.

"I did happen to notice, as a matter of fact," I said. "She was leaning all over me, practically. She was just trying to be nice. I mean, I think she seems to be a nice person, not phony nice but really nice. You can tell that."

I always overflowed with words when I spoke to Peter. I couldn't stop the flood, adding, "And she's very nice to you. You can see that."

This meant, I think she'll sleep with you if you want, and you wouldn't have to do too much romancing. Forget the alleged boyfriend, Brian.

"Too bad she's crazy," Peter said, which meant, let Brian have her. It also meant, ironically, too bad she's a woman. "Much *too* crazy."

This meant, I know I could sleep with her, but I don't have the patience for what I'd have to go through to get her into bed.

"Jackie went crazy when we s-split," Peter said.

I don't like people mentioning others I don't know by name, the way Susan Spiser did on Halloween, but from Peter it gushed like a confession. He was pulling out of the parking lot and accelerating. On Sundays he always drove like a teenager who'd just fought with his girlfriend.

"She just fucking freaked."

"She blame you? Jackie? She make it all your goddamn fault?"

"Lawyers. She blamed herself. She blamed me. No way, my friend."

Other men amaze me with their reserve, their lack of a need to work things out by talking. Sometimes I think they're a different species from me.

"Typical. I guess it's typical. Fucking typical."

"Yeah," he said. "You do amicable differences?"

"You can call it that," I said. "A mess either way. Just no fucking way around it."

We slipped into the idiom of men sharing feelings: boot-camp profanity. It's a secret of male relationships, much maligned of late, how intimate such conversations are.

"That reminds me," I said. "I ever tell you my tit epiphany?"

Peter laughed, tapping the wheel. He loved my theories about women.

"Lay it on me, my man. This t-t-tit epiphany!"

"My breast revelation. So I'm sitting in Central Park one summer afternoon—I used to wander around the city a lot—pining away for some ex-girlfriend. I can't remember her name. Just her tits."

Peter howled, tapping his forehead against the steering wheel. He loved it when I belittled women, especially on a Sunday.

"Anyhow, she managed to let me know she has this brand-new boyfriend, and I was going crazy. That she'd do to him things I taught her, special, secret things. You know?"

"Oh, I know."

"I was imagining him in bed with her, pawing away at her boobs. The little slut. What the fuck's her name? Great boobs, though."

I sounded like a world-class misogynist when I talked to Peter. I was pretty convincing, too. He was rounding a corner, palms spinning on the wheel. He was also reaching under the dashboard to check the heater because he believed it was not working properly.

"Then I look around and here are all these girls strolling, walking dogs, sunbathing on those big rocks. I mean, it's summer, and they're all wearing T-shirts, if you get my drift. So I think how if there's one thing this world has no shortage of, it's female breasts. There're a million of them. Hanging around, so to speak. These chicks!"

"Broads!" he said.

He chuckled, two boys saying dirty words. But it was not yet time for our Sunday night mantra.

"So I think, what makes one pair special? With all the tits in this world? It's when you think one pair is special, there's a shortage, one pair's somehow unique. That's what makes love possible."

He was mulling it over, but, in his fashion, saying nothing. He had his hand under the dashboard to feel if heat was blowing out. He began banging on metal, and through my legs I felt the car floor vibrate.

"Jackie's tits b-belonged to the world."

I was struck dumb by how he said this. He banged under the dash one last time, really hard.

"I found out later."

He turned onto an exit ramp so sharp my body pressed into the seat. I had the sensation that my life had been a buildup for this moment, racing down the highway ramp with Peter. I had been sliding down a kind of chute since I'd left. Words were propelled from my mouth onto the windshield, to burst on the guardrail unraveling beside me.

"There was one guy I knew about."

"A guy you knew about."

"Named Barry Alter."

"Barry Alter."

"Something had to be going on. I found a letter. A fucking letter."

"A letter."

"A fucking letter. Didn't bother me that much, given everything I knew. Kind of knew. Wasn't the first time she did it, you can bet your sweet life. She couldn't really deny it. Although you know they can do anything. Any fucking thing. Any fucking thing they want."

I fell back on our usual practice of making women out to be fantastic creatures, whose traits we classified with the fascination of scientists describing the beauty of a microbe deadly enough to wipe out the human race. It was what made them worth studying, as one might study boa constrictors because they strangle prey the size of a horse.

"And what'd she say?"

"Same bullshit. What they say. What's she supposed to say? What's she gonna say? You know the kind of shit they say."

Peter said nothing. He pulled up to the curb in front of my apartment and shut the lights, but left the engine on to check the heat, which was finally working, shedding furry air in my lap. Once I parked with friends like this for hours, and now I was doing it again. Being men, it would never occur to us to meet for lunch, as surely as it would never occur to us to buy thoughtful little gifts for each other's birthdays.

"Yeah, those chicks," I said, ready for our Sunday night mantra.

"Those *girls*."

"Those laaaayyyyydies."

"Dames. *Damsels.*"

"Babes."

"Broads."

"Cunts."

"Yes," he said. "*Cunts.*"

We let the word wash around in the car until we were spotless clean.

"The funny thing is," Peter said, "first you get really horny. You wanna fuck anything that walks. Even ones like Sandy look good."

"I thought Elaine looked pretty good tonight. I really noticed her for the first time."

He decided to check his tires rather than answer. He got out, leaving the door open and the ignition chiming for him to please remove his key.

"Sandy's not that bad," I said when he got back in. "Like I said, she's not phony nice. I think she's genuinely nice. She just tries to cover it up so men will like her more. Women are weird like that. "

"Yeah," he said, then added, "Gotta take a leak."

We marched together into the empty lot next to my apartment, to a corner that was dark and also had a mound of clean snow around a tree. A secret yet monumental joy for men is urinating on fresh snow. We followed protocol: he turned one direction, I the other, so as to not see each other but not appear to be avoiding seeing each other.

"First you get horny," Peter called from his corner, "then you get lonely. And listen man, horny is easier."

———————————

I didn't go upstairs but back into the empty lot to sit on a tree stump surrounded by snow. I had to think things to torture myself. Am I the only one who does this? I ponder something that I know will torment me, and not only do I do it, but I do it with rabid, masochistic zeal. I recalled details about Barry Alter I hadn't ruminated over for a while. For example, the letter was on a lined hotel pad, sky blue, with "Atlanta Marriott Marquis" on top. It was written and rewritten, with dozens of versions underneath. I dredged up lines: "I keep trying to forget it happened but I can't, you bastard." "I fought with every last ounce of my strength but it was too strong!" And I had forgotten this gem: "I gave in only when I knew it was inevitable, that I couldn't stop our love—we had no right, but we also had no choice!!!"

Melissa had made a decision, that was at the bottom of my pain. She had deliberately let someone into the circle of sexual intimacy that enclosed us, which made marriage bearable, at its worst, and a gift from the gods at its best. Yes, I thought, looking up at the lightening sky, that's why it's called "cheating" and being "unfaithful." It was not that Melissa had been attracted to someone else and wanted to do it; it was that she had thought it over and *decided* to.

The light had seeped down through the bare branches, and the tree stump was a block of ice freezing onto my thighs. For the first time all month I felt lonely, in a way I hadn't since before I met Melissa, a loneliness not inside my head but welling up around me like ocean waves. I had to reach back years to recognize it, back to the days I wandered the city alone, and I did, bit by bit.

I peeled myself off the stump. A mean wind slapped my face. I walked, thinking, I am here, on this street. *I really did it!*

The other houses were like mine, neglected Victorians with wooden staircases zigzagging up to a rented attic room. I passed another empty lot (there are still quite a few up here) and through it I could see the mountain in the distance, since the sky was light and there weren't any leaves. The cold truth is that I never confronted Melissa. I waited for her to confess, prepared to be shocked and deeply hurt. I gave her the chance, no one could dispute that. I don't know why I let it ride. Like running away, it was on the premise that I'd never have to explain, and here I was, already trying to, even though not a soul was listening.

My life was a mess before I ran off, I don't deny it. I don't mean the Barry Alter business, but my whole life was a fake. I lied to everyone. I lied to myself. I never worked for the *New York Times*. I told myself I had, to psyche myself for the interview at *The Journal*. When I decided to run away I actually believed it; in conversations with myself I asked why I was unsatisfied even though I was at the top of my profession. I'm just a pathetic dreamer, that's what I am. Even the night I wandered the city and met Melissa I was probably pretending. I'd imagine I was John Lennon strolling Fifth Avenue incognito. I'd turn in to Washington Square believing I was heading for a gig playing backup guitar for Bob Dylan in a Bleecker Street cafe. I'd pick out a woman on a bench and pretend I had to tell her it was over. She'd plead and beg, but I had to be free. When I spotted Melissa playing that corny snake-charmer melody, I asked how I could give this dark-eyed beauty up. Then I became a Broadway impresario about to pluck a ravishing flutist from obscurity and make her a star.

I was the goddamn Walter Mitty of Washington Square.

And that was the least of it. There's more to my stupid charade. I of course never wrote any best-selling books. I could have, I believe it to this day, but it never worked out. They were fabulous ideas, they really were, but they never got out of my head, my arguments with myself. And I was having one now, a furious debate in my head, alone, walking past an empty lot, imagining I was talking to a woman who was hanging on every word.

The staircase to my apartment clung to the side wall, and as I climbed I could feel the empty lot and the stretch of yards expanding at my back. I got in the door and felt relieved. I had furnished the place exclusively from yard sales and furniture set out as trash. It was necessary to do this. I looked out the window at the yards shuffling off along fences and hedges and haggard, sun-bleached poles. In the hazy morning chill every-thing looked exhausted. I had only this cheesy little radio, which cost fifty cents at a tag sale. I tuned it to the station from the nearby college, and heard the lost song.

I knew the song from Montclair but never caught the name. It's hard to catch the words, but it seems to be about setting someone you love free from her private demons. All I can really understand is the word "surrender," which is re-peated over and over. The song brought back a night I danced with Ramona just weeks before I left. We used to sing along together, I recalled, as I sat heavily on my couch. The fetid cushions responded by exhaling a dank aroma that aspired to be mildew but hadn't grown rancid enough yet.

The night I danced with Ramona I had been debating with Melissa whether to cut down an ancient oak in the yard that was tilting, a rotting tree once struck and scarred by lightning that the kids believed to be haunted. Melissa was afraid it would crash in a storm and hurt the children, to say nothing of us or the house. I knew it was diseased and dying but was hoping against hope there was a way to save it. Melissa ac-cused me of not caring about the children and plunged into her wronged mistress mood. I spoke with romantic fervor of the beauty and dignity of a century-old oak, the magic of a child's imagination, and then with incisive logic about the improb-ability of its toppling onto the house. My speech inspired a mood shift: Melissa turned sad, distracted, a woman of mysterious sorrows. I kept arguing to save the tree, ego being what it is.

I had gone up to the attic with Ramona to study the angle of the tree.

The attic had been my place of dreams. I imagined all my creations there. I had a writing table with papers and books and a mini-stereo to ease the long hours of mental labor I was perpetually planning. The equipment, carted from Greenwich Village, hadn't been used there except for crossword puzzles and conversations with myself, wonderful books that never got out of my head. It was the place where I imagined, the place where I dreamed, the place where I would begin. I read reviews and was invigorated when a book earned a scathing attack. I had even pinned a few on my bulletin board that were deliciously malevolent. Every now and then I read them out loud.

As soon as we got to the attic I turned on my stereo. I pretended to play along on guitar, and Ramona started to dance. I am, I must add, perhaps the finest air guitarist in all of rock and roll. I have a style all my own, bluesy, soulful, ragged, and wild. People jump from their seats when they hear me, and I blow them all away. Everyone who's heard me knows what I mean.

On the floor next to my table was a cardboard box in which I had old papers, also carted from the Village and never opened in Montclair. The carton said "Attic—Big Room" on both sides in magic marker for the movers, Melissa in her organized mode. It held photos, letters, newspaper clippings, old poems, all to plumb for material, to put my chaotic life in order and fashion that order into art. The problem was that when I went through the pile I got so depressed I couldn't do anything. Other people must have mementos like this, but I can never comprehend how they manage to live with them.

Melissa came to the attic landing and called, "You can see it better here." I joined her at the window while Ramona waltzed around by herself. Melissa was in a T-shirt from the Boston campaign that said, "It's Better in the Woods!" She didn't look up. She had sunk deeper into her mysterious sorrows; after Boston she took long swims in a thick, molasses-like misery. I saw it at the airport even before she got into the car.

"That tree has to go," she said, staring into absolute darkness.

I felt some menace in her body's nearness, a kind of erotic threat. I caressed her arm in an effort to diffuse it. She didn't pull away, but it felt like she had.

"Just don't. Just don't ask. I'm terrified of that tree."

Her eyes were hypnotic as they fixed on mine, large and dark, with a truly spellbinding grief. I'm not exaggerating; all this anguish, this *yearning*, was flowing from her.

"I'm so afraid," she said. "I'm so afraid."

She ducked down the stairs. The bedroom door clicked shut behind her.

I went up to Ramona. "It's the lost song, Dad," she said, pointing.

"Gimme mah ax, Babe," I said, suddenly jubilant.

Ramona knew the drill and handed me an imaginary guitar. I played a few fiery riffs, bopping around. She clapped, and said, "Play me, Dad!"

At eight she wasn't easy to lift anymore, but I scooped her up, got her against me like a guitar, and strummed her stomach. My arms ached and I had to set her down. We jigged about the room, which had the sturdy feeling of a solid old house, treetops out the windows, empty sky.

I bumped the radio louder, which Ramona, already half-teenager, loved. Chords squirted out and splashed my chest. Her body got lively and light as we hopped around. We did an elaborate slow dance. I dipped her backward. I was vibrating with love, pulsating through me like electricity, the current flowing from Ramona's eyes, each contact shocking me with how much I loved this other human being. I let it quiver through me, a maddening, monstrous love, a drug so sweet the next hit would kill me, but be worth it, to die like this, cymbal crashing at my back, the bass thundering against my feet.

She faced me like rock groups do, close enough to kiss, singing into a microphone rigged from a vacuum cleaner. As I sat recalling it on my smelly couch, I pretended to play and strummed air as tinny chords scratched from the radio. With Ramona I had gone wild: I slung the guitar on my hips, strutting, prancing, bouncing up on my toes. I spun her off, and as she came back I felt her eager weight in my wrists, the strain of it, and on the creaking wood floor of the house below, where Melissa was waiting in the bedroom for me to end my dance with Ramona and begin another kind of dance with her.

I lived all those years with a fear that I'd burst.

That was clear to me now as I sat on my couch, throbbing in time. Last summer Melissa and I stole into a forest to make love, but did not understand at the time how scary this was. When I danced with Ramona I was exploding with love for the girl who was my daughter, whom I held the first minute she was alive, and who was shoving me off, only to come back, on the next beat, eyes tangled up in mine.

The song was ending, and she allowed a fantasy she alone knew I had: I raised the guitar over my head to swing down like a scythe to signal the band to stop. She laughed. I laughed. The child in her joined the child in me in a game, the game of every dance, the child in her almost gone for good, the one in me daring, impishly, to show its face before running from the room to hide.

I brought down my guitar. On my signal, all at once, the music stopped.

— 5 —

Melissa and I made love in the woods because we had no choice. For close to a month we'd been sharing a one-room cabin with the kids and hadn't had a moment alone. The day before, in desperation, we made an appointment to have sex. We sneaked back according to plan, got inside, and sat on the musty bunk. We felt bashful, pressured. Melissa, nervous Ramona or Zach would wander back, kept getting up to glance through the window. After a while we went out and sat on a rock in the sun. She relaxed and stretched out her legs, her feet childlike in my sandals. The rock was hot and hard. Melissa sprawled out; in the sudden brightness her skin took on a glow. I sat salivating, looking her over as a lion looks over a group of spectators lining his cage, deciding who to bite first. In the end we hatched the plan that had us tramping into the forest, holding hands, and carrying a blanket.

This was last summer. I had just gotten back from my father's funeral, Gideon Bloom had just died, and my alleged career was in its usual comatose state. I don't want to go into all the gruesome details but all I did was sit around and dream. I was also starting to suspect something going on between

Melissa and Barry Alter, although I was still in the beginning paranoid stage. I wasn't exactly feeling like the king of the jungle.

We took a dirt road to the trails. It was very hot, but Melissa never minded the heat. In fact, she blossomed in summer, brimming with color and flush from exercise and fresh air, as opposed to winter when she was always cold. She wore hiking shorts cut from jeans, ragged on her thighs, a Tanglewood T-shirt she had designed herself, which she gave to me but still wore, and new waterproof hiking boots. We were looking for the Lost Mountain Trail because our cover was that we were hiking to look for deer. The real reason was it led to a secluded part of the forest packed with pines, and the ground, cushioned with pine needles, would be soft enough for two lovers to lie down on.

"How're the new shoes, Lissie?" I said. "Getting dirty yet?"

The boots were expensive and she rarely treated herself to expensive things. Although she bought them precisely for hiking trails she was stepping around mud, afraid of getting them grimy.

"So far they're okay," she said, as her feet landed on a dry spot next to a pool of mud. "What's with this Lissie business again?"

I don't know why I called her Lissie; I knew she hated it.

"I don't know."

"I prefer Melissa, thank you. I went to enough trouble to de-Marcia myself way back when. This it?"

We slipped into the cool forest by a tree marked with blue paint.

"Must be," I said. "These blue blazes are what we want."

I always played outdoorsman with Melissa. Every relationship has myths, he the solid rock, she the whirlpool of emotion. One of ours was that I was Daniel Boone, rough, raw, with an instinctive sense of direction.

"We're walking north," I said. "I can feel it."

The trail curved up along a small rise. We stepped on pebbles and twigs in a bracing chill. The air we breathed felt deep as the forest, thick with musk. Our feet flattened twigs, which sunk and nestled, crunching. Melissa wrapped the blanket around her.

"I hope so," she said. "We don't have that much time."

I was feeling pretty good that morning. I had come across a review in the *Times* of a rock concert by a band I had never heard of. (Lately I had broadened my reading to include reviews of concerts as well as books and movies.) To my delight the review had been indignant, smacking its lips as it ground the banal music to bits. I read it twice, knowing every venomous word was true. I asked Melissa if I could read it to her, but she was immersed in a piece in the *Science Times*, headlined "New Puzzle On Sex Life Of Octopus." No one else at the table wanted to hear it. The review gave me quite a boost, though. I looked at the other people and thought, *some day they'll think back to this morning and say, "Can you believe it, Daniel Weil used to come here—Daniel Weil! He'd sit with us in the dining hall. I mean, he was sitting* right *there!"*

As the trail narrowed I let Melissa go ahead. I analyzed the mechanics of her hips, how they swiveled as she lifted her legs to step higher and find a dry spot. She would shove her backside out until the lead foot settled in the twigs, then pull it back in as the other foot caught up. I could see the muscle at the back of her thigh harden into a ridge, then soften, harden, soften.

"This is definitely right?" she said. "We have to pick them up at four."

"Trust me, my love."

The path turned muddy, though it was still well-trod. I thought I should do something romantic, given the nature of our mission, but couldn't come up with anything that wasn't too corny, even for Melissa.

"I feel we're going off on a secret tryst," I said. "Like we're married to other people but sneaking off into the woods to do it with each other."

It was lame but the best I could come up with. As soon as I said it I thought about Barry Alter, which was a real downer since I was feeling so good from the review. I hadn't yet found the letters.

"It does," she said, perhaps too knowledgeably. "Think of the excitement! Forbidden fruit. An illicit liaison. L'aaaizonnn! As they say."

This confirmed it.

"Like us."

She tried to lean back into me as she spoke, but the trail was too steep and she almost tripped. "Has to be an amazing turn-on," she added.

Believing that Melissa had been unfaithful made her repulsive, because she betrayed me in such a fundamental way, yet more sexual because of the nature of the betrayal. Suspecting, without knowing for sure, made her only more sexual.

The denim strings of the shorts, withered white, swung between her legs as she turned to ask, "Are we near Woodstock?"

"Only thirty miles south. As the endangered crow flies."

She laughed; no matter what, making Melissa laugh was a great joy. Her poor sense of direction was another myth we maintained. The thirty miles was of course a wild guess. I wasn't even sure it was south.

"You know, Lissie, we never did it in the woods before."

I don't know why I kept calling her Lissie. She really hated it.

"Or anywhere outside," she said. "One of the few places, I guess."

She pulled herself over a high rock. Her shirt bounced up and I saw a glimmer of sweat-shined back. I considered gripping her hips to help her up, then bringing my hands up under the shirt.

"We were outside at the Reiners' July Fourth party!"

"Not outside in the woods!" she said. "They live on Upper Mountain Avenue!"

"Yeah, but their yard's as big as a forest preserve. That chaise you sat on near the pool that kept making noise!"

"But no one *did* anything. There, in their yard?"

"Who did? Some secret boyfriend?"

"Very funny. What in the world are you talking about?"

It occurred to me that I had no idea what I was talking about. It had started as a joke, but I'd lost track of it.

"I mean the Smucklers," I said. "The Smucklers' noise. Noi*ses*, I should say."

"Oh, *them*," Melissa said. "They were practically *necking*. She said—correct me if I'm wrong—'hot dogs with mustard always turn me on.' What a character she is. Both of them."

She twisted as she said it, swaying as her foot sunk down. Her breasts heaved forward, filling out the T-shirt to what had to be its limit.

"Melissa!"

"Now you're talking weird. I mean, *they* are truly weird!"

"They'd do it on a roof!"

"Remember the recycling meeting? We couldn't get a quorum 'cause they were busy screwing!"

"Supposedly," I said.

"She is a big talker. Everyone talks about it."

"It's all marketing, she always said. I can't believe I once worked for her. She's very into her image. Her whole business is image. That's fashion for you."

"Who isn't," Melissa said. "Why do you think I changed my name? And my image of myself did get better. I hated being a mousy little Marcia."

I wanted again to touch her, but I was afraid.

"I heard she had a kinky affair when they were separated," Melissa said. "On her office couch! She told Carol. Bragged! Nutty."

I froze.

"You're kidding."

She took time to find a place to step, found one, and said, "Anyone roaming around when you were there? Some employee, I heard."

"Could have been a hundred guys, maybe it was a hundred. Probably put out the story herself. Would think it's cool, promote her sex fiend image."

"What sex fiend image?"

"She has this sex fiend image. The whole office talked about it. Why she told Carol? I mean bragging? Can I ask you something, Lissie?"

"Ask."

"Did you do it at Woodstock?"

"Do it?"

"Like, do it do it. In the woods. At Woodstock."

"I told you a hundred times. I told you the big deal I did."

"I want the truth."

She laughed. It had come out as a joke. Melissa never understood the complex feelings I had about her sexual experiences with others. The trail widened and she got next to me.

"Me and Shula—she was Sheila then—we go off into the woods. We take off our bras, stuff them in our pocketbooks, and walk around."

"Wait a minute. With nothing on?"

"Our shirts of *course* we put back on. Tie-dyed. Mine was purple, a huge lopsided peace sign. I'll never forget it. Ugly, but I loved it. I felt hip in it, for a change. Instead of some Miss Goody Two Shoes flutist heading for snooty fancy Juilliard."

"Anyone notice?"

"No one noticed Shula, of course. She hardly had to *wear* a bra. But boys always stared at my boobs."

"You have the most beautiful boobs in the world."

"I doubt it. They're too big. Later Shula got really stoned and did a dance thing topless in some mud. That got a little attention, a little."

"Weren't they once too small?"

"Once they were. Then all of a sudden."

"So they were the right size for about a week."

"About a month. In seventh grade. End of summer."

She was serious.

"You're a riot," I said.

"And you didn't go, of course. Why?"

It was revenge, and I had it coming. I had been teased over the years that Melissa, the straight-laced, classical music student, had been to Woodstock and I hadn't. She loved hearing me explain why.

"Because it was too commercial. Because everybody else went. Another love-in or be-in or protest march that'd be forgotten in a week."

"You sure had that one figured."

The forest opened up, and the trees spaced out. The ground was uneven, like the sea in a storm. Huge half-sunken boulders were all around.

"So never in the woods, not us," I said.

"Not yet. Hey, we forgot camping."

"That doesn't count. You know what I mean."

Ever in the woods with anyone else? I needed to know.

"So, if you didn't do it at Woodstock, Lissie, where *did* you do it?"

"In apartments. I don't know."

Our voices could be heard for miles, like church bells. The woods grew thicker, the ground bumpier, with tree roots gnarled and twisting into others along the trail. The air was brilliant but not sunny. It had a mystical soothing quality, as if the light had no source and we could get lost in it forever.

"The first time you were crazy."

"I'm not talking about *that*," she said, her voice ringing like a bell.

"You've been saying that forever."

"I'm talking before we met. The second time I was crazy."

She had slept around a bit, I knew. It was twenty years ago, and she was a free woman at the end of the sixties. Rationally, politically, morally, philosophically, intellectually, religiously, I had no reason, surely no right, to question anything she had done. Yet, despite all that, it killed me every time I thought of it. I can't explain why. It's embarrassing just to admit it. I mean, it's a political gaucherie to intimate I ever even *thought a* thing like this.

"The famous promiscuous stage?" I said, feigning curiosity. It was one of the few subjects I had Melissa buffaloed on.

"You're exaggerating again. Compared to Shula, I barely did a thing! Little Miss Goody Two Shoes again. Can we sit?"

We sat on a log that was white, had no bark, and felt rotted enough to crumble. Melissa folded the blanket in her lap and leaned on me. I responded by pulling her against me in the romantic spirit I had failed to create on my own. My fingers spiraled down past the crook of the elbow to the underside of her wrist where the skin was tight, soft, and miraculously hairless.

"I was acting out. That's why I went crazy the second time. I was looking for a father's love. Corny, I know. I still do in all my flirtations. I learned that from Dr. Fine and Dr. Felder—Feld. I was looking for it with them, too, which is why I couldn't end therapy with either one."

I felt compelled to chronicle my personal history to Melissa and often went back to describe an experience that was particularly fascinating. She rarely went in for it, but when she did she sounded like an oracle.

"I was acting out the same dynamic when I met you."

"What about that guy in the loft?"

"Loft. What guy?"

"The West Village. The toilet backing up."

"I can't believe you remember that. And I was putting in a diaphragm!"

"I thought you were just using the bathroom."

This was too trivial a distinction for her to bother with. She picked dirt off her shoes with a stick. I could make out the label on her bra.

"Shula once said there's a Zen of putting in a diaphragm. Like believing you can fit it and then everything working perfectly on the first try? The Zen archer doesn't aim, and that's why he hits the bull's eye."

I decided to ask outright if she had ever made love in the woods. But something stopped me. A man and woman were picking their way toward us.

They came to the log and asked, "You guys heading for the waterfall?"

"The pine forest," I said. "We're looking for deer."

"They only come out at dawn and dusk," the woman said in a way that got on my nerves.

"Is that way right?" Melissa asked. "The pine forest?"

I could have strangled her. She knew I would never ask.

The couple disagreed with each other and offered no help.

"Love your shirt," the woman said. "Clever, very clever. The idea that Mozart would say that."

Melissa thanked her, too modest to add she had designed it herself. The man contemplated Mozart's grimacing face on Melissa's chest and the words in eighth notes beneath it. He was one of those jerky guys who has to read everything out loud.

He read, "I composed music early to be at Tanglewood sooner. Tanglewood blah blah blah, Lenox, Massachusetts. Where it's better in the woods! For ticket information call—"

"I think we get the picture, Jerry," the woman said.

The man looked at her, then back at Melissa's shirt, baffled.

"It's so spooky seeing others out here," I said. "It's eerie."

The couple agreed with each other this time. As they shuffled off the man glanced back at Melissa's shirt. Soon the forest swallowed them up.

"I think they were off making love in the woods," Melissa said. "That's why they were so awkward."

Melissa imagined other couples had wild sex lives. I, on the other hand, could never quite believe other people regularly had sex.

"Awkward? He seemed to notice our blanket."

"No he didn't."

We crossed a stream, which purred in our ears on the plank bridge, then faded out.

"Is it at all possible that we're lost?"

"You always think we're lost. I know exactly where we are. Exactly."

I had to select a new trail where two converged. The one the couple came on had to be wrong. It wouldn't have been so dumb to bring a trail map.

"So, any boyfriends you forgot to tell me about?"

"I don't think I told you *every*body. I have to report a flirtation, though."

On both sides of the trail the terrain threw me off-balance. Everywhere I looked the ground dropped precipitously, suggesting terrible falls.

"Who, Barry Alter?"

"You knew? That it was him?"

"You've been jabbering nonstop. I know he's madly in love with you."

"He just *thinks* he is. That divorce of his was so horrible."

"I thought he was just after your ass."

"That's all at first. But his attention is such a turn-on. It's okay if I'm honest, right? He *notices* what I wear. He has a way of *facing* me when we sit together. He really *looks* when he looks at me. It's so obvious."

This was my fear. Melissa's weaknesses were part of her lessons.

"So, what's new with him now?"

"He's trying for this Europe job. Says he can perform again maybe."

All Melissa's associates fantasized about performing again. I kept tabs on who pulled it off and took pride that very few had.

"And he's still after you."

"After me? Whatever I wear, he just keeps staring."

She groaned, shaking her head.

"I know he has the hots for me. But I'm eating it up. I admit it, okay? It's like, okay? *Honestly* okay?"

She could not speak this way if she were really sleeping with him.

"Then we had to review the presentation? And he's talking to my breasts. The whole time. The board noticed, I'm sure. They're very uptight."

"Not very subtle."

"I'll say. Like that guy in the couple was."

"He was?"

"She noticed it, too. Obviously."

"As long as you don't do anything," I said.

"One more thing. I have to tell you everything. After the presentation we're walking in a park in Boston and suddenly he has this straw basket. Wine, cloth napkins, two cute little glasses. To celebrate all the pledges we got he kisses me on the lips, *quick,* but *not* on the cheek. The lips. Smack on the lips."

Melissa was an expert on the precise calibrations of physical affection.

"I want to say outright it wasn't on the cheek. It was very romantic, but I think I drew the line. I know I did."

I was either the most trusting husband or the biggest fool.

This is how it works when you suspect someone of an affair: you choose one opportunity they had and convince yourself that it started then. Evidence uncannily appears, piles up, and proves it beyond a doubt. I had settled on Tanglewood. At the time I had nothing solid, and Melissa had no idea I suspected. I knew men were attracted to her and that she enjoyed it. (I had previously obsessed on an assistant conductor in Los Angeles and a cellist in Houston, among others, both of whom were quite smitten with her, according to her reports.) I knew Barry Alter was also crazy about her, but I trusted her, even though she was alone with him in far-off settings and he pulled the kind of silly romantic stunts Melissa adored. I didn't have a doubt in my mind.

"Let's stop a second," Melissa said. "I have to tie my shoes."

We sat on a rock so ridged it seemed to grin up at us. It was cold as I dropped down. It had ledges, as if layers of rock had been stacked. The view was spectacular, sun sparkling through leaves. I felt the smoothness of the air in a forest, endless trees, the scent of earth rising around us.

"He's also very pent-up," she said. "Egotistical. Such a comedown from his prodigy days. There's something scary about him, like—" she unstrung the lace of a boot "—time bomb-ish."

"As long as he doesn't go off in your face."

"He won't. I'm a big flirt, I know, but I'm in control. Okay?"

"Okay, so," I said. "I finally met Sophie."

"The last of the harem."

Before he died, my father lived with a series of women whose names I didn't know. After his stroke, and after my mother's death, these women had taken care of him. I think there was a woman there cooking for him the day he came home from the funeral. The ratio is about ten women to every man in my father's retirement community. I lost track of who they were, and every time I called another one answered. I talked to my father through them, since after his stroke he couldn't communicate at all. I knew the last one was named Sophie; she had called to say he died.

"You didn't tell me how it went. Did you tell everybody I was in San Francisco, that it was impossible?"

"There's no everybody to tell anything anymore."

I took a breath of sleek, tranquil air. Yes, there was no one left even to make excuses to.

"So how'd it go?" She began working the other boot.

"The house was filled with strangers, all women. She kept introducing me by saying, 'This is the son.' And she kept saying my name was Don. 'This is Don,' she'd say. 'He's the *son*.'

"I corrected her, and she started calling me Ron. She was hard of hearing, and I didn't want to embarrass her. I felt bad for her, and then everybody was calling me Ron, which in a minute became Ronald. I don't know."

I kept thinking about a line I heard on a television show, about people dying of AIDS. The man said that when any human being dies it's a library burning, a voluminous collection of dreams, fears, memories, ambitions, desires, a library of human experience up in smoke. My father's death was this, but quietly so. I never knew what was stored in his library. He never talked about it when he was healthy, and in the end he couldn't talk about anything. The meaning of his death was kept secret from me, like his life.

"I should get a real job," I said. "What am I trying to prove?"

"You don't want to have a mid-life crisis on vacation in the woods."

"With you next to me I only want one thing," I said. "Especially now."

She loved this, and leaned so heavily on my shoulder the ridges of the rock cut viciously up through my pants.

"I don't have to have a mid-life crisis," she said. "I had two already. I can skip it and go directly to nervous breakdown."

She pulled away, cool hands on my arms.

"It was tough in Lenox," she said. "Musicians are all nuts."

"You used to be a musician."

"I'm *still* a musician," she said.

It pleased me to see her become defensive about this.

"And I used to be nuts. And yes, you should get a real job. I thought you wanted to work on your projects. I wish I could cut down on the travel."

"You've been saying that for years."

"I don't mind paying for most everything, Daniel."

"I worry about things I know can't be true. I think my ship's finally coming in—I mean, my whole life's one, it's just one, one big, *almost*."

"Shhhh!"

I felt her fingernails tease my neck. She was directing my attention to a deer browsing under a tree. The deer raised its head, gave us a serious stare, then skittered off, bounding over a series of logs. The click of its hoofs kicked a hole in the stillness, squeezed through, and shouted back to where we sat.

"Just look," Melissa said.

"So much for only dawn and dusk. They said on that nature walk I took that there were too many and they were starving. Monie started crying."

"She's getting so tender," Melissa said. "So vulnerable."

She held the blanket around her shoulders. "It's cooler. Feel it?"

"I actually can, Lissie. If we put the blanket on pine needles we won't be cold. Although I hope to find better ways to warm us."

This was further effort on my part to be romantic, but in the setting it sounded like a practical tip for surviving in the great outdoors.

"We'd better get going," she said. "I'm getting cold again."

We stood, legs aching, and went back to the trail. We were uncertain which way to go. I made a decision and hoped it was right.

"Under the pines will be best," I said. "You'll see."

"Remember those other summers?" she said. "I'd sneak into your sleeping bag while the kids were asleep. Or vice versa."

"How could I forget."

"If Monie woke now and saw you in my bunk it would be horrible," Melissa said. "She'd know."

"She'd know?"

"Kids know," Melissa said. "On some level."

"Are we talking about your first crisis? In college?"

"You need lines between some things. Are we there yet?"

"It's down this trail, I think, beyond those trees. It looks like the pine forest I was tracking for us. I smelled pine. I *knew* I smelled pine."

"Delicious smell," she said. "I knew you'd find it."

"Pine needles are the softest thing around. I slept on them camping."

My hand was on her bare shoulder, under a damp film of heat.

"With who, the famous Suzy Q.?"

"Yeah, Suzanne. Suzy. How did you know?"

"I know everything about you. You told me *everything* about that relationship. The famous sleeping bag acrobat." She bopped me with her hip. She did it too hard, and we lost our balance for a second, because we were walking flat against each other. "And I probably smell. I mean, I haven't had a real shower in a month."

"You're so romantic."

"We're not lost, are we?" she asked. "Remember, the kids are at four. Four-fifteen to pick them up absolute latest."

I realized I wasn't sure where we were.

"Got to be this way," I said.

"It better be."

"Can I ask you something, Lissie?"

"If it's not my crisis, sure."

"Did you ever make love in the woods? I mean like with *anybody*?"

"In the woods. I don't. No, I don't think so."

"What do you mean, I don't *think* so."

"I mean, I don't *think* so. I don't know."

"Did you ever want to? Fantasize?"

She drew a lazy breath. "Not till now," she said.

The trail veered right. The blue blazes led upward, beside a squat boulder, and the ground got rocky. Melissa used my arm for support, stirring me to insanity by brushing against me. She seemed unaware. According to her lessons, that was impossible.

"These trees remind me," she said. "I worry about the tree in the yard, the haunted tree, as the kids call it."

"We're still not sure, right?"

"I'm just asking around. The way it leans scares me."

"There's something so sad about a big beautiful tree being cut down. Like that one." I pointed to a massive oak hanging over the trail, cracked at the base. Its broken spine was bursting with jagged spikes.

"Sad, yes, but the children getting hurt is sadder."

"If," I said. "That's a *huge* if."

"Gideon Bloom scares me."

"Yes," I said. "Gideon Bloom scares me too."

I stroked between her shoulder blades. She responded, closing her eyes and moaning. Her weakness for physical affection was amazing. Her shoulder rose smartly against me as she stepped on a rock, hard, then soft.

She stopped and said with excitement, "I see those wild-flowers down there!"

She had been searching for certain wildflowers for days. She shoved the blanket in my hand and clambered around the wrecked tree. The ground sloped abruptly, and she dropped from view.

Her voice called through the hollow space between us, "I've been searching for them all month."

Her head, then the rest of her, rose up. I watched her grab-bing the spikes of the shattered trunk, legs sideways, denim strings dangling. Despite her doubts, Melissa had perfect breasts, from a man's point of view, which means just a trifle larger than they need to be; she seemed to use them for bal-ance as she hauled herself up. In the Village she wore long dresses that shaped her like the flute she carried. She swayed so much as she walked that she seemed on a tilt. Back then I saw her as a woman struggling to keep her sexuality under wraps but whose hot-blooded nature was impossible to hide. She always held back, as people seething with anger will hold to a whisper to keep themselves cool.

I pulled her against me. She gave me her Village hug, brash and full on the chest, shy and wide at the hips. I could tell by the lack of totality she was still disturbed from talking about her crisis.

She snuggled my arm up around her and said, "Where are we exactly?"

"I don't know, to be honest."

"Now I'm scared. We have the kids."

"Melissa, we have plenty of time. We're not lost."

"I hope not. I want us to have time."

I realized the air was enormously sweet. We were inside the pine forest. I had found it.

"This is it," I said. "We're here."

"Finally."

"Native Americans thought pine forests were haunted," I said. "Because the light is so odd."

The light was indeed strange, slashing the pines into a menacing weave. The earth was black and broke into dust on our ankles.

"Pines are a climax species," I said, using the remaining fact I had acquired on my nature walk. "After they come nothing else grows. Look at the ground."

We had entered a section of the pine forest where the trees were thin and the light was even. The air, with room to spread out, turned luminous.

"There's a great spot," I said.

The ground swept away but leveled off into a ledge. After that it fell frighteningly on every side.

"Too steep."

"Just let go, Melissa. Let's take a chance."

We scrambled down. We began to slide, Melissa clutching the blanket to her chest, I behind her, high on my heels, skidding through pine cones and pine needles that swirled up to our knees. Our shoes churned up flakes of root, twig, very dry dirt. We landed in a secluded crest on spongy ground that released a syrupy fragrance that seemed locked in until our feet kicked it free. We couldn't be seen from any trail. From under a rock grew a weirdly shaped tree, branches twisting like snakes, drooping, dipping, finally rising in a manifold struggle for the sky.

"My God, it looks like an octopus," Melissa said.

"What's the name of that song Monie loves? Ringo?"

"I was thinking about the sex life they have. That thing in the *Times*."

"Typical *Science Times*. Sex life of an *oct*opus."

"Don't get started on the *Times*, Daniel. It was interesting."

The air was transparent with brightness, as if clarity could actually be seen, not seen through.

"I only hope we can climb back out," she said.

"We'll make it, don't worry. We'll manage."

I had never been so nervous with a woman in my life.

"So," I said. "You never made love in the woods with anyone?"

"I said I don't think so."

She scraped her thigh with a pine cone and said, "I keep thinking about what I told you."

"You mean . . ."

"Yes. I mean my first crisis. This *man*. My mother'd go out. I was twelve, I never told her. I wanted to, but she liked this guy, this creep, this neighbor. She'd talk about him, and I'd just sit there. She had a crush on him, I think! She was all alone remember and he was some kind of father—"

She fingered the whitewashed strings on her shorts.

"— father figure, to me, to us. The bastard," she said. "He was *nice!*"

I waited a moment. "I thought it was in college."

"The crisis was in college because I was like, *with* guys then, and I was with guys so it, I'd think of *it* in the middle."

"How many times, the neighbor?"

"Not once. I was a child. I trusted him. He was *nice.*"

"I thought it was once. Every time you talk about it it becomes more, I don't know, *bigger*. Did you complain?"

"To who? It doesn't occur to you. Daniel, Monie's my age."

"Your age?"

"I mean almost my age then. I tried to wash it out, a filthy stain, it cuts at such a private part of you. Your heart, I mean, a woman—"

There came a moment of silence, in a forest, in a marriage, in a life, that must finish by itself.

I felt the vastness of the woods around us, how they went on for miles and miles. Out of it, it seemed, Melissa crept over and onto the blanket under the snaky limbs. Before we kissed, before we took off our clothes, before we did what we had come to do, I stroked her arms and neck and legs. She lay there with a smile I'll never forget: she looked delirious, deliriously *something*, but I couldn't for the life of me figure out what.

— 6 —

It hit me so hard I had to sit. I ducked into a restaurant I hadn't
eaten in for a few days, sat at a table I liked, near the bar, where
I had a good view of everything, and thought, *nothing's changed.*

I got through the first month watching television.

I went on a junk-TV bender, holed up in my apartment,
leafing through *The Journal*, and staring at a color television, my
first major purchase. Sunday news shows, daytime talk shows,
cotton-brained sitcoms, ecstatic infomercials. Once I watched
American Gladiators from beginning to end.

The second month I walked. I paced Lincoln Avenue
through the old downtown, from the Sears and Woolworths
to the new age health food store. More than once I thought
Melissa had tracked me down and was stalking me. I spotted
old girlfriends, even followed one thinking she was Suzy Q.,
revered acrobat of the sleeping bag and fantasy of the afternoon.

My children haunted me.

"Shie shie poop breath!"

"Shuck muck you kango butt!"

I'd turn, heart leaping, to two strangers speaking a foreign language.

I was shocked at the physical adjustment. I was braced for a cataclysm but crashed instead into kitchen linoleum and an empty bed.

I'd wake up remembering things like this.

Melissa was flying to Toronto. I served dinner, supervised homework, and packed lunches, as she dressed for a late flight. When the kids got lost in a TV show I raced upstairs. I found her in the bathroom in my robe. I latched the door, the only one in the house with a lock. I took the brush from her hand, pushed her against the tiles, and unbelted the robe. "They'll hear," she said. I spun the shower knob until it was on full force. "Before you go," I said, and kissed her throat, through a forest of sopping hair. I ran my fingertips down her neck and inside the robe. Her lips went soft and loose, as they did when she got very turned on; her nipples were hard as acorns. I kissed her breasts, along the slope of her stomach. "Hurry," she said, craning her neck at the ceiling. I didn't. I was in control, and she was *mine*. She cradled my head and twined my hair. Through her legs I could feel the hard tiles rolling.

Peter and I met for drinks. We never talked about Melissa, against the bathroom wall or otherwise, his ex, or our kids, the subjects that tormented us. We swapped sex yarns, like what Suzy Q. once did to me on her knees in an elevator, and what he did on his knees to someone named Betsy Bender against an office photocopier. We analyzed the war in Kuwait and a *Geraldo* on which couples explained why they had never consummated their marriages. We voted on which women in the newsroom would be easiest to get into the sack—best while there, easiest to get out after.

They were blissful nights. We got a little loaded, talked of sex and war, and floated home to sleep, alone, yet with ease.

I tried half-heartedly to pick up women.

In the book aisle of Sears I got into a conversation with an anorexic redhead buying an Anne Rice paperback. "You work at *The Journal*? That must be so *interesting.*" I followed her to the register and watched her pay. I told her I hated Anne Rice, which I do, even though I've never read a word she wrote. It didn't matter. It meant we'd have a lot to talk about. I knew I should ask her number or suggest coffee, but it seemed so obvious I would be picking her up that I couldn't get the words out. She waited, longer than she had to.

Another time I started talking to a single mother (I know because she announced it in three seconds) whose stroller I helped carry down the steps at the lunch counter of Woolworths. Her daughter was hugging a Barbie, and I said my daughter also loved Barbie dolls. It was my first mistake. I started blathering about my kids and couldn't stop once I started. There I was at the revolving doors, weeping inside, holding her stroller and eyeing the voluptuous Barbie boobs her daughter was fondling. "She really loves that Barbie," I said like an idiot. The woman, meanwhile, was throwing on her coat, and she was pretty busty, too. Not like Barbie—no human female is—but enough to be self-conscious. It became one of those hideous encounters between a man and a woman where you both want to flee but the awkwardness itself is a glue that grips you together. "Oh, you work at *The Journal?*" she said, as we struggled to break loose. "That must be so *interesting.*"

During a freak ice storm I found myself in the frozen food section of a supermarket. It was ten on Saturday night, when a supermarket's the loneliest spot on earth. With my head inside a refrigerator, fingers freezing on a package of peas, I listed what I had come to dread about living on my own.

- Supermarkets at ten on a Saturday night.
- Turning on the television as soon as I wake.
- Jumping for joy when the phone rings. Racing for it.
- Seeing a movie to fill an afternoon.
- Taking walks to change a mood. Choosing streets with crowds.
- Having too much time to do things (instead of too little).

- Deciding again that my down feeling is just self-pity.
- Rotating the places where I eat out alone.
- Something always spoiling in the refrigerator.
- Supermarkets at ten on a Saturday night. Worth mentioning twice.

———————————

I began flirting with Elaine. I hinted in screentops about getting together, but she never got it. My Melissa schooling told me she definitely got it but had no patience for a man who couldn't seem to decide if he really wanted to ask her out.

She got sexier every night. Her hair was incessantly long and black, and her green eyes were lasers that aimed at me when I glanced. Some nights we played peek-a-boo looking back and forth. She wore high heels with jeans, but once a week she'd be in a skirt, those short ones women have to keep tugging down. On those nights I felt she'd undressed for me. She'd sit sideways and her legs were just out there.

I observed her closely and developed a theory. Like all newsrooms, *The Journal* had an unabridged dictionary on a wooden stand, near where Peter and I sat. Elaine and Sandy used the dictionary on a schedule. Sandy went only on nights Peter worked and late in the week, after he had recovered from visiting his children. With Elaine, as far as I could decipher, it depended on what she was wearing and the degree of sexual tension between us.

One night I was editing a "bright" about a customer in a massage parlor in Thailand who paid to have sex tied up in a tub of hot cooking oil. But the prostitute was his wife, it said, and she was so enraged at him for visiting the place that after he was roped up she boiled him slowly to death.

THAI PROSTITUTE BOILS
HER STARTLED HUSBAND
IN VAT OF COOKING OIL

I read it out loud. Elaine and Sandy found it hysterical; they treasured any story in which a woman wreaked vengeance on a man who wronged her. They especially savored it if some kind of mutilation was involved.

Elaine was in an oversized yellow sweater, and every time she flicked it back her naked body would flash before me. *She crawled on top of me, dangling her breasts in my face. I felt how cool they'd be. She'd drag them across my cheek to my mouth. I'd reach up with my tongue and—*

The real Elaine's head snapped up. I flew back to the poor slob stewing in oil. Elaine stared, arranging her sweater. She yanked each sleeve flush and checked her chest, examining one side, then the other.

One morning, when the ice storm eased a bit, Sandy had the idea that we should all go see it. She managed to corral Peter (who was still dazed from having just seen his children), along with Elaine and me. We had breakfast at a diner that had just gotten its power restored and argued about daytime talk shows. Copy desks are filled with overly educated people who relish explicating these shows with reverence, as if each were a bold, new, and brilliantly eccentric interpretation of *Hamlet*. It was accepted without question, as one accepted Peter's Mickey Mouse ears.

I still didn't have a car (I was nervous about registering it), and Elaine drove me home because it was on her way. She walked me up the outdoor staircase, over crackling sheets of ice. She hadn't put her boots back on and her heels kept jamming. I pulled her up with playful chivalry. I felt the bones of her hips through her coat. She seemed to want me to feel them.

"Your kitchen's definitely as small as mine," she said, once inside. "Definitely as tiny. You can't deny it."

"Yes," I said, witty conversationalist that I am.

It all had something to do with a pretend-argument we were having over who was the better cook and who had the smaller kitchen. She stood at the door, car keys in a gloved hand.

"Just look at your stove! Case closed."

"Yes," I said. "Case closed."

"Then I guess I'd better be going."

"Yes," I said, continuing my imitation of Oscar Wilde.

"I'm always so exhausted in the mornings," she said.

"We're both exhausted," I said, one clever repartee after another.

Should I grab her? Why were her gloves on? Melissa informed me that although Elaine may not want to be ravished on the spot, it was impossible she wasn't aware of the sexual tension in the room.

"There's a fantastic *Sally Jessy Raphael* in an hour," Elaine said. "Men who've been raped by women. The women'll be there to describe it. In detail, no doubt. Sounds like a must-see."

"My reception's lousy on that channel," I said.

She hesitated and said, "You mean you don't have cable?"

"You have to, up here," I said. "To get anything."

She hesitated again and tried to feel the key's teeth through her glove.

"I'll guess I'll see you then."

"Yeah, tonight," I said, Sir Rapier Wit to the bitter end.

Her heels punctured the ice on my stairs. It was hard to get each step unstuck. She took a long time starting her car. Engine trouble was just an impossible dream.

I had a brainstorm: leave a cute message on her machine.

I was told what number I reached by Elaine's voice and was urged to leave a message at the beep. I tensed up. The voice had that guarded geniality peculiar to answering machines. It's as if the very silence is out to trick me, laying in wait, as I pause, fumble, and say something ridiculously stupid for posterity.

I lost my nerve and hung up.

"You call? You too? My machine decided to, like, die, for a change."

The next night Elaine had stopped on her way to the dictionary. She was busy making sure her hair was even on her back. The conversation (which she was only half tuned in to) allowed me to wrangle a date. I cornered her when she again bragged about her cooking. I'm a pretty good cook, but she never took me seriously; I have no idea why. She was to show me the "real way" to make tofu with broccoli in spicy peanut sauce. There would also be basmati rice and a mystery vegetable, meaning something whose name I should have known but didn't. Sandy and Brian were supposed to come, and it was unclear where it would be. It ended with the two of us at her place. She was obsessed with proving she was the better cook. I didn't care. I knew what I wanted.

Let me issue a warning to all married men. Listen carefully. It's too depressing to say more than once.

For years you've fantasized about being single. You believe that with all you know about women you'd be a world-class lothario. Who knows better than you what women want? You'd be sensitive yet rock-solid, romantic yet tough as nails. You'd be "there" for her, a wise, witty, irresistible rake who listens to NPR. You'd buy impulsive gifts, send roses, make her laugh, and—need I mention—be the most sensational lover who ever unbuttoned a blouse.

Then, when you finally get your chance, you're no Casanova, not by a long shot. You're Woody Allen, on a really, really bad date.

As soon as I got to Elaine's I realized my first gaffe. I had asked if I should bring anything, and she insisted I didn't need to. I assumed this meant that I actually shouldn't bring anything, forgetting everything Melissa taught me. I could tell by how Elaine looked at my hands as soon as she opened the door.

She took my coat, clutched it to her chest, and had an awful conflict over where it should go. She gripped the doorknob of a closet, cleared a table, then put it on a little stool where her pocketbook was, toppling both. "The floor's okay," I said, with my flair for turning an awkward moment into a social fiasco. We stormed into her bedroom. Above her bed was an iridescent poster of a rain forest. It reminded me of a book I read to Zach about a kapok tree in the Amazon that someone wants to chop down with his ax. The sheets were conspicuously fresh. My coat, as she dropped it, didn't make a dent on the bed. We hurried to the kitchen; it seemed to take a full two or three minutes to get there.

Elaine immediately went to a kneading board and began to beat the living daylights out of a slab of writhing dough. She was in an apron striped like a candy cane over black jeans and high heels.

"You had no trouble finding me?"

"No," I said. "I know the block," which was certainly true, having walked it a dozen times plotting to run into her by accident.

The way she worked was fascinating. A mean streak came out, and she pounded the dough like she detested it, with the kind of sadistic fury I often show in dreams where I pummel someone without mercy. (I've had these dreams a lot since leaving Melissa.)

"Your place is about the same size," I said.

"Exactly the same, I think."

Silence held the room in that iron grip it has when you are struggling to make conversation. No even faintly appropriate words existed.

"I love your poster. Those animals are so *real*."

"It's supposed to be the Brazilian rain forest. Supposedly."

"The Amazon. The snake is scary," I said. "Right over your bed!"

"Yeah, right over my bed. Right over it. It's funny."

Scary snakes in her bed. Brilliant.

"I mean funny when you think about it," she said.

"Yeah. But only when you think about it. That's a kapok tree, right?"

"Might be. Might be. So how'd you end up at *The Journal*? Married, too?" She did a quick tattoo on the dough. "Right? Were? That's a dumb question. I mean like where'd you work before, before the *Times*?"

I waited while she took a few more whacks, aiming her blows with cold-blooded precision, rising in her heels for leverage. I heeded a lesson from my attempts to pick up women. Corny is fine. So is obvious.

"Tell me about yourself first. I want to hear about you."

This inspired her to give the tortured dough some time to think it over, and she pulled herself out of the apron. Under it was a thin green T-shirt. She sat across from me, realigning the collar. The T-shirt matched her eyes exactly.

"Not much to tell," she said, which always means a long story is on the way. I learned that Elaine had an eclectic background, like people on copy desks everywhere. She had been a social worker, a waitress, a graduate student in classics, did a tour as a suburban housewife, had an ex-husband somewhere (no children), had lived on an organic farm and also in Brazil, perhaps at the same time. She did not eat red meat, at least on a regular basis, was a devoted cook, and made perfect romantic dinners for herself alone. When she mentioned eating alone she pinched the T-shirt at the shoulders and lifted it an inch, then let it billow down. I made it clear I was listening intently.

She got up to test the dough with a finger, and climbed back into the apron. It took so much twisting she smeared her cheek with a chunk of dough.

"I don't believe you live here without a car!"

"I like it," I said. "I'll get one eventually. I'll have to."

"Borrow mine, really, any time you feel like it. Just take it. How in the world do you survive without the mall?"

"I hate malls. I love old dying downtowns. Lincoln Avenue?"

"Lincoln Avenue."

"Lincoln Avenue. Malls killed those old downtowns, slaughtered them. I love this one fighting to survive, even though it's hopeless. I walk there all the time. The Sears? The old Woolworths with its lunch counter? How about Holistic Health for Humans?"

I knew Elaine had zero interest in the old downtown, but I couldn't stop. "So what you're saying," I said, "is that you don't give a damn about little stores like Holistic Health?"

"Of course I care. I care very much. You know how I feel when I cook?"

"With its shiatsu massage aisle? Its vitamin of the day? Its vita pet display?"

"Like my mother," Elaine said. "I feel like my mother when I cook."

I took a breath.

"Well, I feel like John Lennon. John Lennon baking bread? Which shows what few role models we men have for anything domestic."

She hesitated, kind of missed a beat. She was taking it very seriously. I had learned about Lennon's alleged bread-baking from one of Ramona's books. The memory—reading to Ramona while curled up on a rainbow quilt, her collection of dolls at my elbow—didn't hurt. It just made my upper body start to melt.

"I hope the broccoli is up to your standards," she said.

"I'm sure it will be."

Her hair was wild from her assault on the dough. She put her knuckles in her mouth, as if nursing a bruise. She sucked them as she said, "I hope so. For such a gourmet. Ex, your ex, she mind you cooking?"

"No. She loved it, believe me she loved it."

Elaine found this funny. She patted the dough.

"How long ago are we talking?"

"Year or so. She traveled a lot. Her job. Her boyfriends."

She found this even funnier, and said, "So, you quit your wife *and* quit the *Times*?"

Because I was with a journalist the second fact was the intriguing one.

"Yes. All of a sudden everything changed. My life just changed."

My working for, and having left, the *New York Times* had become office legend. I was asked how the *Times* would play a piece of news, and everyone would put it down, saying how stodgy the *Times* was.

"So we're talking a clean break?"

"Very clean. The lawyers squabbled. I had to get out. And I did."

"You mean no children. Same as me? Same as mine?"

"Two," I said.

This was unethical to fudge.

She went to the counter and gave the dough a truly ferocious thrashing, bare fists flailing over her head, Slap! Slap! Slap!, then lifting out of her heels and coming down with a real haymaker, her body behind the final smash.

"What age?"

"Two and seven. Actually, four and eight. Now."

She adjusted her hair, spread it over the apron. She seemed to do it every minute. She eyed the dough. Her hair had gotten messed up from the last exertion, and her breath was quicker. Her fists were clenched at her sides, clotted with dough. Her slender body, propped up on the heels, was designed to wrap around a man, to give him pleasure.

"That's a nice age," she said. "When was the last time?"

Melissa had alerted me to these subtleties, that Elaine was adroitly probing for information. I reminded myself to be on the lookout because I was being gone over by a pro.

"I never see them," I said.

"Oh, that must be so tough." She rinsed her hands and dried them by gathering folds of apron and making fists.

"Don't ask. The joint custody thing wasn't working, and I don't feel like going into it. Don't ask if I miss them."

Elaine now felt like a fool. She knew children were not a footnote on a wrecked marriage, like your wife having been a nag. It was like the old joke, "Aside from that, Mrs. Lincoln, how did you enjoy the play?"

"Let me tell you a theory of mine about men these days," I said.

"Wow, sure. Go ahead."

"Since I've been on my own I've learned a lot. I learned I never got the hang of *being* on my own. Men like me, with mothers like mine, they planned to take care of us and then turn us over to another female."

She hesitated, listening closely, and said, "Another female."

"Yeah, so here's the problem. If you're a home-and-hearth kind of guy, like me, who loves to cook and all, it goes against your image of what a man should be. The prevailing image in society. That's why men resist domesticity so much, even though we're hooked on it and utterly helpless at creating it for ourselves. We're trained from birth to expect someone else to provide it."

"A woman, that is. You're so right Danno. You're so right."

I waxed poetic. "We want to be warmed by a cozy fire, Elaine, but we also believe we should be out there, in the cold wind and the hard rain. No one talks about the conflicts of men. Our pain. How men suffer."

"Try being a woman. But I truly understand what you're saying. You're really very sensitive."

This meant I was talking about my feelings, which supposedly men never do; my problem is that I hardly like to talk about anything else.

"Can I help?" I said. "Something? I don't want to just, you know, *sit*."

She hesitated again, kind of skipped a beat, and said, "No, I'm fine."

She got the apron off, then squirmed back into it. Her long hair dangled over striped shoulders as she pivoted this way and that in her heels to swing her kneading board, serving bowls, and assorted contraptions. I pretended to be curious about books stacked under the telephone, cookbooks like *The New Hampshire Women's Collective Cookbook, Tofu for Two, Broccoli of The Gods*. I slipped behind her. She was thin as a toothpick, just enough breast and hips to announce *woman*. In homage to her beauty, I stroked her neck. She did nothing. I gave her neck a massage. She cooed, but stayed focused on her work. I felt I loved her. I honestly did.

I knew I had to plan. I had to get everything in motion before it got late, when I'd have to grab her. It can be quite nerve-racking. I'd have to reach across a couch or something, which at a time like that feels like the Grand Canyon. It's even worse if she's just sitting there waiting for me to make my move.

I kept my hands on her neck and kissed her hair. She ignored it, as if men always kiss a woman they're standing behind. I knew from Melissa that she was as likely not to notice this physical affection as not to notice me setting fire to her clothes. Yet all she did was stand there and thump down the dough, first with one fist, then the other. She was beating the poor thing senseless.

"Can I tell you something really honest?" I said.

She checked her knuckles. The dough on the counter had passed out in an exhausted clump. She flipped off the apron again and evened her collar; she pushed her bra strap over, but pretended she was just scratching a shoulder. She sat at the table and had trouble finding a place for her chair. Her green eyes blinked, uncannily mirroring the T-shirt's shade of green.

"I want to say something special about you that I just want to say, like say upfront."

She was licking a finger where a clot of dough was stuck.

"Elaine, my whole life, especially since my marriage ended, I see women I want to go to bed with. I mean . . ."

She hesitated, about to speak, then said, "You mean . . . ?"

"I mean, I'm not saying this right. I'm saying there are women I just want to sleep with. But none I want to *make love* to. Like explore every nook and cranny of her flesh. Just hold her for hours, *hold* her, for hours. I mean, one of the shocks of becoming single is so many women I *could* sleep with, but I'm not interested in that, even though it's out there for me if I want. Elaine, what I'm getting at in this stupid clumsy way is that you're the first woman in all this time that I, I mean, being with you, and . . . It's more."

Her bracelet got stuck on her wrist, and she was trying to work it free.

"I want to make *love* to you, Elaine. And it scares the hell out of me. Someone so beautiful, you really are, so nice. I meet so many people up here who fake being nice, but you're *genuinely* nice."

She broke the bracelet free so she could twirl it, which she did.

"I was very hurt once, and I'm terrified of caring for someone again. It's scary, wanting to make *love* to someone. Make *love*. To really *make love*."

She pondered this very, very seriously.

"It scares me too Danno. If you want to know the honest truth."

"You too? You feel it?"

She gave me a fierce, green-eyed stare, a glance that said something so obvious it was silly to put it into words. I didn't have a clue what it meant.

"You're so sexy too, if I can say that. The way you move? A sensuality. A womanliness waiting to be released. You also have about the most beautiful eyes I've ever seen. So green! You must hear that all that time."

"I get compliments. I don't care. Like so what? Like how I was born?"

"They add depth," I said. "And sensuality, richness. So your eyes aren't just pretty. They're more than pretty."

She blinked, checked her arms and her chest, and blinked again.

"Like you."

"We'd better have dinner before I overcook it. You just sit. I'll serve."

"If I must," I said, though it hadn't occurred to me to help after she said no once. "In fact, they were the first thing I noticed. Across the newsroom."

"I need to finish the rolls first," she said, standing up. "I can't believe you remember when you noticed me. That I want to hear. In detail. It's so *funny!*"

She swiveled to the sink and punched down the rolls with a barrage of ruthless *thwacks*. In bed her thighs would curve in delectable ways. She would be an adventurous lover, I decided, as the rolls deflated, sighing, and were left to grow fat and plump, swelling in readiness for us like remote sexual organs.

———————————

There were so many aromas the tiny kitchen was too small to contain them. They burst forth, and dinner was served. It was excessively lavish and indulgent, too spicy, too saucy, too pungent, and too exotic—in other words, it was what everyone these days considers a palate-thrilling Epicurean delight. Elaine stayed on her feet, on the prowl for flaws. She would only nibble, she said, because she had already eaten too much that day.

There was only one problem. Something was wrong with the broccoli. I don't mean just not good, but dreadfully, sickeningly wrong.

"How's the broccoli?"

"Delicious."

She had a load of ego riding on everything, that was obvious, so I made a heroic effort to gulp it down, as if it were foul-tasting medicine I had to take to live. It had a texture like wool, a decayed-fish flavor, and an aftertaste that was keenly, sweetly, metallic.

"At least the broccoli's decent. At least there's one thing I didn't *totally* ruin. The sauce is polancioni, from *Tofu for Two*. It's terrible. I think I added too much ginger."

"I love it," I said. "It's delicious. I never had it this good."

I know I should have said, "I'm not in the mood for broccoli," or just left it on my plate. But I knew how disappointed she'd be. She was at the sink with her back turned. I had a second. I speared a chunk of broccoli to stash it somewhere. If I hid it under a newspaper she'd find it later. The floor was out of the question. I had to hide it temporarily. I grabbed my belt and underwear waistband and slipped it in. I nearly stabbed myself in the groin, I was moving so fast. It settled in hotter that I expected. The sauce kept tingling.

She turned, and it was worth it. "You like it!" she said, radiating joy.

"It's *very* good. I mean *very very!*"

"You look flushed all of a sudden, Danno."

"It's just absolutely delicious Elaine. Hot, but good."

"Temperature hot? Or hot hot?"

"Both," I said. "It's just terrific."

Then I had to embellish, of course, and dig myself into a hole.

"It just feels so nice here with you. You're a *fabulous* cook. I admit it."

Her whole face started smiling. Her eyes were green flares. She took on a sexy glow, ecstatic because of what I had done. Still smiling, she waltzed over and deposited two more gigantic broccoli spears.

"Eat as much as you want," she said. "I'm really not hungry at all."

She turned. I put it in my pants.

I went to the bathroom to dump it. But I was afraid the toilet wouldn't flush. There was no window. I know. I looked. I worked off the porcelain top of the tank with trembling hands. But what if she discovered wilted broccoli stalks floating in the water? What if it clogged? I was also worried about the polancioni sauce, whatever the hell that was. The inside of my crotch looked like a green fungus had sprouted.

When I came out I squished as I walked. I felt warm, squirmy liquid oozing. Keep in mind that I was already in the mood for sex.

As soon as dinner ended Elaine went into a flurry. She bounded about the kitchen making coffee, even after I said twice I didn't want any. The beans had a name like Brazilian kumanansa triple decaf.

"This coffee will be perfectly perfect," she said, bouncing a bit, her body out of kilter from the angle of her heels and the success of her dinner.

"I smell the rolls, Danno. I think they're ready."

She was at the oven. "I *ruined* them." She was practically in tears. "I'm making a wreck, I'm *wrecking*, just about everything."

I couldn't get up to comfort her. She sat across and told me how she had made a mess of her life, her marriage, all her relationships with men, her Brazilian wackamacaca rolls. I suggested that the evening was perfect, so perfect we shouldn't overdo it.

"Listen, Elaine. I think we should go very, very slowly."

She hesitated that way she did, and said, "Yes. I definitely agree with that."

"I think it could easily get too hot and heavy for both of us."

"Yes. It could."

She came around and rested her head on my shoulder. Half her body was on me. I had to put my arm around her.

"I thought you thought we should stop, that it was too heavy."

"I said I thought it was scary," she said. "I didn't say *stop*."

She started speaking again and hesitated. It was like a nervous tic.

"Daniel. Danno. What you said rings so true, the idea of making love *with* somebody. The way you described it. Dan, if we ever make love, ever do, it'll be so *beautiful*. I didn't think I was ready. Now, I'm not so sure."

"Elaine, you have to understand. Tonight may not be right."

She straightened into her chair. She rearranged her T-shirt then stood and got the coffee. In a suicide move I got up too—

it hurt too much watching her—and we stood sipping coffee. I kept trying to turn away. She kept trying to nuzzle.

"It's not that I don't want you," I said. "I want you too much, actually. I should head home. I really should. For tonight, I mean. Like maybe now?"

"I'll be gentle with you, Danno," she said, trying for a joke.

She gave me that mystery glance; it had something to do with our feelings for each other and how much we were sharing. I had to kiss her. She worked it into a kiss to lead us into her bed under the rain forest. When I peeled myself off my jeans were green at the crotch, which was swollen, who knew from what.

"Elaine. Please understand. I have to go."

"Sure, you wanna go," she said, her thighs sinking onto mine.

I knew the risk it took to do this. It broke my heart.

"Elaine, I can't stay because I want to so much."

"I promise," she said. "I won't *eat* you."

The unintended double entendre humiliated her.

"I can't figure you out, Daniel. I just can't. So help me."

Her green eyes were dulled by a film. She reached under her T-shirt and shoved the bra strap over, not bothering to disguise it this time.

"I mean, *go* if you have to so much. First you come on like gangbusters, then you're disappearing on me. I wasn't planning to *rape* you."

"I know you weren't. Honestly. I just have to go, right now."

The film on her eyes collected into tears. She retrieved my coat. She took my quickly donning it and opening the door as further insult. Icy air roared in and attacked my wet crotch with a vengeance. She hugged herself in the skimpy green T-shirt. The cold brought out a hint of nipple on one side.

"I can't stay, Elaine, because I want to so much. You don't know how much I want to. Please say you understand. You understand?"

I was half out the door.

"I guess," she said.

— 7 —

I walked home from Elaine's through the old downtown, hoping to pass a few people. It was deserted. No one came here at night anymore; the old downtown was just fading away and nobody gave a good goddamn. I'd bet anything that the mall out on the highway would be packed all night.

That I had sabotaged my evening with Elaine was nothing new. My whole life is a joke, a cosmic goof, a slapstick tragedy. I take off on a quest to discover the meaning of life, settle a score, and test the limits of personal freedom; I end up scurrying down a freezing street in the middle of nowhere with my crotch turning into a green block of ice.

I'm the guy who never asked, "Why did you go to bed with that creep?"

And with Elaine it was simple. All I had to say was, "Food's great, Babe, specially the broccoli, but get that apron off!"

"What?"

"You heard me."

She takes the apron off. "What's going on?"

"This is going on." I take her by the hand. "You're coming with me."

I lead her into the bedroom. She allows herself to be taken.

"I told you how much I want you" I say. "To explore every nook and cranny of your body."

She pretends not to understand, but lets me ease her down, under the rain forest poster. I spend a long time stroking her arms, in the flimsy green T-shirt. I make sure to look into her eyes very meaningfully as I do. She takes on a delirious look.

I leave her lying there and return to Melissa.

"I didn't do anything."

"Don't lie to me, Melissa. I saw the letters. 'I overpowered you with my hunger, Barry. With my lust.' Sound familiar?"

"Them! You saw the letters!"

"And that mark on your neck when you got back."

Her hand flies to her neck, although the wound has healed by now.

"I gave you plenty of time. You kept it a secret, and that's worse. We should talk. Right now."

"You think it's a hickey, or something?"

"I'd just like an explanation. And for how you've been acting."

"Acting?"

"All of sudden you're never in the mood. Then suddenly you can't get enough. You talk of monsters. You're fixated on that stupid tree. You're terrified, Melissa. Something's going on!"

"Hold me, Daniel. You don't understand. Please, hold me. Please."

She did say something like that when she got back from Boston.

"What is that, a hickey?" I had said, as a joke.

"Believe me, that's one thing it's not."

"What is it then?" I asked, heart pounding.

"Nothing," said my lovely, faithful wife. "It's just *nothing*."

That was all she said, but with such volcanic emotion under the surface—it was a kind of violence, how she said it—that I backed off and let it go.

A couple in a car twisted their heads. I may have been shouting. I gave up Melissa. I squeezed out Elaine. I forgot my frost-bitten crotch. I turned to Suzy Q., my sexual muse. Cooperative as always, in a moment she was before me whispering, "This you're gonna like."

Once, before Melissa and *The Journal*, I really was a full-time journalist, for a sleazy little daily in New Jersey. At first I was a reporter, then a copy editor. I was glad to get out of reporting because I knew I'd get nailed big time for what I was pulling. When I wrote stories I couldn't resist making details up. You can't imagine how hard it is to keep every tiny fact straight. It was, however, a slippery slope. Soon I found myself inventing personalities and fabricating events. I wrote follow-ups on meetings that had never happened. It was like living my fantasy life but in public. The editing job saved me from myself. (I was awarded it, of course, because I was considered so conscientious and reliable as a reporter.) That's when I learned to savor the poetry of a good headline. I also got involved with a photographer named Suzanne Quinlan. The first time we slept together was the night a notorious criminal was arrested.

SUBWAY STRANGLER NABBED!

We called him the Subway Strangler even though it happened on a PATH train under the Hudson River, and no one was strangled. In the office we dubbed him the Path Pervert, because all he really did was expose himself as a train door closed in Hoboken. The victim (a homeless woman with a long history of mental illness) told police it made her feel "strangled and jangled."

Suzy covered his arraignment with two reporters (one now at *Time* magazine, the other writing on national affairs for the *Washington Post*) and I was editing a special color foldout section on his capture. I was working with Steve Glickstein, my equal then at that rag. (Yes, he exists, and I knew him; for years I used him as a reference. Last time I asked him to say I worked at the *Times* because I was applying at some cruddy newspaper. He was such an egotistical sap he'd laugh it off and go along, or so I hoped. I also calculated, correctly it now seemed, that *The Journal* was too disorganized to check.)

Suzy was ecstatic: I was playing her pictures up on page one as if they showed a second gunman aiming at JFK in Dallas. She came to where Steve and I were laying out pages. She had a blond ponytail and wore tight tops with about five cameras dangling on thongs that crisscrossed her chest. He was the only married guy there. He used reading glasses (which no one else did yet) and snazzy fountain pens. Suzy flirted with him. Always.

"I know the one you're gonna like, Steven," she said, flicking her hair like a horse flicks its tail.

He tapped the desk with his flashy pen and kept editing a story, still on paper then. She tossed her hair back once or twice then dropped the contact sheet where he had tapped and sauntered off.

"Tits," Steve said.

"Suzy Q.?" He always made me say dumb things. He scowled and gazed over his glasses, watching her promenade back to the darkroom.

"Ass."

"Yeah, nice," I said. "See Chaiken's piece?"

Jeff Chaiken had done the lead Strangler story. He's the one now at the *Washington Post*.

"Scumbag," Steve said. "Sucks. Shit sucks."

The guy was so articulate no wonder he landed a job at the *Times*.

He slid his glasses down and read: "The yearlong reign of nighttime terror ended yesterday with the dramatic . . ." He shoved his glasses up. "Sucks."

"We still need that strong vertical from Suzy Q.?"

"Fuck," he said.

It meant yes. It also meant what he wanted to do to Suzy Q., what he thought she needed, what he couldn't do because he was married, how he felt about that, Chaiken's story, his job, life in general, and the things no one, especially me, could ever do right enough for him. It had a haiku-like brevity. The man was a poet.

I played servant, as usual, and went to the darkroom for the photo.

Suzy and I studied a contact sheet. She was stimulated from shooting what she saw as her first big story, and I put my arm around her to calm her. Her ponytail whipped my hand as she whispered, "Soft, but a great shot. Nice, tight. Steven'll like it, won't he?"

I told her he would. I wasn't annoyed that she sought his approval, even though he and I were equals—one of those work situations where everyone confers authority on someone who doesn't officially have it. She was so happy we shared a kind of victory hug. The press of her breasts scared me, the way she deposited them on my chest as if to say, "Here's something special I want you to have!"

I scratched her back. Her shirt was danskin, popular at the time, which is as thin as a T-shirt but silkier. Her bra strap, when I crossed it, was remarkably taut. We kissed, and with the sleepwalk jerkiness of a kiss-blinded grope, I felt to where her jeans held everything tight, and around to where her breasts could overwhelm my hands. She had that knack of making something sexual just *happen,* with neither person seeming to initiate it. I felt that giddy panic, my first taste, but didn't understand how addictive it would be. I was astonished, frankly, that Suzy would do this in a darkroom. I don't know why I am always so surprised. Other men seem to take this sort of thing in stride.

After the paper was put to bed the staff went to a bar. We all felt triumphant, real journalists. Steve Glickstein and I chatted about our layout, equals, *exact, perfect equals.* We were all hopeful, today a big story, tomorrow the big time. (Steve was gone in a year; Suzy soon became a photographer for the *Daily News.)* At two Suzy took me to her room in Weehawken, with lens caps and cameras on bureaus, film canisters strewn like bullet casings after a calamitous battle. We started to neck in the elevator. We undressed in the foyer. As we dived into her bed, I nearly castrated myself on a huge telephoto lens hiding under the covers.

She made up for it in a way new to me then: a strenuous effort to be a superb lover. Suzy did not want to be romanced or comforted or worshiped or drawn in to a serious relationship. She wanted simply to be a great lay. That was her sole ambition, and she achieved it. Making love to her was weightless flight, sex as sport, sex as theater, sex as religious epiphany. After reaching its soul-shattering, revival-meeting climax, I didn't want to cuddle or joke about how we met. I wanted to leap off the bed and shout, Hallelujah!

We became an item. I was the guy with a woman half in his lap at a movie or pawing him in a restaurant. More than once she unzipped me in her elevator and dropped to her knees. She lived on the third floor, and she'd finish the job (thankfully) behind her door, with me against a table where she kept tickets for the Lincoln Tunnel. We went camping. She performed breath-taking feats in a sleeping bag. She'd talk dirty, out of a male teenager X-rated fantasy. She was the sex partner I had dreamed of since puberty.

It was amazing how quickly I tired of her.

Every relationship cools, but with Suzy there was no other level for us. Our main conversation was her orgasms, which could have been measured on the Richter scale, stupendous, earth-shaking, apocalyptic—unless it was a *really* good one. She was a woman brilliant at starting a relationship but incapable of sustaining one. Her full-throated sexuality was irresistible at the outset, but soon I dreaded being alone with her. The odd thing was, even before we broke up I began to fantasize about her. I'd wander the city recalling her sweetest moves. She had become my sexual muse.

Terrific sex, of course, never goes unpunished.

Is there a moment every married person would be unfaithful? Self-doubt, a low ebb in the marriage, that inexplicable attraction for a stranger? Say the stranger is available, pursues you, and you have the opportunity? How many would walk away?

I got my chance the circuitous way I get everything. First my career had to self-destruct, for a change.

When that crummy scandal sheet-wannabe converted to electronic typesetting I was offered a job as the computer company's "liaison" between their nerds and our editors. I took to computers, meaning I picked up the lingo of those with genuine expertise. But after six months the company that hired me was taken over by a bigger one, which was taken over by an even bigger one. I had no idea how volatile the computer field was, even then. I was never fired during these corporate evolutions, just phased out. I had no real computer experience and ended up a consultant for the company in its last incarnation, which wasn't bad until that company was absorbed into a holding company in California. This left me a consultant for a company that didn't exist in a field I knew nothing about. That's when I began to write press releases, first for an underfunded ecology group, then for anyone who'd have me —boutiques in the West Village, witchcraft stores in the East Village, third-rate politicians, small service companies. I tried to work a day a week as a copy editor and told myself I was honing my skills for the *New York Times*. But I never felt confident enough even to send my résumé, with its gutter-level newspaper and obscure computer jobs and, worst of all, experience in public relations, which to journalists is one notch above being a child pornographer.

The situation enabled me to be home with the children while Melissa traveled, to be a liberated father without a straight job. It helped when Melissa's career took off, as government funding dried up and orchestras were crying to raise funds. Friends saw me as a new-age father, a man whose wife has the "real" job. I saw myself as a man without a career, who started this and started that as I turned forty with the simmering ambitions and paltry achievements of a twenty-year-old.

That's when I bumped into Suzy Q.

I had seen creditlines on *Daily News* photos that said "Suzanne Quinlan Daily News." I didn't admit to myself that I wanted to see her, but when the *News* went on strike I began hanging around with the pickets on 42nd Street. I would have killed to work at the *News*, but being a strikebreaker was wrong. The pickets were glad for anyone to join, and I did, many times. One night someone next to me was snapping her ponytail. It was Suzy Q., in a tight top like she always wore, but this time of fancy cashmere.

I've become something of an expert on failure over the years because I've had the opportunity to observe it firsthand. I was even a flop at being unfaithful. I was at an all-time low that night, and despite how I felt I was able to reach down inside myself and find a new bit of weakness to keep me from getting what I wanted. I was planning something, I admit it. The next morning Melissa was flying to Los Angeles, on one of her first projects with Barry Alter, of all things.

"Hey," Suzy said. "Let me show you my place. I'm two blocks over. No kidding."

"I'm here just to show solidarity. And taunt the scabs. But hey, sounds great."

Her apartment was like the Weehawken one, cameras and lenses and film canisters everywhere, but on curvy white metal furniture. She must have seen my ring. According to Melissa, there's about as much chance of a woman missing a wedding band as missing that a man has one leg.

We sat on a couch, and with my usual Don Juan savoir-faire, I managed to impale my thigh on a flash assembly tucked under the cushion. I gave a fiery defense of workers' rights. I presented it as if I were picketing with the strikers in principle rather than because I dreamed of somehow finessing a job at the *Daily News* without compromising my beliefs, and faulted myself—saw it as yet another sign of failure—that I would not bend my principles.

We started necking. She was at my belt.

To this day I don't know why I stopped her.

"I can't go through with this," I said. "I want to, but I can't."

She didn't bat an eye.

"I saw Steven a month ago," she said, flicking her hair. "He hates it."

We chatted about how Steve Glickstein hated the *Times*, with my pants at my knees.

"I saw him in the Village. He lives in Chelsea. I forget the street."

"Really. I can't believe it."

"Yeah, he does. He's got two kids now. Can you believe it? *Two!*"

We said good night. We fixed our clothes. We were at the door.

Then I did the kind of stupid thing I specialize in when everything is going well. I kissed her, to thank her for understanding. She was very brusque about it. And, given how battered my ego was, I felt rejected. So I kissed her again, a deep, enthusiastic kiss. I really wanted her now, and we pawed each other like in the old days. She fell to her knees and unbuckled my belt. She nibbled my stomach. Her head inched down.

"This you're gonna like," she said.

There is no man alive who could stop a woman doing this. Except me. I gripped her shoulders and pushed her off. I zipped back up and left, feeling like the biggest jerk in the world.

When I got home Melissa was sleeping. I was relieved to find that she had not programmed herself to wake. I couldn't lie to Melissa, but like most married people, I could omit part of my day if I had to. For the first time I seriously considered if she was having an affair. I put my arms around her, cradling her into our sleep position, one hand on her shoulder, the other finding a breast. There is a particular sensation, I discovered, in touching your wife after touching another woman: Melissa's body, oddly, seemed the newer one. I might have tried to wake her to quench the wild flames her body sparked (the back of her thighs on mine, squirming, her hair in my eyes) but common sense prevailed. Instead I held her tight and summoned up Suzy Q. against the door, whispering, "This you're gonna like."

A hot shower took care of the last of Elaine's broccoli. I had half a mind to go back, but given how I left, I decided to leave well enough alone for once in my life. I was certain I wouldn't be able to sleep. I was nervous about facing Elaine at work; facing people is one thing I'm not good at. I got up more than once to look out at the mountain and remind myself that I had wasted my life. I had time to work out seventeen more tricks I could have employed to sidestep the broccoli and get my hands on Elaine. In my sleep, it seemed, I charted Melissa's affair with Barry Alter. I speculated on others—the many lovers I knew, at that moment, that she had definitely had. It gave me a fresh arsenal of stilettos to twist in my guts. I recalled her moods after the Boston trip. I considered that she'd never slept with him. The mark on her neck and the moods were circumstantial, but how could I explain away those letters?

I muddled into the next day. Around six I got comfortable on my reeking couch and flipped on the news. It's even more vacuous up here than in New York: the inane banter over the weatherman's haircut, the phony joviality. Nothing's worse than some dope trying to act cute and being too much of a nitwit to pull it off.

By now he's there a lot. He plays piano for the kids, yucking it up, a goddamn friend of the family. He pounds out Beatles songs for Ramona. He might even change Zach's hat while he sleeps.

I got off my stinking couch. Lincoln Avenue was still busy, and there was a restaurant I hadn't eaten in for almost a week. I wanted to review the slimiest thing I had ever done. Here's how tacky it was. Melissa got me the job, and our trysts took place in her office.

I could smell my couch all the way to Lincoln, even in the cold.

Melissa met Ellen Smuckler at a recycling committee meeting, and learned she needed someone to write press releases. Ellen had remade herself, with the addition and deletion of one letter, into Elena, of Elena Fashions Ltd., clothing for the thinking woman. Her marriage was on the rocks because she and her Park Avenue lawyer husband worked ungodly hours (and made ungodly money, I might add). I had done a presentation for Bloomingdale's, and we were in her office reviewing it. We were on her leather couch, and she teased me into massaging her neck because she was tense about her big chance. Remember she not only knew I was married but also knew my wife. I was working the muscles in her neck, which were knotted like steel wires, when she said, "You'd better lock that door."

Right then I could have stopped it, but I worked for her, and needed the job desperately; if I could believe what Ellen promised I would soon no longer be contributing just petty cash to the household. It's hard to explain how much that meant to me. When I got back to the couch I was resolved, and she was ready. Her dress crinkled as it came off, and she laid out all her clothes on an antique table and the arms of the couch. Our lovemaking was formal, an extension of office activity, its passion circumscribed the way lunch is confined between twelve and one. It even felt timed, because Ellen was a devotee of time management programs. She taught me about managing my time, making lists, doing the hardest thing first in a day. She also taught me about women's underwear. Ellen's were purchased from a place with a name like Patsy's Panty Paradise, whose designs she was more or less planning to steal.

It lent our sessions the sultry beat of a lingerie fashion show with Ellen as model strutting down our leather-cushioned runway.

"They have very pretty things," she said, and decided to show me the catalog, the way another woman might start off with a slow dance alongside the bed. She sent me traipsing across her elegant office in my underpants to fetch the catalog. Looking over the catalog underscored the business nature of our activity ("Isn't this enticing?") the way executives might refer to a sales campaign during lunch ("Yes, that's the spot!") to allow them to deduct the meal as a business expense ("Don't stop. *Oh God please don't stop!*").

Ellen saw herself as a savage sex animal, a ravenous tigress always on the prowl for fresh meat, although she was obviously inhibited, too concerned with managing her time and how everything looked to appreciate sex. She was most stimulated by clothing, perfume, lingerie, the outer garments of sexuality. For example, she was most eager on days she was wearing something special underneath that she wanted to show off. Once she stopped in the middle of everything to show me how this gauzy bra with something called an under-wire slipped off, and how it "supported you," as if it were a rich uncle. She hooked herself back in with little shrugs of her shoulders, then sort of kneeled into me sideways so I could un-snap the back and she could stare down fondly at her pushed-up then pulled-off self. As the bra trailed down her arms she looked not at me or herself but at the bra as it skated past her elbows. Her eyes asked "Well?" as a woman will ask during lovemaking if her new position is exciting. And like at those times, I had to feign being very turned on by what she did; I didn't see myself as having much of a choice.

It was Ellen who ended it. I got fired and dumped, simultaneously. She hired an outside advertising and public relations agency, due in no small part to my success with Bloomingdale's. She also reconciled with her husband. I tried, with her recommendation, to get on the staff at the agency she hired, but I had no real advertising or public relations experience. I also had serious moral qualms about the field, which began the second I was refused an interview.

I'll never forget the morning I got the ax. Ellen told me early; I was the difficult chore she wanted to get out of the way first thing. I got home to find Melissa having an absolutely lovely morning. She had an afternoon flight to Chicago and was lolling in bed playing the flute, a rare indulgence. Beside her was a mug. Melissa brewed gourmet coffee constantly, poured it in a mug, and let it get cold. She panicked when she heard me. I forgot how unsafe she felt when she was alone in the house.

"What's going on? Oh, I didn't know *who* it was."

"I got fired."

"You got *what?*"

"Ellen decided to go with a regular agency."

I sat in the rocker, facing the bed. Melissa threw the covers off with her flute and sat on the floor. She was wearing a plain white T-shirt; it was startling to see her in one without corporate or symphony logos and slogans from fund-raising campaigns. She held my hand. I drank her coffee, though it was stone cold. I really needed to talk. I find it impossible to cry. Melissa didn't cry either, but started sniffling. She had to keep reaching into her Boston Symphony bag for tissues.

"I know how much it hurts, Daniel. It seems the end of the world. But it's a blessing in disguise, I think."

"Melissa, it just feels there's no point in me even trying. I try this, I try that. None of it's what I really want anyway. Won't you miss your flight?"

"Chicago can wait. It's not going anywhere."

"I just can't seem to find my spot."

"You wanted out anyway. You don't need *her*. You're *too* good."

"Gideon Bloom is also bothering me," I said. "You spend a little time with him and nothing else matters."

"Last night I talked to Carol. It's getting very bad."

"I feel petty and stupid having these problems when I'm more than forty fucking years old. Between Gideon on one side and Ellen on the other, I feel crushed in the middle."

She shifted into her oracular mode. It was something she could do.

"Zach's okay. Monie, our children, are safe. It's tragic about Gideon, but there's nothing we can do. You help more than most, by the way. Spending all that time with him? And you'll connect with what you want. It's near. I feel it's very near. I can sense it."

"I really believed Carol. What she promised me."

"Yes. I know."

We had the house to ourselves, but all we did was talk. Finally, she picked up the phone in her organized mode, canceling one flight, booking another, remembering to coordinate frequent flier miles. We chatted as she stuffed clothes into her Boston Symphony bag. She pulled off the white T-shirt. "It's dirty," she said.

"I'll clean up," I said. "You can't miss this flight." As she tossed it on the bed I regretted she would not cross the room naked to the hamper; through all our changes her body never failed to pack a sexual wallop, as it did now, while she stood before a drawer pondering the sweater to reach for. At last she was layered into her public self, Ms. Melissa Weil, Juilliard flutist and fund-raiser par excellence, and we drove to Newark Airport. We kissed until a cop banged on the hood. She went off, swinging the Boston Symphony bag.

I raced back to Montclair just in time to meet the school bus. After the kids had a snack I did the dishes, straightened up the bedroom, and collected a light laundry. Before adding the white T-shirt, I pressed it to my face.

— 8 —

why do women have vaginas? (PETER)

eternal mystery (VEIL)

so men will talk to them (PETER)

guy choosing among 3 women to be new viceprez. one italian, one greek, one polish. which one he promote? (PETER)

afraid to ask (VEIL)

one with biggest boobs of course (PETER)

speaking of boobs and vaginas, have question for u on "them" (VEIL)

on boobs? or on vaginas? (PETER)

owners of both, ya goddamn sexist misogynist clown! ya know: THEM (VEIL)

oh, THEM! whaddya need to know, my friend
(altho thot u was expert on this subject) (PETER)

can't stop thinking about the S word. only thot
of sex for last 48 hours, old girlfriends, my ex, etc
(VEIL)

dinner with elaine that good? (PETER)

dinner with elaine that bad (VEIL)

Peter was bitter after visiting his children, but this Sunday his humor had been singularly vicious. Curiously, I had heard the vagina joke before from a woman, as "why do men have penises?" Same anger, same loneliness, different anatomy.

I got into Peter's creaky but smooth-running Honda. He wore his Mickey Mouse ears, which on Sunday nights he kept on. I had come to cherish these rides, hurtling together in a mass of steel, the heater blowing on my knee, the dark road pushed so hard it kept splitting open before us.

He still had some venom to spew.

"Question," he said. "What do you call the piece of useless skin outside a vagina?"

"I give up."

"A woman."

He really liked this one. I could tell he'd been saving it to do in person.

"Hear about the w-woman who went to a sperm bank?"

He was working himself out of it.

"Yeah?"

He gargled, cupping his mouth.

"Wa-wa-wa—" he slapped his face. "Wa-wa-where do I deposit this?"

"Where do I deposit. Very good. What's this?" I pulled a plastic Ninja Turtle from under me. "Which guy's this, Raf?"

"No, Michaelangelo," he said. "He must've left it. Of course Jackie'll kill me. And he'll notice, since Mike's his latest new favorite."

"I didn't recognize him."

"It's a new model. Their weapons are locked in their shells."

"I should someday tell you this great idea I had for a toy, called Happy Singing Killer Frogs, but the Turtles stole it. Anyway, screw it."

Peter drove with one hand, staring straight into the hole his headlights were boring. He fit the Turtle into his shirt pocket and said, "So I show up."

"Yeah? What shit she pull this time?"

"Just fucking unreal."

"I can believe it."

"She always w-wears something weird. I show up Saturday night and she's in this slinky evening dress. 'I *love* being able to go out,' she fucking says. 'I can't believe the whole night's mine!' the whole f-fucking night she says. So of course I pump the kids and she's seeing *Ghost* with her fucking friend Doris. What's insane is she must've known I'd ask."

He was becoming animated, a good sign.

"She's blinded by passion for you," I said. "You know they're crazy."

He made our usual illegal left turn with glee and said, "Once they were staying home to watch *Shining Time Station*."

"I know it well. With Ringo Starr as Mr. Conductor. My daughter got into the Beatles because of it."

"Once she was in a bathing suit, and I know for a fact that she thinks she looks f-fat in a bathing suit. Who can understand how they think? It has to do with how she hates her thighs?— how can you *h-hate* your own thighs?"

"They have a very intense relationship with every part of their body."

"Relationship? You're kidding me."

"No. Ask a woman what she thinks of her kneecaps or her earlobes and you get a considered opinion, like you asked about the reunification of Germany."

"They *are* amazing," he said.

That was all he said. I really loved this guy.

"You don't visit, right?"

"No," I said. "I don't."

"In a way you're lucky." We watched a light change. "L-lucky."

"Yeah."

"She looked pretty-sexy though that *Shining Time Station* time," he said. "Last night she was just ugly-sexy, if you know what I mean."

"I know exactly what you mean."

He was better. We roared up the highway ramp. It was time.

"Yeah, those chicks," I said.

"Those *g-girls*."

"Those *mizzes!*"

"Bitches. Dames."

"Damsels. Babes."

"Babes, *yeah*. Broads."

"Cunts."

"Ah yes," he said. *"Cunts."*

Elaine slipped off the yellow sweater and looked up. "Just lie there," I said. "Let me give you pleasure."

I kissed her breasts and tugged off her jeans. A high heel fell, the other dangled from her raised leg. She shuddered under my masterful fingers, green eyes ablaze. She seemed delirious, shivering in ecstasy. I owned her.

The real Elaine looked up.

Hi. I think we should talk (SPERLING)

Maybe it's only me, but every time I see or hear those words I break out in hives. It reminds me of an old Peter Sunday night joke.

What are the four most horrible words in the English language?

We have to talk.

sure (VEIL)

at least yr speaking to me (SPERLING)

i mean u owe me the chance to explain (SPERLING)

stop pretending everything's ok. ok? (SPERLING)

ok (VEIL)

can we at least have breakfast? i'll treat. one of those places you love on Lincoln. order ANYTHING! (SPERLING)

up to $1.15 (SPERLING)

even $1.50? $1.75??? (SPERLING)

$2. FINAL OFFER! (SPERLING)

pretty please (SPERLING)

am i being silly????? (SPERLING)

absolutely not. it's a date (long as u pay) (VEIL)

As soon as we sat down she said, "Danno, we have to talk about our relationship. I know why you took off like a bat out of hell."

"Why I took off?"

"Yes, took off. I blew you away. I came on so strong."

"Oh, that take off. I felt bad, too."

"Not as bad as me. I not only ruined the dinner, I *made* you go."

"You don't have to explain."

"The broccoli was the only thing that was decent. And when you talked so beautifully about making love it—" she looked around, but the place was empty "—I guess it just seduced me."

"I hope that's a compliment."

She hesitated and said, "It *was* seductive Danno. Not the sex, but to have a relationship. For *us* to. I did a lot of thinking. About me, about *us*, about our relationship."

The food came. The waitress, whom I had tried without success to flirt with when I was alone, was very solicitous. Elaine waited for her to leave.

"I didn't even realize it till you were gone. I know I made you go by pressuring you. It's that romantic dream, that's what seduced me. I mean, I don't mean that *you* didn't. I mean, my own *fantasies* did, really. And what makes it so lousy is we really deserve a chance, our re*latio*nship does, to move ahead, slowly, see where it leads and all. I'm talking too much I know."

She had not taken off her coat, and now she did, slipping it around her like a shawl. She made adjustments to her hair, fluffing it out. She picked at her eggs, saying she never ate breakfast. She just broke the yolks and watched them run.

"This isn't what I had planned to say. I had it so com*pletely* planned. You know what I'm saying? I shouldn't have brought up your family. I know that, Danno. I really understand that. Believe me, I do."

She yanked the sweater under her coat to fit her shoulders. The gesture somehow told me I'd have a second chance. But I knew Elaine wasn't in it for a quick roll in the hay. I wanted to bring up Melissa, Barry Alter, my children, even Gideon Bloom, but I knew I couldn't. I felt the loneliness of a date: something was eating me alive and there was no way I could talk about it.

We finished eating—she didn't touch hers—and decided to go for a walk. She insisting on paying. I tried to catch the waitress's eye, but she was busy checking out Elaine.

We walked together, picking our way through a radiant landscape of ice-encrusted trees, leaking bark, and watery slush. The streets sparkled as we strolled. Icicles melted off roofs and splashed into holes in the snow.

We talked about how beautiful the storm was, and I told her my theory about beauty. According to my theory, beauty has an element of danger, of pushing you beyond a limit. Every time I look at the ocean, for example, I feel not only its beauty but also a kind of fear. I related this to the ice storm, which everyone agreed was lovely to look at even though it had disrupted countless lives and caused incalculable damage. I found myself saying that every time I was happy, like in Montclair during hopeful times, a part of me was screaming. I don't understand it, but I think it has to do with the terror that lurks in all eye-blinking gut-wrenching beauty. In a stroke of genius I added, "and in our relationship."

I realized right then this was an important moment for Elaine, a very romantic event in her life. I heard it in her voice as she said, in a happy singsong, "You're such a mystery man, Danno. I can't figure you out nohow."

---

*what do saddam hussein and sandy
have in common (PETER)*

can't imagine (VEIL)

they both want amman (PETER)

*who are u? just saw yr message from last nite on
silly woman in combat piece i had to write (SIMON)*

*i new person on copy desk. finally allowed to
handle real stories, like yrs (VEIL)*

u a man or a woman? (SIMON)

checking . . . (VEIL)

*two men on commuter train.
first one: "Got a dog for my wife."
second: "Good trade!" (PETER)*

. . . have just confirmed i indeed a man (VEIL)

*that fabulous! entire features crew in stitches. know it
busy there but wow, not that bad! is u guy who worked
for infamous ny times? (SIMON)*

fraid so, in earlier life (VEIL)

*u going to end of war party danno? i exhausted,
4 day shifts, romantic walks in snow, etc (SPERLING)*

*wilt thou be available for autographs at end of war party
later? & offer thrilling tales, i.e, inside look, at the
Kingdom & the Power? (SIMON)*

will stop by. promised mickey, i mean peter (VEIL)

*will stop by. promised mickey, guy you see on desk
with ears, a.k.a. peter (no one at the times ever wore
ears! that one story) (VEIL)*

*it at seedy (but legendary) Lincoln Ave Tavern.
be there—or we'll gossip about you! (SIMON)*

*i going home to bed but will prolly be up late cooking
(she added, batting her eyes) (SPERLING)*

I didn't answer Elaine's last screentop. We had become
pretty much Platonic friends, and this kind of kidding was typical, especially on Saturdays when we worked a late afternoon
shift for the Sunday edition. I was busy putting a cute angle
on a story for the bold-face box on page one alerting readers to
turn clocks ahead later that night. It had been written straight,
and Charley had called out before the whole desk for me to
"punch up the lead"; it was not the first compliment he gave
me. He complimented my work a lot.

TURN YOUR OTHER CHEEK
IF THE PAPERBOY FORGETS
TO TURN HIS CLOCK AHEAD

DON'T BE ANNOYED AT YOUR PAPERBOY IF HE DELIVERS
THE JOURNAL LATE THIS MORNING. HE PROBABLY FORGOT
TO TURN HIS CLOCK AHEAD AT 2 A.M. AS THE NATION—
EXCEPT ARIZONA AND HAWAII—GOES FROM EASTERN
STANDARD TIME (EST) TO EASTERN DAYLIGHT TIME
(EDT).

I was so absorbed I didn't see Elaine leave. Only after she
was gone did I see the message she sent, which she must have
thought I had ignored.

I in the mood to make
the coconut pudding you like
Stop by and lick the pot? (SPERLING)

I felt sufficiently guilty to stop at Elaine's before the party, but on the way to her apartment I got into a debate in my mind on the politics of the Gulf War. As I passed her house I was evaluating the historical necessity of violence and devising a four-part test to apply to the invasion of Kuwait. I couldn't be interrupted, and by the time I brought my argument to its dramatic conclusion (there wasn't a dry eye in the house) I was already on Lincoln.

Out of nowhere I felt dizzy and thought I was having a heart attack. I held myself up on one of those peculiar bulging-in-the-middle parking meters that run along Lincoln. I've heard that people's lives flash before them when they think they're about to die; immersed in obituaries for months, I saw only this headline:

> HEART ATTACK FELLS
> DANIEL WEIL, 44;
> BROCCOLI BLAMED

And then it got complicated. Even at death's door I can find a way to trip over my feet.

> BROCCOLI VICTIM
> LED DOUBLE LIFE,
> WEIL? OR VEIL?

In a minute I was better. It was the pressure; I was feeling guilty about Elaine and going crazy over Melissa. I had proven my point by now, but just what the hell was my next step? My brush with death (in my mind, of course) made me think of my father. I looked around at the old, faded downtown and saw it through his eyes. I tried to conjure up his glorious New York. I came closer than usual but not enough to keep it shining before me.

"When I was young, Elaine, my father would come home at night and say, 'I walked through Rockefeller Center today past the ice rink. Skaters were doing figure-eights.' Or he'd say, 'Today I was in Battery Park. A big ship was passing.' Or, 'I went to the Empire State Building. I was on the twenty-third floor.'"

"You know, I was never in the Empire State Building. Why didn't I ever go, I always ask myself. I mean, I was right there!"

"Elaine, listen to me. As a boy, my father's New York was the most glamorous and exciting place I could imagine, an empire that would one day be mine. To experience it daily was beyond anything even I could dream up. There was little more to seek in life than to leave my family every morning, explore this always-amazing city, and return at night with stories to tell.

"And Elaine, I came over tonight to talk to you instead of going to the end-of-the-war party because I suddenly remembered the way my father talked about the city and how fabulous it seemed. And how I searched for that New York, his lost, glorious New York."

"My father never talked about anything. Really, it was the craziest thing!"

I tried again.

"When I worked in Manhattan years later I searched for it." (And when I wandered the city the night I met Melissa.) *"I never found it, Elaine. Until just now on Lincoln. And that was only a glimpse."*

"Lincoln? Are you serious? It's so depressing there!"

"I know, I know. But I saw a glimpse. And maybe once or twice before I glimpsed it, back in New York. I'd look out an office window on a drizzly morning and it would be there. Or a subway would switch tracks, the lights would blink, and it would be there. Once, I was swept up in a theater crowd near Broadway, and I had this inkling—only an inkling, mind you—of fathers and time and cities and my place in an ever-changing flux."

"You must have loved him very much. Have some coconut pudding. I'm afraid I put in too much sugar."

I gave up. Even though I was heading for her house, I gave up.

I went by myself to the hospital room where my father lay last year. We both knew he was close to death. I remembered —there, on the cracked pavement of Lincoln Avenue—the shape his body was in, this guy who used to hoist me on top of his head and run up and down the stairs.

I had to tell someone.

"I tried to tell you, Melissa, how lonely his death made me feel—how even though I rarely spoke to him I suddenly missed speaking to him. I'd wake in the morning and say, 'I don't have a father.' And the crazy thing was, I felt it meant much more than anything I'd ever said before in my life."

It meant so much, in fact, that I didn't know whom to tell: that when I try to figure out why I ran off, my father's death always comes to mind. And so does what happened to a kid we knew, Gideon Bloom. I don't know why the whole death business should throw me for such a loop. Years ago my mother died, a pioneer, so to speak, of Alzheimer's disease. It took ages to figure out what she had. We watched her go from wearing her clothes a novel way to not recognizing her own face in a mirror. It took nine or ten years; we don't actually know when it started. How can I deal with these things? When I sat with my father he'd look away, scrunch his face, and whisper, "Ow!" It was the most heartbreaking sound I'd ever heard, his crying "Ow!" like that. I had imagined pain from cancer to be different from how it hurt when I banged my elbow or stubbed my toe. Not just worse, but a different kind of pain; even death had no mystery, when I got close enough to really see it. Only something as miraculous, as exuberant, as powerful, and as passionate as human life and the love within a family could end like this. The naiveté of his cry, its rawness.

I was in front of Elaine's house. The windows on her floor were flooded with so much light that it overflowed onto the trees in her yard.

I was alone, and I just kept walking.

— 9 —

As soon as I stepped inside the Lincoln Avenue Tavern I was staring into Judy Simon's eyes. Instantly, we both blinked away.

I strolled to the bar where Peter stood holding a glass.

"Who's the one with the tits?" he asked. I thought he might be drunk, but the guy was so laid back it was impossible to tell.

"Beats the shit out of me," I said. We ordered fresh drinks. I got the vodka tonic Peter had, slugged it down, and ordered another.

"You gotta choose between booze and broads," I said. "Who ya pick?"

He thought it over. "Broads I'd give up. You can live with booze without broads but not broads without booze."

It was the type of remark that made us laugh.

"I have a theory about people like Sandy," I said, knowing he loved to hear my theories.

"People who never had to take care of anyone but themselves. Who never had a family, I mean, their biggest sacrifice is should we have Italian or should we have Chinese? They have no idea how much you can have to give up. And it shows in how they complain, of tiredness, I'm hungry, headaches."

"Jackie was like that when we were together," he said.

"Self-absorbed?"

"I guess you could call it that."

I let the subject drop. Peter had the quiet intensity that made me afraid of some people. I returned to eyeing Judy Simon. She was in a sleeveless black dress that fit badly and gave her a street urchin look, as if she were beautiful but too poor to afford anything nice. It hung like clothes on a doll, not fitting as much as wrapped over and snapped in place. I couldn't tell Peter about her because she was the object of such scorn on the desk, which, in the perverse way of all flesh, made her more sexually appealing.

"I keep noticing how self-absorbed everyone is," I said. "Maybe because this generation never went through a war or a Depression and is really pretty affluent. You talk to people and in ten seconds they're talking about themselves. You can test it."

"You might be right."

"I notice it at work on Saturdays when we see all the day-side people." I was keen to explain. "You say you're thinking of buying a car, and in ten seconds they're talking about needing an oil change. I call it the Self-Absorption Theory."

"Self-Absorption Theory."

"Just so incredibly self-involved it drives you crazy."

I was starting another rampage. I'd been doing it more lately, and Peter didn't always have patience. Elaine, on the other hand, was enthralled by my Self-Absorption Theory; she had turned it into a discussion of herself, whether she was too self-centered.

"Perverted," Peter said. "Can you imagine setting oil wells on fire?"

"No military advantage," I said. "None. After we fight to make the world safe for monarchy."

"For feudalism."

We got into a conversation about the Gulf War. Other men joined, an instant round table on missiles, ground war, how tanks made cavalry obsolete. We advanced on Judy. She and I nodded, but I stayed in my conversation on how technology had sanitized death on the battlefield.

Judy detached herself from her group.

"I'm Judy Simon," she said, in my group now, disregarding what we were talking about. "Your message was absolutely hy*sterical.*"

The men stopped talking. They smiled, studying Judy's naked arms. (It had turned quite warm that weekend and women were suddenly in sleeveless tops.) She described our exchange about being a man or a woman, getting most of it straight, but neglecting the skillful pause that made my joke work. I guessed she was in her twenties, with sharp features, high cheekbones, and almond-shaped eyes. Her jaw was so tight it looked hewn of sheet metal. The vertical strength of her face was emphasized by earrings, greenish, long, and pointed, like snakes that slithered as her jaw bent up and down. Her lipstick was heavy and cherry-red. It brought out her doll-like quality, as if she were experimenting with lipstick for the first time and hadn't gotten the hang of it yet.

"What do Saddam Hussein and Little Miss Muffet have in common?" she asked, bringing the joke over from her group.

The two women she was with, including the one whose chest caught Peter's eye, were probably reporters trying to get into features. I could tell by how they took in every word. One held a small silver package.

"They both have Kurds in their way," Judy said, earrings wiggling.

The women laughed. "Kurds in their way! Curds in their whey!" one said. She opened the silver package, which I thought might be cocaine. She peeled the wrapper, with precision, to reveal a stick of chocolate.

"I hope we didn't disturb your big macho discussion," the one with the chocolate said. She appeared to delight in being hostile to us.

"So, they have parties like this at the *Times*?" Judy asked.

Everyone stared.

"Only when wars end."

On her arm was the fleshy scar of an inoculation. Spotting this minor blemish made her even more attractive.

"You worked at the *New York Times*?" the one holding the chocolate asked, looking me over. Among journalists, this is

like saying you were there when John Lennon met Paul Mc-
Cartney.

I nodded as she added in her belligerent way, "So then
what the hell you doing *here?*"

I finished off my drink. My head had turned pleasantly
soft.

"It isn't professionally satisfying in a big place," I said,
repeating what was, in effect, fifth-hand gossip about the early
days of the Beatles. "Everyone is really competitive and there's
a lot of favoritism. It's hard to deal with all the political
garbage."

"That's what everybody says," the woman responded, her
need to appear in the know overcoming her need to challenge.
She presented the chocolate to Judy like a lady-in-waiting.
"Isn't it terrific?" she asked.

Everyone watched as Judy took her time to finish chewing.

"I thought it was maybe cocaine," I said.

"No one does *that* anymore," the belligerent one said. "It's
Belgian, a special kind. I brought it from my secret stash."

"Omigod!" Judy said, as if in terrible pain. "Omi*god!*"

She swayed, eyes shut in voluptuous release. Everyone
politely waited for her soul to ascend, with her face screwed
up in ecstasy.

"Luscious, incredibly *luscious*. Absolutely in*credibly.*"

Her eyes opened a sliver. "This stuff should be illegal. It's
too good."

Her lovely jaw was vibrating. Everybody watched as she
bit a chunk, nibbling the tip before taking it all in her mouth.

"I think sex, you know, sex? Just a sublimation for food,"
she said.

The women laughed. The belligerent one said, "Don't you
mean—," caught herself, and added, "Oh, that's so *funny.*"

The woman whom Peter had commented on stepped out
of the group and led him, carrying his drink, into the conversation. The rewards of silence.

I headed for the bathroom. Peter did too, and we had no
choice but to go together. We followed men's room etiquette.
There were four urinals. He took the extreme left. I took the
next-to-far right. We stared straight, as if at attention. I

studied a drip off the lever that's pushed to flush. We zipped up, eyes on the dripping beads of water.

As soon as I walked out I was buttonholed by two reporters who had heard I had worked at the *Times* and had to enlighten me on what they didn't like about the paper. I looked between their sputtering heads (foaming at the mouth with *Times*-bashing fever) at Judy's legs and worked my way up. Before I met her glance she turned away. Our eyes never met but I felt they had, as you see light in a room after a lamp is shut.

About half past one Judy asked me how I was getting home. She knew I didn't have a car. She asked if I'd had a lot to drink, which you always deny even if you've just chugged down three bottles of Scotch and can't pronounce the word "no" without slurring its many convoluted syllables.

Judy sat at the wheel. Green neon light from the tavern sign glowed on her earring. Her hair was brown, with the light spinning out hints of red. She could be twenty-five, the new young, which was accentuated by a childish barrette she wore. I reminded myself I was drunk, which made me pat the fleshy scar. She didn't move. I took her face in my hands, turning her prow-like chin around, and kissed her on the mouth. I needed all the available slack in my seat belt. Even at forty-four, after reading her signals all night, I am still surprised when a woman lets me kiss her. Me, the guy kissing the girl in the car. I was smothered in cherry-sticky lipstick. Right then we signed a sexual pact, a pledge to sleep together later. It's a tacit agreement, but I always know it when I make one. I kissed her again, with teenage extravagance, with deadpan, stare-in-the-eyes tenderness.

Judy lived in a modern apartment with a balcony facing the mountain. I stood on her elevator with my hands in my pockets while she tapped number four, which lighted at the edges as the elevator hauled us up. I resolved to do something amid the elevator's eerie seclusion, with its motionless motion and soundless sound, but before I could decide what everything jerked to a halt, and the door glided open on a shiny hallway.

We walked through her living room, passing posters of a tarot deck flipping open and a map of the solar system showing which moons were in ascendance, and went out on the balcony. It's still cold here at night and there were no lights, just the mountain's shadow. She took me through a sliding door into her bedroom. The glass had an orange sticker that said SAVE THE EARTH. She toyed with the digital clock on the glass night table as I took the chair; there was no other place to sit. It was complicated to arrange my enormous feet.

"It's almost exactly 2 A.M.," she said. "Spring ahead, fall back."

She stretched out on the bed, the dress over her knees. It reminded me of how I used to sit on the rocker with Melissa on the bed. I looked at Judy's baby barrette, the way it held her hair like a dam where it split and burst in reddish spirals that splashed across her neck.

"So now's the witching time of night," she said. "An hour that isn't really happening."

"Before changing the clocks?"

"Forget about the clock. Every year I do this, every year when the clocks change. An hour that doesn't exist, a different dimension to explore. You can do any crazy thing you want. Say anything. I love magic. Okay?"

"Okay," I said. "Way back once I screwed up when the clocks changed. My daughter had a pottery party, an hour-long party. She was about five. It's so crazy when you have kids that I, we, I forgot the time change. I got there when I thought it was ten, and kids were leaving clutching knickknacks they had made. I can still see them walking out of the Y with their stuff. And her expression."

"She must have been really pissed."

Five-year-old daughters don't get pissed. They get hurt, angry, maybe traumatized forever by what you did.

"She probably still hates me for what I did."

It seemed, objectively, the saddest thing that had ever happened to a father in human history. I did one of those dumb things I do, I mean, I knew I was rambling and boring Judy silly, but I couldn't put the brakes on.

"What really pissed me off was what my wife did."

"Wife?"

"Ex. Ex-wife."

It had been easier to learn to say "ex" than it had been to start saying "wife" or, especially, "son" and "daughter."

"She was a fanatic about changing the clocks. Drove me up the fucking wall! She'd start Friday night. Different clocks in the house would change different times. By Saturday night I couldn't tell what the hell time it was except by my watch, which she'd *also* change if she could get her hands on it!"

"I just mean we can say anything we want."

"Okay," I said. "I think I wasted my life. I made all the wrong choices. I wrecked whatever nice things I got on a silver platter. I just totally blew it."

I knew I was acting like an idiot, but Judy seemed oblivious.

"I should have slept with Eddie Matson," she said. "Way back when."

"Eddie Matson?"

"I should have. I know *he* wanted to, even though we were so young."

"I guess you weren't ready."

I didn't feel like hearing about Eddie Matson, which was probably when she was eleven. I wasn't finished talking about Melissa.

"Oh, I was ready," she insisted. "I got fitted for a diaphragm."

"I guess it just wasn't your karma to do it."

"You know that's it *exactly*," she said.

I knew she'd lap it up if I used an expression like karma.

"I once heard there's a Zen of putting in a diaphragm," I said. "Like believing it'll fit and everything working perfectly on the first try. The Zen archer who doesn't aim so he hits the bull's eye perfectly."

"I'm very, *very* into Zen. Where did you hear that? The *Kama Sutra*?"

"My ex said things like that." I wished I could stop babbling about Melissa. "I think she stole it from somewhere."

I was drunk, I reminded myself, and terribly depressed. I knew a sexual pact was in force. I fell across the bed and onto her.

But only in my mind. Instead, words were tumbling from my mouth.

"Can I say something honest? You're *so* lovely. It's scary to want someone this much. I don't just want to like, *sleep* with you, but I want to make *love* to you. Explore every nook and cranny of your gorgeous flesh, your sexy bod. Why don't you slide closer to me right now."

I kept the eye contact going. It also helped me keep my balance.

She extended her arms. The scar wrinkled. The earrings wiggled. When I managed to find my way across the vast chasm of the bed and flap my arms around her she embraced me with readiness, like an engine catching on a well-tuned car. Her barrette scratched my nose. She lifted her hair so it corkscrewed over the pillow, as if she had made me come so she could pose, reddish hair spraying over the immaculate white pillow, fine strong chin, eyes looking up at the slightly tipsy man who was droning on about his ex-wife but who also wanted her very, very much.

"They're amethyst," she said, meaning her earrings. We lay side by side, stroking each other and continuing the eye contact. I understood at once I was forbidden to look away.

She began to gossip about the copy desk. It seemed to turn her on.

"You know Sandy's always prattling on about some boy-friend, Brian something?" Her eyes were frozen on mine. "He doesn't . . ." Her eyes were glazed but stayed on mine. "He doesn't ex*ist!*"

She had begun to hiss.

"What?" I said. "The guy who, who works at the college? Teaching young girls, girls who, who all want, want to sleep with him?"

It was hard to form sentences without looking away.

"A fantasy of hers," Judy said. "Based, I figured out, on a professor she had the hots for. I have it on the very best authority."

"But she talks about him, him all the time. What she made for dinner? For dinner. A fight they had? How he wants to start, start living with her?"

"Trust me," she said, her pupils gleeful and locked in mine.

"Who sends her those flowers? Roses? I saw, saw them, delivered?"

"She sends them to herself!" Judy dropped her voice. "He exists only in her imagination. He's *never* there. She never shows with him anywhere. No one's ever *seen* this guy. They were supposed to come for dinner once, and he had an emergency, or so she *claimed.*"

She took my hands and pressed her palms against them, comparing our hands without looking, then put my hands back on her dress.

"She once, once, did the same with me. And someone," I said.

"Sure. You know about her and Peter, of course."

"Her and her and Peter? Her and Peter?" From the corner of my eye I saw her earrings do a sensuous wiggle, and behind them I noticed how clean her sheets were—they looked new, but whiter. "It's a, a, Dickensian universe," I said. "Everybody turns up sooner or later. They all turn up. Everybody."

"Like in *Great Expectations?*"

I glanced away, but she was too agitated to care.

"They used to be an item, but he couldn't hack a relationship at all," she said, hissing again, her thighs grazing mine. Her dress seemed tailored to fit a woman lying down, the way it flayed out over her legs.

"She said all he could talk about were his kids."

Her eyes were shut and her face screwed up, as when she'd swallowed the chocolate. She did something with her body, moving without seeming to, so her breasts jutted out more, her thighs crowding mine, the dress staying draped perfectly at her knees.

She said, "I never repeat gossip. *Never.*"

The statement was so heartfelt it suckered me into reestablishing eye contact. "So you better listen careful the first time."

She liked her line so much she kissed me, twirling under me with one knee raised, like a dance step, all while staring into my eyes.

"Sandy hates me. Everyone hates me."

"How could they?" She was really getting on my nerves.

"Elaine's nice. Very intuitive. She does so much with herself. Bea*utiful* hair. She's supposed to be this in*credible* cook? I love how she looks in those tight jeans. The way she runs around with those please-fuck-me shoes? I should wear them. But I'm not sure I'm the type?"

"I wouldn't worry about being the type if I were you. You give off tremendous sexual energy. It pulled me toward you. From across the room."

"I know," she said. "I felt us connect. I knew we'd be like this. I'm psychic, I have second sight, I'm a telepath. Can you believe I saw us *exactly* like this at the party? A vision. Exactly like we are this moment."

She was awe-struck at this revelation, as religious fanatics are when they announce the world is going to blow up the following Tuesday.

"I'm very into amulets and magic spells."

"I was attracted to you right away," I said, because I knew she'd love hearing it, and also because I didn't want to hear about her magic spells any more than I had to. It seemed time to shed our clothes. No matter how young and modern Judy was it was still the man who would reach first for the zipper.

Which was what I did. Her dress was unzipped and put aside.

She had worked herself into a tremendous heat. *"On! Put it on!"*

"Put what what?"

"You really *are* drunk. Or just a *dinosaur*. I just hope I have an extra."

She yanked the glass night table drawer open and found a condom, which she shoved angrily at me after ripping the wrapper a hair. I was amazed she could be hostile at a time like this. She hung the sheet on her shoulders and went into the bathroom. Her thighs were ignited by the hall light, swinging, ruddy flesh. I was perceiving what was probably her worst fear about her body, and it felt good because she was bugging me so much. My Zen comment went right over her head. Melissa heard it from Shula. I know it's bizarre, but I felt an ice pick of jealousy imagining Melissa putting in her diaphragm for that creepy Casanova in the West Village loft, my sweet lovely wife just getting *laid* and being happy about it. It was twenty years ago, before we met, and it was cutting me to shreds. Go figure.

"The first thing I heard was that you were into astrology," I said, when she had settled back in her sheet. "Tarot cards? Biorhythms?"

"They hate my stuff on the fucking desk," she said. "Everyone does."

We were both getting pretty nasty. "Think so?"

"*Know* so. Astrology, hey! Women're a lot more open to the moods of the earth. Don't laugh at biorhythms, please. I don't want snickering from you."

"That is totally *untrue*. Men are at least as open. And no one hates your stuff. No one. I know that for a fact."

"Are you serious? Are you fucking serious?"

"I think men're getting a bum rap lately. They're at *least* as sensitive as you are. We just show it different ways."

I peeled the sheet off her. She shrugged, helping. I really didn't like her.

"Are you for real?" she said. "Now *that's* a crock!"

We were arguing, me fully clothed, she in that ridiculous half-off sheet. It melted into teasing, and we started kissing and squeezing, a little game.

"Dinosaur," she said, rubbing my stomach. "Dino-*saur!*"

"Dinosaur? I'm as hip as you!"

"Hip, the guy says. *Ha!*"

She laughed, and her body crept the rest of the way out of the sheet. My hands were all over her. She did a little jig under my fingers, grinning to say "Gotcha!" It had been a long time, and I couldn't get enough. I was awash in that sly, honeyed pleasure of great sex with someone I didn't like.

"So, there's life after forty, huh?" she said. "This a good party?"

"Wonderful party. Worth turning forty. So much to *eat*."

I nibbled every part I could get to. I was practically de-
vouring her. God, I love women's bodies, even this woman's
body. I undid my clothes, the sheet coiling under me, and
resumed the ritual of staring into each other's eyes. I had to
say something, she was giving me such pleasure.

"The dinosaur says happy birthday" I muttered, back to
our silly game.

She answered by clamping her arms around me and
adding a second clamp with her legs. I was welcomed, gra-
ciously, into a spacious room where a surprise party was waiting, that I'd known all night was being organized, but had
never in my wildest dreams expected to be so grand.

— 10 —

"Remember," said Melissa. "We're dressing for dinosaurs."

I had come down from working at my desk in the attic and I was loaded for bear. I had stumbled on a review of a first novel in the *Times* that gushed over the "luminous surface," the "hypnotic prose," the "erotic intensity at once haunting and heartbreaking." I mean, it blathered on and on until I went stark, raving nuts. Even the photo enraged me, all dark, sultry eyes and rippling black hair. I shouldn't have read it; I know myself, and I should have known what it would do to me.

It was an ominous start for an evening. Later that night I'd find the Barry Alter letters.

"And guess who's in for Ed's big four-oh. Joanne's sister, the other Melissa, the famous Lissie Meadows, world famous violinist. I'll catch up on all the latest Juilliard gossip? Anyhow, *dress*. It'll be dinosaurs. Okay?"

I had chatted with Lissie Meadows when she visited Joanne and I called on recycling committee business. I told her how I loved classical music, and we definitely connected. I knew she had never married and saw herself as a failure because she never made it as a soloist, even though she and her string quartet had toured the world and been written up more than once in the *Times*. Of course Melissa sensed my interest; she could divine my slightest attraction for another woman, even before I was aware. In fact, I'd been secretly in love with Melissa Meadows (Lissie was a stage name she invented) for years, even though I'd never laid eyes on her. In my mind she looked just like the writer in the *Times* photo, the same eyes full of dream, the same mouth full of lust.

"Gimme that back, quiche face!" Ramona shrieked.

"No way!"

"Kango butt! You're dead. Count on it, pal!"

"No way! Shie! Shie! Shie!"

"Get dressed. I'll handle this," Melissa said. "It's been going on all day. And the Philharmonic found my check. Someone has to deposit it next week."

I went upstairs, still seething over the review. I put on a grudging sports jacket over a nice shirt, good jeans and, in a concession to the dinosaurs, my "man" shoes—I think they're called wingtipped Oxfords—that remind me of a real man's going-to-the-office shoes. Melissa had started packing for a trip, and left her underwear drawer open. I was forever cleaning up after her, so I fished a bra off the music stand and put it away, making a mental note that she was running low on underwear. As I closed the drawer I saw the Boston Symphony bag on the floor and kneeled to dig out the Philharmonic check. Under a cardboard folder pantyhose is sold in I found a sheaf of stationery from the Atlanta Marriott Marquis. The first page said, DANIEL-ABUSE.

The one under it said, "It was so romantic in the woods, Barry. I know I was flirting. I know I was asking for it."

There was more. ("That kiss was the biggest mistake of my life.") ("I gave in only when I knew it was inevitable, that I couldn't stop it—you had no right, and you gave me no choice!!!")

I read carefully. Then I put everything back in place and went down.

I caught my breath on the landing. Melissa was in the kitchen in her organized mode, phone under an ear, balancing the checkbook, and shouting compliments into the living room where Ramona was practicing piano.

"I'm not telling anybody anything," I could swear Melissa said on the phone. "Not yet, anyway. I'm almost there. *Very good, Monie!*"

I couldn't really hear, especially with the piano. But my brain was on fire, and I believed I could make out every word.

"Oh, he senses something, definitely. Europe, *Yes!* the bastard gets off *scot-free!* That *fucking* bastard! Excuse my French." She stroked her neck with her flute, then scratched her back with it. She thrust out her chest, squinting her eyes and rocking in a kind of autoerotic trance. (*"It was not my fault! I am not to blame!!" "That kiss was the biggest mistake of my life!"*)

Meanwhile Ramona, who needed nonstop prodding, started fooling around. She began to improvise, turning one note into a trill and the next into a staccato, and backing it up with whimsical chords, her own lilting, jagged-edged, idiosyncratic song. I was suddenly inside the nightmares that made her call out about monsters in the haunted tree. I studied Melissa swaying in pleasure and was thunderstruck at what a beautiful woman she was.

I walked in as she hung up. "I can't find thirty-two cents," she said, pounding the checkbook with her flute. "It gets me so up*set!*" She blinked away a threat of tears. "You look good. Good. Carol'll be there. That was Carol. She knows Joanne's pregnant. She *seemed* okay about it. God, Gideon! Did I mention Joanne's sister? *Enough fooling around, Monie!*"

"You mentioned Lissie Meadows, I think."

She looked at me longer than necessary.

"I have to get dressed. *Great! Do it again.* They need dinner, too."

I rubbed her as she put the flute down. Melissa always turned me on, but now her flesh injected me with some kind of sexual adrenaline. I nearly cut my hand on the edge of the counter.

"Remember Caitlin's at seven-thirty. *We can't do a duet now, Monie.*"

Ramona's scream blurted out. "Shie shie quiche face!"

Then Zach's. "Flongo pie head. *Mongo* pie head!"

The riot was started by Zachary, who had sneaked into the living room and cruised by the piano with Ramona's doll. "I got Samama. She's miiiiine!"

"Now's your turn, okay? Me? I'm getting dressed. Dinner, don't forget. Someone has to give them dinner."

I followed her angling up the stairs. She leaned forward to generate power as she climbed, elbows tight, as if lifting herself breasts first.

"You can't just *take* Samantha!"

"Count on it, pal!"

"Daddy, Zach hit me."

"She asked me to, Dad."

I surveyed the field of battle. I was an enlightened parent, equipped with psychological skills to deal with sibling rivalry in a manner that addressed each child's needs in a firm but loving way. This meant, of course, I would use the time-honored method to get children to behave: bribery and intimidation.

I bribed Ramona with two extra cookies and threatened Zach with no television. I was too stressed out to cook and threw together a clever dinner of leftovers jazzed up a way they liked. They soon became human again, even speaking in English. I had them chilled out, and I was chilled out too, the horror of the letters drowned in the flood of exhilaration I always got from outwitting my own children. Time tripped to a stop, as it does when rowdy youngsters are stilled. I heard Melissa upstairs stomping about with the self-contained tantrum she threw when she had to dress for a party. I sailed into a moment with my children when I wanted to weep for all I had, and stared into the yard, at the haunted tree, even though it was too dark to see it. *I saw you looking at my body and I liked it, Barry. I dressed for it! I fought with every last ounce of my strength but it was too strong! For sex, pure and simple, I did it, a quick lay on a hotel bed.*

Melissa came bounding down the stairs, looking spectacular. She had settled on a new outfit, a short gray skirt with black tights, and a black mesh sweater over a camisole, also black. She eyed herself suspiciously in the hall mirror while I let in Caitlin, the babysitter, and gave her instructions.

"Remind me to do a wash," I said, as we pulled the car doors closed around us. "You're running out of underwear."

"I promise," she said, as she lowered the window. Lately, Melissa would never ride in our car without a window open at least a crack. I decided to take a roundabout route.

"So, you're finally going to meet the famous Lissie Meadows."

"I guess so," I said. "So what?"

"So what? You *love* talking to her on the phone. You never
talk to *anybody* on the phone."

"Maybe Barry Alter'll be there."

"He's in Europe."

She reached in her coat to feel the mark on her neck, now
just a scratch.

"Maybe he'll make a surprise appearance, being so head
over heels in love with you."

"Yeah, right!"

We were coasting down the wide hill of Lorraine Avenue.
Despite everything I was enjoying the wintry streets of my
town, how the headlights shook the trees and stood them tall,
how they rose over the windshield in salute, as I paraded along
between them.

"You look great, by the way," I said.

"Thank you. I'm feeling much better."

"Better?"

"Daniel, I know you know I've been acting funny."

"Yes. You *have* been acting funny."

"I *know* I've been acting funny."

The branches around us were lush, even in leafless Decem-
ber, and they mingled overhead to form a canopy for us to
drive under. Lorraine feels very broad in that stretch, because
the houses are so set back.

"Please hold on. Just hold on. Okay?"

Beside us ran a wall of piled stone and lawns as deep as
fields with hedges zigzagging. I made a right on Grove, past
the light at Bellevue, and up Summit or Cooper, one of those
sinuous streets near Brookdale Park. I was steering through one
of the things I loved about Upper Montclair, how the streets
wave and wind as they roll off the mountain. They bend like
a woman's leg, in this case Melissa's, in the black tights whose
knee she was pinching in the dashboard light. (*I dressed for it!*)

"Does my friend Barry Alter have anything to do with this
new mood?"

I was waiting at the stop sign on Park. An eon went by;
the air in the car turned cold, then warm again, as if an ice age

passed. It was like when Sophie said, "I have bad news about your father," or when Melissa gripped my shoulder and gave birth to our first child.

It seemed natural for Melissa to ignore my question.

"I saw no problem with Caitlin this time around," she said. "I don't think she'll try to get Zach to go to sleep without his cap again."

"Yeah, smooth as silk. She learned her lesson that famous last time."

I felt the burden of our twin secrets, mine about hers, and hers about herself. I finally thought of something to say. "You know what I heard on the radio? I heard that twenty-five years ago this month the Beatles released *Rubber Soul!*"

"Aren't we going out of the way? Isn't this *way* out of the way?"

She was almost teary. Since she'd slept with Barry Alter she turned teary at the craziest things. Before tonight I wrote it off as a mood.

"I just wanted to take a long way around," I said. "If it's okay."

She made no reply. I said, "And by the way, we should definitely not cut down the haunted tree. I was studying it when I fed the kids. It's not that close to the house. There's no danger. Nothing's falling on anybody."

She still said nothing, which sorely disappointed me. It was one of those times in my marriage when I was desperate to argue about something. She just twisted her legs and made the kind of alignment to underwear she did only in cars as we drove to parties, elastic snapping. She raised the window, which had been blowing frigid air on our faces.

"Oh, you know who said she knows you? Who joined the committee?"

Melissa arched her shoulders for something that wasn't quite in place. It always took a while to fix her clothes on the way to a party. The better she looked, the longer it took.

"Who?"

"Susan Spiser? You were at her house on Halloween. She recognized Zach's cap, and came over and introduced herself. I think she's nice, but she's definitely a little spacey."

"I vaguely remember. Who else?"

"Ed's brother David and his latest girlfriend. You know that Joanne's pregnant, right? It's still a secret. God, I haven't seen Lissie Meadows in years."

I parked at the Reiners' on Upper Mountain Avenue behind a Volvo wagon the same color as ours with a bumper sticker that said, "Arms are for Hugging." The house was festive, with spotlights on the lawn shining up to the copper tower that jutted over the roof. The porch needs six lights for all of it, and the corner came to a point, like a whirling cap that mimicked the shape of the tower. Ed Reiner owned a business that manufactured those pieces of molded plastic we grip at the end of a Venetian blind cord. It was an inconsequential object you never think about, but someone else did, and he made a fortune. America is filled with people who pocket millions by creating essential items that are nearly invisible and, I might add, not especially uplifting spiritually. But it freed Joanne to earn peanuts as a freelance writer for obscure environmental publications, which gave the Reiners impressive credentials as a couple committed to social activism. Theirs was the perfect Montclair marriage: liberal politics wedded to a liberal income.

I looked at the porch twirling up toward the tower, and all I could think was that Lissie Meadows was inside waiting.

We passed through several doors and doffed our coats in one of those superfluous rooms huge houses always have tucked in corners. We strolled through the hallway, past a poster that was a play on a famous *New Yorker* cover (it showed Brooklyn as the center of the universe instead of Manhattan), and into the kitchen, which was the size of my entire downstairs. One wall was floor-to-ceiling glass, and there were two tiled islands with sinks. Over the table was an Astrodome-size skylight, and from it dangled a pelican, or some other endangered bird. Three jugs of bottled water stood against the wall. Above them was a calendar showing a whale turning joyous backflips under a blood-red sun.

Joanne was holding court and fussing. With one hand she was putting a pot of water on the stove (those commercial stoves people insist they need) and gesturing with the other as she told a story of an anchorwoman she had interviewed on the media's treatment of recycling.

"So you wouldn't believe it," she said, a hand on her chest to clamp her necklace in place as she reached over the pool table-size stove. "She thinks she's Walter Cronkite. She sits there intoning, pausing, between words? Mega ego trip! She wants to do lunch, to get me on board, to gossip about Jane Pauley bonding with her baby. Or *not* bonding. Blew me away!"

Joanne and Ed Reiner spoke their own idiom, expressions from the sixties mixed in with phrases made popular by the last issue of *People* magazine.

"But it was a trip, doing lunch at this yuppie cafe, pseudo yuppie, and *oh, so Soho!* She orders Diet Coke! In her office, Styrofoam cups. *Styro*foam! And heaves the cans. *Heaves* them. Imagine!"

The story, ostensibly to poke fun at the celebrity, had the more urgent goal of revealing that Joanne Reiner had been in this well-known woman's office, gossiping cattily with and, now, cattily about, the rich and famous.

She lifted the pot aloft. A coffee filter, beige and un-bleached, was skirted out and readied for its baptism of fiery spring water.

"I can tell we're getting old," she said. "Everybody drinks decaf. The wild, woolly days are over. No more sex, drugs, and rock and roll."

She put down the pot, looked up at the ceiling, and said, "Hah!"

This was the Reiner host laugh. It required her to flop her arms at her sides, gaze at the endangered bird in the skylight, and let out a hoot, which exploded like a warning shot and advised you to start having fun, if you knew what was good for you, now that you're in Reiner territory.

"At least no more drugs and rock and roll," Melissa said.

Joanne repeated the phrase to see what Melissa had left out, looked up, and said, "Hah!"

"You know in the business they're called hairdos," I said. "They play this game that they're real journalists, but they're just pretty faces."

"I thought they write their own material," said a woman I couldn't place, who had glasses, a lot of lipstick, and a perpe-tually puckered expression. At least it had been puckered (lips in a little knot, as if the heavy lipstick had glued them) as long as she had been standing there. "They don't?"

"First of all," I said, "it's a fact that all the words spoken on a television news show'd barely fill a single column of the *New York Times*. And second, what they say is so dumb. They're all goddamn morons. I wouldn't care about their fat paychecks if they just accepted they're entertainers and that's it."

"Decaf, you're so right," Melissa said. "Years ago no one drank it. We'd laugh. Now everybody does. Or tea. Remember Lucy?"

I stood there holding myself back. I had erupted like a volcano, lava-hot hatred flowing. I didn't know why I was getting so worked up about television news. Of course everything I said was true, but I didn't want to look like some lunatic with an ax to grind.

"But they *have* to know what they're talking about," Lucy said. "Don't they?" She was wearing a fancy red dress with a bow over the neck. Melissa was right. There were going to be dinosaurs here.

"Most of them couldn't write a news story if their fat bloated contracts depended on it," I said, calm, yet putting the matter to rest. "Each show has a team of writers. Check the credits. Take a look."

"I will," Lucy said. "Thank you. That's really very fascinating."

"Decaf, I almost forgot," Joanne said. "I'm making two kinds. Hah!"

She peeled open a brown, wholesome-looking package of Colombian coffee, which she explained had been grown on a cooperative plantation where the laborers weren't exploited. She sprinkled the beans into a hand grinder, watched them bounce, and cranked the handle, trying again to hold her necklace so it wouldn't get caught. Joanne didn't wear clothes as much as costumes, which made her look not like a well-to-do suburbanite who shopped weekly for clothes but a penniless free spirit with an uncanny knack for dressing. She was in blue cashmere, a stretchy outfit that's a sweater but goes to the knees, over turquoise tights, and speckled shoes that about twenty people had commented on. Swinging on her neck was a long necklace of bone-colored objects resembling elephant tusks.

"So I think it's actually happening," Joanne said, as she dumped the coffee into the beige filter, using a fingernail to scrape out the bottom. "I can't believe it. I am psyched. I am ready to rock."

"Yes," Melissa said. "You're tanned, fit, and four months late."

Joanne rubbed her stomach, looked up, and said, "Hah!"

She flicked grinds off a fingernail and wiped her hand with a washable cloth napkin (no paper was wasted in the Reiner kitchen). Joanne was finally having a healthy pregnancy after a series of early miscarriages. Melissa had been her confidante through it all. She gave Melissa the lowdown, hoisting the pot high like a winner's trophy. "Hah!" she said, and poured. Water cascaded into the filter, turned it brown and steamy, and a delicious aroma wafted out toward us, rich, delicate, and politically impeccable.

They talked about ovulation, biological clocks, and whether Joanne was "showing." I drifted toward the dining room, on the prowl for Lissie Meadows. I stopped at an oak table overflowing with food, all vegetarian.

"Hi!"

I turned to find Susan Spiser in the same black dress from Halloween. The same black bra, too, I couldn't help noticing. "So how the hell *are* you?"

She stood in that eager way of hers. It flattered me.

"As well as can be expected," I said, which is what I always say. It's a line I picked up somewhere. "Under the circumstances."

"What's the matter?"

I thought I might actually tell her everything that was wrong. It was her full attention, her focus on my eyes. It's disarming, having someone really look, really listen.

"Nothing," I said. "I was just joking around."

"This paté is *sinful*," Susan said, sucking in her cheeks as she munched a whole-wheat cracker with something brown smeared on it.

"Try some! You *have* to! Oooh! God! *Mmmmmmmmm!*"

She shut her eyes and tensed her shoulders. Her neckline popped outward, and her coy wink of cleavage broke into a lewd gaping grin.

Her eyes opened, and in the languid afterglow she asked, "You ever get to doing anything with those frogs?"

"The Happy Singing Killer Frogs? No, nothing, I'm afraid. Too much else to do."

"Tell me about it," she said. I liked her saying that. Melissa gave me a hard time when I said I had too much to do.

"And since then the Ninja Turtles became so big, stealing my idea. All my ideas, just stolen."

"Well, it was the highlight of my night—Grongo, Jongo, Rongo, and what's his name?" She started giggling, bless her, a throaty, female giggle.

"Pongo."

"Pongo. You were terrific."

"Thank you. That means more to me than you realize."

"By the way, which one's Ed Reiner? I think Lou knows him."

"Lou knows him? It is a Dickensian universe. The guy near the stereo."

"A little too Dickensian if you ask me."

She pulled herself up ramrod straight and marched over to Ed. She waited, shuffling, at the edge of his group, and announced, "Happy birthday, Ed. I'm Susie Spiser. I'm new on the committee. Louis my husband tells me you know him from the train? So, how does it feel to be forty?"

"Lou!" Ed said, slapping his hip with a compact disc. "I talk to that guy all the time! When he's not on the road. A wild man. Lou Spiser? Lou-ee Lou-i himself? Wild-man Lou? Hah!"

His version of the Reiner host laugh was more militant, a strict order to laugh, or we can't be held responsible for what may happen next.

"He's in San Diego," she said. "He's always—but Lou a wild man?"

"You know what this guy tells me?" Ed asked, drawing in the group, whom he'd been addressing the whole time. He's always more at ease with a crowd. Even when he talked just to me a crowd seemed to be nearby.

"What did my wild man say? This I gotta hear."

She was smiling lavishly; he hadn't been all that witty. She drew her body into her tight way of standing, hands clasped over the black bodice of her dress, as if preparing for the first step of a dance—if only someone would ask.

"Hah!" Ed said, his eyes on the ceiling, the arm with the disc recoiling.

"He tells me," Ed said now to one and all, raising the compact disc back up and flipping it around like a Frisbee, "he's into running. Eight miles —"

"I re*mem*ber," Susan said, adjusting her body to better face him. "The running craze. He went totally psycho! *Psychotic!* Till his knee gave out."

"A wild man," Ed said. "A goddamn wild man. And listens to what on his Walkman?" He started nodding.

"Oh," Susan said, dropping one shoulder so her body would fit into his, the dance about to begin. "On his Walkman. Of *course.*"

She laughed, following his lead, nodding her head in time until they were engaged in a kind of nodding waltz, which they kept up while the crowd watched, eager to take part but unable to break in.

"To Pink Floyd," Ed said. "Only to Pink Floyd. Pink Floyd only. And only *Another Brick in the Wall.* Hah!"

The group lunged at the opening and started nodding. But Ed wielded the compact disc like a nightstick. It was not yet time for others to join.

"And why?" he asked, staring at Susan, nodding again.

"I know, of course," Susan said, as they did a suave two-step with their heads, bobbing up, and freezing.

"Some argument he had in college, right?"

"You got it," Susan said.

"If it's *brick* in the wall or *break* in the wall. He said it psyched him to run, proving he was right. He tells me he went to some psychedelic room in his mind where this guy was always sitting smoking a joint and scored debating points. Made mincemeat of that stoned sucker. Stoned mincemeat! *Hah!*"

At the signal everyone picked up the rhythm, nodding at the joke. But Susan pulled back, stopped nodding, and drew extremely erect.

"He's *very* competitive," she said, which managed to hold Lou up to ridicule while also flaunting her inside knowledge of his idiosyncrasies.

"That was Mitchell Lowery," she added. "The big argument in senior year. Lou hated his guts. He even said the album cover was wrong, a hoax. A sort of Paul is dead joke. Paul is dead?"

"I think I have it on disc somewhere," Ed said, backing into the gleaming black boxes of his stereo as Susan closed in.

"He was a man po*ssessed*," Susan went on, as Ed ran his thumb over a rack of compact discs, gliding one out, then shoving it back. *"Totally* possessed by the whole thing!"

"Now, here's an incredible gift," Ed said, holding up a boxed collection of music by the Byrds. "The best part is the live version of 'Tambourine Man.' Where Dylan shows up and sings along. He's just *horrible."*

"He is *so* out of it," said a man Ed had been talking to, a skinny guy whom I immediately disliked.

"Wrecks the goddamn song," the woman with the skinny guy said. She was even scrawnier, and all in black, with a cape. She had that vulture Tribeca look. "I think poor Roger McGuinn tries to shut him up."

Ed held up the disc, but didn't disagree. He liked debates.

"Well, you know he did write it," I said.

I didn't like them taking pot shots at Dylan, who is one of the few famous people I respect. When I lived alone I had only classical music in my apartment, except for Dylan, a place of honor, I used to tell anyone who'd listen. (Lissie Meadows did, twice, on the phone.) He said the things I wanted to say, yet it didn't drive me crazy somehow.

"He is a total, total *dodo* head," the man with Ed said. He was not only skinny but wore a sports jacket over a turtleneck sweater. I despise men who wear sports jackets over turtleneck sweaters.

"You hear him at the Grammys?" the Tribeca vulture said, flicking her cape. "He makes like this goddamn mumbling speech. No one understands a goddamn word. *Redemption?* Who the hell knows. High as a kite. Just out of his gourd."

I had a murderous thought: the viper in black could be Lissie Meadows! Then I realized the skinny guy was Ed's brother David. He always tilled the voluptuous garden of New York single women and came up with weeds. Melissa and Joanne gossiped about it all the time.

"The point is," I said, "he's the one who went alone into a room and came out with 'Tambourine Man.' If not for him there'd be no song. People think they own him. He goes electric or on a religious trip and it becomes a personal betrayal. The depth of his music is amazing, starting way back in the sixties, the folk stuff, powerful lyrics, real poetry. It speaks to me, it still speaks to me."

I was going off on a tirade. I was furious—at the Byrds, at Tribeca, at compact discs, at men in turtlenecks and sports jackets, at women in black with pretentious capes, at anyone who didn't love Dylan, and anything else I could come up with. But Susan, sweet Susan, was taking me by the eyes and starting a dance. It lasted a second, enough to cool me down, before she turned to face Ed with the brazen interest she had begun showing him.

"So, Ed," she said. "Speaking of age, how does it feel to be forty?"

This time Ed took the cue. He waited for his audience to quiet and said, "In a word, in one word, un-fucking-real."

"Un-fucking-real," he repeated for the few who hadn't heard. Everyone agreed, chuckling, the fuse of laughter lit. His timing would have to be perfect.

"*Hah!*"

Laughter detonated instantly. Ed flinched, ducking away, and his guests, laughing too much to remember what they were talking about, dived toward the table of food.

A voice hit me from behind. "So, I hear Melissa's pregnant!"

It was Alice Metzer. There were only two things everyone knew about Alice: that she worked for the *New York Times* and that she had taken so many drugs in the sixties that she once had to be hospitalized. She was equally proud of both.

"News to me," I said. Every time I looked at Alice I saw the *New York Times*. Of course it didn't help that she found a way to slip it into every conversation, between boasts of illegal substance abuse. Not only did she love to drop that she worked at the *Times*, she loved to rub my nose in the fact that I didn't really work anywhere.

"Well, I *know* I'm not hallucinating. I know I heard she and Joanne in the kitchen."

Joanne and her, I corrected in my head, but of course didn't say to Ms. Newspaper of Record, as she slithered in next to Susan. The three of us settled in together after Ed's joke, Susan because she didn't know anybody, and Alice because she was put on earth to torture me. We were having the fragmented conversation of people stuck together at a party as they silently map out a means to escape.

"We're not pregnant," I said. "For sure."

"The husband's the last to know, you know," Alice said.

"I wonder what this stuff is?" Susan said. She took the food very seriously.

"Everyone's pregnant," Alice said, too full of herself to continue needling me. "It's all everyone talks about. Like people used to talk about the good dope they scored. This yellow? Guacamole?"

"I never eat food I can't pronounce," I said. "Or food that looks embroidered." Both lines were stolen, but Susan smiled.

"But isn't it funny how you hear something everywhere?" said Alice, oblivious as usual. "I mean, isn't it just truly *amazing?*"

She was speaking with staged enthusiasm because, I knew, she was trying to maneuver the discussion around to herself.

"It looks like some kind of mousse," Susan said. "Like the way this month every radio show in the world's saying John Lennon was killed exactly ten years ago. Can you believe it's been ten years?"

I tried to come up with a food comment or something about the Beatles, but I was never that fast on my feet when Alice was around.

"Anyone know if Joanne's sister is here?" I asked.

"The famous Lissie Meadows?" Alice said. "I don't have the foggiest. And the old memory's kind of blitzed, if you know what I mean."

"I heard the violin beauty was in," Susan said. "What the heck's this?"

Alice glanced at the creamy stuff Susan was pointing to and said, "I mean, like, just last week, I was working on the national desk—they needed people, you know, with the stuff in the Gulf with Iraq?" She paused to ensure that the vital part had registered. "I was like so wrecked! And I had to go in! Anyway, everyone was talking about getting pregnant. That's it. That's all I heard. Fertility. Adoption. Baby hunger. It's like become the latest craze."

Alice was so self-absorbed she could make deciding to start a family sound like trying transcendental meditation or eating oat bran. But it conned Susan into popping the question Alice had been longing to hear.

"What desk? Where do you work?"

Alice made a face. "Oh," she said, "the *Times*."

"The *Montclair Times*?" Susan said. "That must be so *interesting!*"

"The *New York Times*," Alice said. "Unfortunately."

I nearly blew a gasket. I was afraid I'd fire off another harangue so I made my escape as Susan bent to prod the creamy stuff with a hairy whole-wheat cracker, and Alice, addressing her cleavage, said, "Everyone's very competitive and there's a lot of favoritism, political garbage. You know?"

I took a glass of wine (there was only wine) near a cluster of people guffawing at a story Ed was telling. I ran a Lissie Meadows scan and spotted Melissa talking to Carol Bloom. Everyone else had embraced Carol then staggered off to a less hazardous conversation. As a result, Carol was marooned with Melissa on their own island of grief, from which Gideon's death emanated like radiation. Unknowingly, Carol's friends were adding the insult of ostracism to the devastating injury of Gideon's death.

I was scouring the room now for Lissie Meadows. My eyes flew over Melissa, and I turned to look back. It took a second, but before it snapped in my head that I was looking at my wife I felt a yen to know her. It took me into a game I had fun with—I called it the Daniel Weil test: I'm deciding which woman to move in on at a party. (I'm quite debonair in this fantasy; at the time I was still certain I'd be a veritable robo-Romeo if unattached.) Every time I tested it Melissa won, hands down. How many men can say this about their wives?

I studied Melissa as she inhaled, a sigh of empathy, a breath of compassion for a friend. Her willingness to share Carol's sorrow was in the tension of her posture. Her legs, sleek as steel in black tights and riveted to the floor, shot up into the circle of the skirt, where the black mesh spread another circle around it. Sympathy rose through those circles, gaining intensity as a camera sharpens focus through a progression of apertures. I was thrown by the breadth of her compassion and the darkness of her eyes, the angle of her hips, the nasty sweep of black mesh around her expanding chest.

Another man's hands.

"It was so romantic in the woods, Barry."

My shoes clomped the floor as I made my way to her, hands in hip pockets, a very casual gait. Lately Melissa and Carol had been on the phone for hours. With every step I felt more panic, sizzling hot, more like lust than like anger. My shoes stopped on the lustrous wood. I stood as if listening to Ed's brother describe a problem his computer was having.

"Don't you work with computers?"

It was Alice Metzer, and I had walked right into it. She always started conversations calling out, and I had to turn to see who it was. She was, as usual, badgering me for not having a real job; she really got off on bringing up old jobs I no longer had.

"Not anymore," I said. "I don't anymore."

Susan, still stuck with her, was cradling a cracker with purple buttery mush. They came over (detouring around Carol and Melissa like they were something spilled on the floor) as I reached into my haphazard computer knowledge for an idea.

"The solution is rather philosophical," I said to Ed. "It's about the spiritual essence of a computer."

Susan laughed. She laughed at anything with the rhythm of a joke.

"I think what you need is a path," I said.

"I have a path *command*," the skinny brother said, in his exasperating way. "In my autoexec *dot* bat file. Root directory, of course."

His voice was pinched, as if the turtleneck squeezed his vocal chords. His vulture girlfriend tossed her cape and glared.

"Well, I just do my stories," Alice said to Susan. "And worry about keeping up my supply. I don't worry about what's inside a computer. Just those *dead*lines."

But, triumphantly, no one asked what she had to be supplied with or which deadlines she was talking about.

"Finding a path?" Susan said. "What is that exactly?"

I blazed ahead.

"A computer mimics life. You have to give it a path, to look for what it needs to handle commands. So if it doesn't have a path, it's lost. Doesn't know where to look. It just can't find the meaning of its life. It's *very* existential."

I knew just enough about computers and existentialism to know this had nothing whatsoever to do with either, but Susan laughed. The way she looked at me was unnerving, like she loved me passionately, or was on heavy medication.

Ed's brother insisted my solution wouldn't work, but fell into the trap I sidestepped by using such technical jargon that no one followed him except his skinny vulture girlfriend, who was no doubt putting on an act. And even she was left in the dust when he said, "and, to make a long story short," which people say only when they're about to make an already interminable story into something even more excruciating. Ed tried to bail his brother out by kidding him about software piracy for taking a file from work. I was sorry that Ed had to see his brother embarrass himself silly by boring Ed's guests until they were practically in a coma. I wanted to rescue Ed from his blowhard brother, and I wanted to rescue everyone pretending to listen, even Alice and the skinny vulture girlfriend. But most of all I wanted to rescue Ed's blockhead brother from himself. I don't know why it kills me so to see someone make a fool of himself in public, even someone I can't stand.

I jammed a fresh idea into the first open space David Reiner yielded.

"You know, that word itself is very interesting," I said. "Piracy, I mean like in software piracy. It shows how we don't think it's that bad to steal software. Or tapes. Pirates have a mystique. As did bootleggers. They're folk heroes."

There was silence—everyone was in such a stupor from David Reiner's monologue.

"Hah!"

Ed's voice slammed in like a rocket. He had backed away to position himself to pull the plug on his brother and get the party going again.

"So, where the hell did the sixties go?" he was calling out.

"Sixties?" Joanne said, making a dramatic entrance from the kitchen. They moved about so nimbly it had an air of theater. "What happened to the seventies? Tell me that! Hah!"

"*Hah!* And the nineteen-eighties are history, too."

"The nineties'll go like a flash. You'll see!"

"Ten years since Lennon was shot."

"Twenty since the Beatles broke up."

"Dylan's pushing fifty!"

"He sounds *ninety!*"

"Hah!"

"*Hah!*"

I went along the table into another room. Behind me the group had begun a ragtag version of the Beatles' "Birthday," and tossing birthday gibes. The cracks were in Reinerspeak: turning forty was "a mega-heavy trip," Ed was being a "wuss," a "dorkwad." As I left the room Joanne yelled, "*This* is freaky! In ten years you'll be fifty! *Fifty!* Think about *that* if you wanna totally blow your mind!"

"Major bummer!"

"Major downer!"

"Hah!"

"*Hah!*"

I came across Ellen Smuckler talking to Mike Berkoff next to the poster of Brooklyn as the center of the world. Ellen had been there the whole time. She looked different every time I saw her.

"Terrific," Mike was saying, "everything's incredibly terrific."

Mike's life was always going fabulously well. He had been through two divorces, his children were scattered, and he'd suffered at least three unplanned career shifts. He always said how his life improved after the last change. He was pretty convincing, too.

"It's amazing," he said. "I took over the recycling newsletter, and I have time to do some real writing finally. To expose the hypocrisy of government, a book, *The Vicious Cycle of Recycling,* or maybe *Psyching Out Recycling,* even better. I planned it out. Bought a new computer. Set up a study in my new place. I look forward to getting up in the morning just to work, if you can believe that."

Ellen was checking out the room. Her earrings, a purple spoon on one side and a purple fork on the other, chattered as she swiveled her head. "You know I saw Melissa near Boston, don't you?" she asked.

"You saw her near Boston? No, I didn't."

"She didn't say anything? That she saw me? I was near Tanglewood on a shoot. She was with a guy carrying a straw basket with wine and bread. It must have been for a shoot, too. It looked too fancy for real life, and it's *very* pretty there. A rose, too. I guess for her job? I didn't know she did commercials. They took off before I could say hello. They were in a big hurry to get *somewhere,* that I can tell you. I was there for a lingerie show. A *fabulous* lingerie show!"

"What was going on?" I asked. "What exactly did you see?"

"Absolutely *fabulous* lingerie. You and Mike would love it! The new look's so *frilly!* Very, *very* feminine. And *very* sexual. A whole new sensual way for a woman to—"

"I mean, what did you see Melissa doing? I'm curious. I think I know the guy she was with."

"Oh, they were talking and laughing a lot. *Something* was hysterical. That I can tell you. And the *colors!* Pink will be huge this season. *Huge!* Daring colors, *daring!*" She looked first at Mike, then a bit longer at me, and said, "You two will like the new look. I think I can safely say that for a fact."

She began nodding like mad, until the sections of fork and spoon in her ears went *clink-clink-clink.*

"Anyone know if the famous Lissie Meadows is here?" I asked.

"The violinist? The famous gorgeous sister?" Mike said. "I'm afraid I have no idea. Although I wish I did."

"The single one?" Ellen said, and shook her head, earrings going wild.

Ed Reiner drew up to my elbow. "Melissa Weil just threw away a perfectly recyclable bottle. Your wife is a criminal. We have the evidence. Hah!"

"Scandalous," Mike said, as Ed scooted over to a group at a white baby grand in their cavernous living room.

"That doesn't sound like Melissa," Ellen said, in a way that irked me.

"Fred says to dust the bottle for prints," Ed shouted from the piano.

I turned to the table with the wine to refill my glass and suddenly I was staring right at Lissie Meadows. Then in a crazy instant everything shifted and I was confronting Melissa. "Daniel?" she was saying.

"Yes."

"Daniel!"

"Yes?"

"Daniel, Daniel, we have to talk, Daniel."

"Sure."

"I mean, we *have* to talk."

"Here she is!" Ed shouted. "We nabbed the perp! The *guilty party!*"

He led her away. "The guilty party at the party. Hah!"

He released her at the foot of the stairs. The action had established itself there, the way gatherings take root in stairway landings and kitchens.

"You have the right to remain silent," he called to the crowd. "Hah!"

Melissa swirled her white zinfandel and said, "I throw myself on the mercy of the court. I am guilty of no crime but the crime of love. And if you don't buy that, I want a lawyer, quick."

I had never seen her in action like this.

Her body fascinated me. Each time she swirled the wine she shook her hips in a little jiggle that bounced up her arms to the glass. Then she'd consider the wine and shake her hips again. I watched in a kind of aesthetic rapture, as if she were a painting I owned.

"I am this woman's attorney," Carol said. "May I address the court?"

"Watch out," Melissa said. "It's 'Hang 'em High' Reiner."

Ed was pleased; like all natural hosts he adored it when guests took on the merry-making themselves. "Go for it," he said.

"Our defense, the love thing Melissa meant, is that we love gabbing with Joanne, the court's wife, *hint hint*, and she told us news so exciting we threw away said bottle. She confesses all her sins. Is contrite. Well, sort of."

"I vote for acquittal," Mike shouted.

"Hold your horses," Alice said. "Once you do it once you can't stop."

It seemed to bug her to see Melissa escape punishment, even in a game.

"It was my wife's first offense," I said. *"I forgive her."*

"That's the last thing *he'll* ever do," Melissa said, which got a big laugh. "I can't forgive myself."

"Love your outfit," Ellen, typically inappropriate, said inside the laughter. "That length just is perfect for you, Melissa."

Melissa, slouching immediately, mouthed, "Thank you."

"Hey, I'll visit you in the Big House, Babe," I said.

"Only if it's a conjugal visit!" Melissa said, with a look—dark eyes teasing, legs drawing erect—that tore me to pieces. "And don't bring the kids. I'm talking all night, no kids!"

She had regained her composure and her posture.

Mike picked it up, I think, and said, "I certainly hope so. For his sake!"

"What did she do exactly?" Susan Spiser whispered to me.

"Your honor?" Carol was saying.

"Speak!"

"I am an eyewitness, and I will testify it was an accident. We can just dismiss the charges right now."

Carol thought Melissa was getting uncomfortable and wanted the spotlight off her. There's so little generosity of spirit in this world it's a wonder to see it. I feel like bowing down before it when I do.

But Ed was having too much fun to stop.

"I think we should sentence her to the chair," he said. "I mean chair of the recycling committee, of course. *Hah!*"

"I'll take the electric!" said Melissa, completely in control.

"You do not deny you saw the green bin?" Ed asked.

"Objection! It's too far away, your honor," Joanne said. "Way too far!"

"I confess," Melissa said. "I confess everything I did."

She looked right at me. I swear she did.

"Give her another chance," I said. "Sentence her to life with me with no hope of parole."

"She's already serving *that* one," the Tribeca vulture said, hovering on the stairs, then flying up with two glasses of something pink, cape floating.

It was Joanne who got her off. As if rehearsing for motherhood, she distracted the group as if it were a four-year-old.

"That's why we're redoing the kitchen," she said. "Before the baby comes. Which by the way is the gossip that made Melissa turn to a life of crime. I hereby announce I am pregnant. Four months, and lookin' good."

It worked like a charm.

Joanne's long-sought pregnancy, rumored on the recycling grapevine, was now public. Joanne cut off the cheers, either out of sympathy for Carol or fear of jinxing something that still had a way to go.

"I love my kitchen, but everything's in the wrong place," she said.

"Just what we need," Ed said, affecting annoyance at having to rebuild a perfectly good kitchen. "Major construction, gutting the room and building out. And we're talking big bucks. Megabucks. Joanne's *very* into it."

He mentioned the cost not to brag, which wasn't in his nature, but because he was embarrassed to be spending gobs of money on something he did not truly need.

"If our karma comes through," Joanne said, crossing her fingers.

"Our karma and our contractor."

"Hah!"

"*Hah!*"

Melissa fled into the kitchen, talking to Carol, probably asking how she felt about Joanne's announcement. (The other guests were listing what they hated about their kitchens.) Melissa took Carol's arm, and Carol put her head on Melissa's shoulder, then took it off. Soon they were laughing and touching each other, with Carol pointing to the green bin with the words "We Recycle." I had to talk to Melissa, and cut through the arms and legs between us. I got caught in a stampede, a moment when a party relocates and everyone rushes to the new hot spot. As I was swept away I heard Carol above the chaos. "The fact of the matter is I had to recognize his condition was hopeless and Gideon was in pain. Melissa, ugly, ugly things happen, and you have to accept it. Daniel, he—"

A ruckus broke out from the hallway, where someone was on trial after confessing she didn't demand paper bags at the supermarket. The next thing I knew Alice Metzer was calling, *"You're* home a lot."

"Ed's going to help *hugely*," she was saying, lecturing Joanne about her own husband. "I guaran*tee* it. He's the type. You won't be as lucky as Melissa though. I mean, her and Daniel have it just *perfecto*. What are you doing exactly now jobwise, by the way? I think you told me once, but the old memory's applesauce these days. I had this flashback when my editor . . ."

I pretended to be heading for the piano, faked left, then charged up the stairs. I hid in the bathroom. I thought I'd unhook the toilet paper and make a big deal that the Reiners were wasting paper. I could hurl the roll so it would unwind over that jumbo baby grand, as evidence. I could put Joanne and Ed on trial. They'd eat it up.

But I wasn't up to it, so I wandered down the hall, past pictures of endangered creatures looking cuddly. I passed what the Reiners called the "media room." The door was half closed, and I heard a television or a tape with a basketball game. "Yes! Yes!" someone was shouting. I saw in silhouette the heads of people, including David Reiner's sticking out his turtleneck like a potted plant. His girlfriend, nearly invisible in black, was jumping up and down. They were before a screen the size of a movie theater's. Frosty blue light flickered on their faces. They shook their heads but could not escape.

Then I heard the violin. I could make it out clearly between the TV and the racket thumping up along the stairs.

I followed it past another bathroom. Something was going on in this one, a couple kissing. And they weren't just kissing but doing some industrial-strength smooching, the woman's back shoved against the wall, the man pawing at her while closing the door. He shut it over her earring, which got caught because she was arching her back in a swoon. Crushed in the door was the last section of a purple spoon, wiggling happily.

I eased around the turn. Above the raucous laughter I could still hear the violin. I inched up the stairs to the attic.

Here the music got louder and more beautiful. It was wiry and tight, the strings coiling around me and pulling me up. I knew the piece, from Bach's "Sonatas and Partitas for Unaccompanied Violin." It had to be Lissie Meadows, playing alone, choosing that instead of the mindless tumult below. She would have haunted, coal-black eyes. Her hair would flow over the grainy wood of the violin and down her shoulders.

I traced the music to the end of the hall where I found a staircase to a second attic. I tiptoed up. The violin was coming from a room at the end of the hall that I guessed was the tower I'd seen from the street. She was on the Chaconne, the last section of the second partita.

I had located the exact door behind which the violin was playing, the door to the tower, and it was ajar. Through its opening I heard the violin as she got to a harder variation, where the melody scales up a frightening crescendo, leaping to more beauty than I could stand, then stepping up yet another rung.

The violin stopped. I froze. Strings were plucked.

With fresh determination I felt her raise the bow. Her playing took on a lustier spirit, that savvy sensuality all music yearns for but rarely achieves. The violin vaulted high, setting free a melody that unfolded another melody inside it, which fluttered in the air above our heads. I saw her draw the bow, eyes closed, head bent. There were tears on her cheeks.

Then it struck me. I was snooping. I was trespassing. She'd think I'm some kind of psycho to sneak up here and crouch outside her door.

I peered through the crack and saw a woman, but the light was wavy, as if from candles. I could make out a domed ceiling, a circle of windows, and floor planks running crosswise toward me. I saw her elbow rocking, the tip of a bow jabbing, a slash of dark hair streaming. I felt her breathe, knew the pain from which her music was made. I shuddered at being granted such intimacy with her.

I struggled for the word to describe it. And found it: Terror.

Or at least that's what I felt, huddled outside the tower door. I clenched my fist. I calculated my knuckles would rap the middle panel.

I thought, as I often do, of a joke. This guy goes into a bar and sees a woman he wants to meet, but asks himself: Does she want a man to approach her? Is she there to meet a friend? Why do humans have an urge to connect? Is it an innate impulse with a genetic basis? Meanwhile, as he's working himself into a metaphysical quandary, some half-drunk bozo walks over to the woman, introduces himself, and the two stroll out arm in arm.

And I stood there, mired in my own metaphysical quandary. Then I did what I always do, what I secretly knew I'd do all along. I stole across the hall and down the short flight of steps, then the longer flight to the bedroom floor. The violin weakened above me and broke apart. Rock music came lurching up toward me on the stairs. I could hear the crowd, all my friends, snickering, shouting, and singing along.

— 11 —

GYNECOLOGIST
PATIENTS LOVED
HAD NO DEGREE

BUENOS AIRES—AN ARGENTINE WITH NO MEDICAL DEGREE WORKED AS A GYNECOLOGIST IN A TOP HOSPITAL FOR 12 YEARS, EXAMINED HUNDREDS OF WOMEN, CHAIRING A SPECIALIST CONFERENCE AND CO-WRITING A POPULAR BOOK ON WOMEN'S HEALTH, LOCAL MEDIA REPORTED YESTERDAY.
JUAN VILONIA WORKED AT THE RIVADAVIA HOSPITAL IN BUENOS AIRES FROM 1978 TO 1990, ACCORDING TO THE CLARIN DAILY.
HOSPITAL OFFICIALS SAID THEY BECAME SUSPICIOUS BECAUSE OF CONTINUOUS REPORTS THAT VILONIA MADE "INAPPROPRIATE REMARKS" DURING PELVIC EXAMS. THEY WOULD NOT ELABORATE.
VILONIA, 44, WAS DESCRIBED BY HIS FORMER MEDICAL COLLEAGUES AS BOTH "BRILLIANT" AND A "PSYCHOPATH," CLARIN SAID.
SEVERAL WOMEN WROTE TO THE MEDICAL BOARD IN SUPPORT OF VILONIA AFTER HIS ARREST. ONE DESCRIBED HIM AS "THE GYNECOLOGIST YOU DREAM ABOUT, GENTLE, THOROUGH AND WITH A VERY LIGHT TOUCH."

why does it take 2 women with pms
to change a light bulb? (PETER)

why? (VEIL)

IT JUST DOES! (PETER)

why did they send women with pms
to fight in the iraqi dessert? (PETER)

? (VEIL)

cuz they retain water & want to kill (PETER)

very good. can i ask you a question? (VEIL)

blast away. i ain't called stormin normin for nuttin
(PETER)

u going home with peter? (SPERLING)

yeah. OK? (VEIL)

sure. just we haven't talked for ages (SPERLING)

& famed lincoln diner has its b'fast special
(SPERLING)

but really, no sweat (SPERLING)

i feeling really bummed about my ex
like all of sudden. (VEIL)

the wise man sayeth: thou needest to get laid (PETER)

did! (VEIL)

and... (PETER)

all i got was someone to add
to our ugly-sexy hall fame (VEIL)

when a good fuck doesn't help
you passed the horny stage my friend.
u about to become a lonely old man (PETER)

Gregory Gregory glided by and dropped a news clip for a story I had handled the night before. *The Journal* library was computerized, and any clip was useless after deadline let alone the next day. But Gregory Gregory insisted on supplying day-old clips on paper. It was about a fund in memory of a boy whose obit I edited on one of my first nights up here. I became "the expert," as they say on copy desks, so I was given the fund story.

BOY, LOCKED OUT,

FREEZES TO DEATH

OUTSIDE HIS DOOR

I wrote the headline and knocked the story into shape without having to think; I had been there long enough to be able to do this by now.

When Peter drove me home he took an especially long way. He didn't say a word and stayed on the highway two exits past the right one. I couldn't get the boy who froze to death out of my mind. I kept seeing his parents finding his bed empty in the morning, wondering where he was, and opening the front door.

"Did I ever tell you about Lissie Meadows?" I asked.

"Doesn't ring a bell."

"The famous violinist? I thought I saw her on Lincoln last night. I followed her two goddamn blocks, but it wasn't her."

"An old girlfriend?"

"No. I secretly loved her for years. She's the one—how can I put it?—if you had her, you'd be happy."

"Oh, now I got it. You know, once I was in this office, the Betsy Bender office, and this woman comes in for a job interview. Sits across from me. She smiled. I remember that smile, really warm. I was going through shit with Jackie. I mean, like incredible shit! She goes in for an interview, she isn't hired, and I never see her again. But I think about her a lot. To tell you the truth, Daniel, she's always on my m-mind."

For the first time in my life I knew not to say anything. I mean, I often know it, but I say something anyway. This time I kept my mouth shut.

"I did a story tonight on that kid who died," I said. "The one who got up in the middle of the night and accidentally locked himself out, whose parents found him frozen in the morning outside their front door."

"Yeah," Peter said, twitching his head to check the side-view mirror even though the road was empty. I had accidentally reminded him that he was not around for his children. As I reached for a way to undo it, he punched on the radio to the college station.

"Okay?"

"Sure."

He tuned in as one of the twenty-year-old deejays was crowing, "And here's a cut you won't hear Linda McCartney on," and started playing the songs near the end of *Abbey Road*, just before "Golden Slumbers." I had a hundred theories about what the Beatles meant to our generation and why that made us resent Yoko and Linda. I knew (from Sandy) that Peter had some association with Jackie and the Beatles. But despite my urge to talk, I managed to keep my yap shut for probably the second time in my entire life.

Peter pulled over, right there on the empty highway. He didn't even bother getting onto the shoulder. We sat in silence to listen as Paul McCartney lamented the loss of the way back home.

"Bitch," Peter said. "Fuck."

He slapped the steering wheel so hard the car frame jolted. I didn't say a word.

I went into the empty lot and sat on the stump. I started with the boy in the story I edited, but soon I was on Gideon Bloom.

I see it as a defect in my character that I have problems with death; other men seem to accept it without flinching. I just can't make peace with the fact that someday we will all die. I mean, an uncle dies when you're a kid and it's a minor event. Then you grow up and discover its nasty side, the way you discover the limits of your parents' patience or the general lack of justice in the world. When you're an adult, it's got you by the throat and it won't let go.

When Gideon was first diagnosed my reaction was pretty shameful. I avoided the Blooms' street when I was out with the kids, as if walking by their house (an elaborate Tudor on Highland Avenue) we could catch their misfortune. I remember how the house looked once on a snowy night, cozy and bright, with the fireplace puffing smoke out the chimney. Only when the recycling committee organized to help did I start spending time with Gideon. We hiked the backyard hill that went up into a wilderness-like field. He had strength to climb, but I would have to carry him down. His eyes would wander as I held him in my arms, to a sky that was invariably blue and cloudless.

Carol and Elliot would come back and we'd talk about the property revaluation then under way, or how to get the town to accept plastic jugs for recycling. Once Carol had a paperback on children with brain tumors, but I was afraid to ask about it. She enjoyed light, gossipy chitchat; Elliot always had something in the house he had to fix.

The reason I could go so much, of course, was that I didn't have a real job. Toward the end I visited him in the hospital when everyone was too busy or depressed by it to go. I sneaked over, juggling babysitters as Melissa flew all around the country to raise millions for world-class orchestras. I felt guilty because my devotion was what I believed I should give to my uncompleted (unstarted, to be truthful) projects. We'd watch cartoons on a TV bracketed up near the ceiling, blitzkrieg after blitzkrieg of violence that hurt no one.

One morning with Gideon on his hospital bed, I had a shattering insight: There was a monster inside him, the monster kids are afraid of, that haunts their dreams and calls out from backyard trees. They were right: the monster was real, it got inside Gideon's brain, and it was killing him.

At a committee meeting a few days later, during a vote on separating polyethylene from other plastics, someone announced that Gideon Bloom had died, his remission ending as mysteriously as it had begun. His seven-year-old consciousness had been wiped off the face of the earth, and with it the hope against hope of his parents and the never-enough efforts of their friends.

That night Zachary and I were having one of our talks. In the kind of coincidence that occurs with children he was asking about monsters.

"There are monsters in your mind, right Dad?" He pointed to his temple, beneath his railroad cap. "Like sellekins in your body?"

"Monsters in your mind? Who told you that?"

"Monie told me. Sellekins are in the body, and monsters are in your mind. Not only what I hear creeping in the haunted tree."

"It's true about skeletons," I said, pronouncing the word in meticulous syllables. "It's the bones everyone has, these."

I squeezed the luxuriously healthy flesh of his forearm.

"Yeah, but Monie says monsters are in the mind. They're not real, she says, they're only in your mind. In your mind, Dad."

"Oh, she meant your imagination. That they're only in your thoughts."

"You can turn off the light," he said. "And you can go."

He often dismissed me like that. I stayed outside his door, stamping so it sounded as if I had gone. I needed to be near my son. I accepted that need, sitting on my stump in the empty lot, a fence outlined behind me, the rocks starting to shine with dawn. *You're right, Zach, monsters are real. They got in Gideon Bloom's brain and they killed him. I can't explain why. You can't trust people, you can't trust yourself, and you don't know what life has in store. Zach, my love, there really are monsters out there, and in the end they'll win. The bastards always win.*

I woke up cleansed. I decided to cook something nice, instead of the crap I'd been eating. It was lovely out, early May, and for the first time I heard the evening echo of children, that floating sound, hard on the edges, soft at the core. They'd be playing in the yard on a night like this.

I had some business with Melissa to take care of. I got into my torture chamber, that stinking couch.

She goes to his hotel room in Houston, the new city where I decided it began. She is still disturbed about my disappearance. She's in her sex fiend mode, in which lovemaking is the elixir for everything aching in the soul.

"What are you doing here? The board's waiting."

"You'd better lock that door, Barry."

"You know, I still can't believe he didn't ask anything later in the car."

"No, Barry. That was how he was. He sensed something, definitely."

"What was he again?"

"Nothing. I mean, he was this, he was that. Yes, like that. He didn't have a real job."

"So, he knew but he didn't ask? You started telling him you said."

"He just asked about Lissie Meadows. She was at the party."

"Lissie Meadows was at that guy's fortieth? Wow! You knew her!"

"He had the hots for her. I knew her from Juilliard. But do you want to talk, or something else you'd like. Yes, yes! That is perfect."

"It's my pianist's touch."

Elaine and I were having Chinese food. After the broccoli debacle (which we each blamed on ourselves, instead of having a normal relationship, where we would blame everything on the other) our Platonic friendship had continued. We spent time together, but nothing more. We shared her car, which she encouraged me to borrow, teasing me about not having my own. She got chatty while we waited for the table, as she often did in restaurants. I'm very picky about the table I get, and she kept asking, "Are you positive this one's okay?" in the deferential manner she took on whenever we were out in public together.

When we got a good table she said, "Poifect," just like that, "Poifect," sort of cute. I couldn't stand it. I suddenly hated her. Then she stood and shook herself. She grabbed her hair with both hands, jabbing furiously, shaking like a dog.

She sat, stared, and said, "Alone at last! I really like being here with you."

"I like it too," I said. "I'm glad we finally worked out dinner."

"You have to admit, Danno, we have one crazy relationship."

"Yeah, I suppose we do."

"I suppose too," she said, and gave me another look that said something so obvious about our crazy relationship that it wasn't worth putting into words. (Why did we keep our distance? That was my best guess.) Then she did something vigorous with her hair as she stared at me. The waiter appeared. I ordered hot and sour soup because Melissa and I had it. We also had dumplings all the time. Elaine said she didn't want dumplings because "I'm not a dumpling person." That's what she said, "I'm not a dumpling person."

The next night I went to the Lincoln Diner because I hadn't eaten there in three days. Unfortunately, there was this very arty type from the college in a booth facing me scribbling in his cute little journal. I detest people who sit in restaurants and scribble in journals. Once I watched a guy in Washington Square writing music. He'd gaze up at the arch, nibble his pencil, jot a note. No one paid him any attention but I could have rung his phony neck.

In the restaurant I worked on my latest list. She did it because:

- I wasn't good enough to her.
- I was too good to her.
- I didn't fulfill her emotionally.
- I didn't satisfy her sexually.
- I did, but she is insatiable, both areas.
- She wanted excitement, romance, a one-time fling.
- She wanted excitement, romance, but it became serious.
- She was drawn to him against her will.
- I am a failure and she wanted a success.
- I am a really a success but she wanted a failure.
- It just happened.

---

*how many women does it take
to screw in a lightbulb? (PETER)*

??? (VEIL)

*none. they'd never screw in a lightbulb cuz
they can't make you stay there all night (PETER)*

*how many ex-wives does it take
to screw in a lightbulb (PETER)*

??? (VEIL)

*one. she just holds the bulb and the ladder turns
cuz the whole world revolves around her (PETER)*

I was editing the letters to the editor column.

JOURNAL IS GIVEN
TIMELY REMINDER

To the Editor of *The Journal*:

Shame on you! Don't you realize that if the paper-boy forgot to set his clock ahead he'd deliver *The Journal* an hour early, not an hour late (as you erroneously informed your readers). Here's why: if 2 A.M. springs ahead to 3 A.M., and our hypothetical paperboy forgets to perform his little task, his clock will read 7 A.M. the next morning when it should say 8 A.M. Ergo, he will deliver the news an hour early.

Below it was another letter on the same subject.

GIRLS ALSO DELIVER

To the Editor of *The Journal*:

I don't ordinarily think of myself as a feminist, but your advice about changing the clocks contained an insult to those girls—my little Heather among them—who deliver *The Journal* each and every day.

Come on guys, give us gals a break! Sometimes your "paperBOY" is a GIRL!

I kept trying to figure out if the first letter was right, but I went in circles, time being as confusing as it is. Finally I just assumed I was wrong, that I had put an embarrassing error and a sexist slur on page one.

But because of General Disorganization, no one connected the letters to me. No one even cared. I know because I kept trying to confess and couldn't find anyone who would listen.

One night at the Woolworths lunch counter I bumped into the single mother whose daughter loved Barbies. "It's me, Vicki," she said, which was weird because she never told me her name. This time I asked what she was doing for dinner, and we ended up agreeing to meet the next night.

She showed up in a dress that looked just wretched on her. I smelled perfume. She said she had hired a baby sitter. I was on a date.

I launched into the Chronicle of Daniel the Younger. In the middle of the first episode I got so bored I couldn't go on. I just didn't have the stomach to go through it one more time. Everything I said to Vicki was in the past tense: I did this, it felt like that. Everything she said was in the future tense: We would take this drive, see that movie, I would teach her to program her VCR. I kept trying to tune in to a conversation two tables over, where a couple was having a really interesting fight. Finally, she had to get home for the babysitter. She told me she did nothing on Sundays, when her daughter was with "her father." I said I worked Sundays. "Wow! *The Journal!* I think of you every time I read it. It must be so *interesting!* I saw your byline, I'm certain."

People always say that because I work for a newspaper, even after I tell them a million times that I never write anything for print.

The next week I got a card saying, "Thinking of you—Vicki. P.S. I got the VCR to work........then it went crazy!! HELP!!!!"

I stopped going to Woolworths. I was even afraid to walk down Lincoln.

"I'm absolutely *dying* for dumplings."

I could swear Elaine hadn't liked them before. Her tastes seemed to keep changing. She asked me what was wrong and I said I was preoccupied. She assumed it had to do with my ex and my children, which she always assumed. Every ex-wife, I've learned, is ipso facto a bitch on wheels.

"I guess it's about my former life," I said. "I'm worried about some things with my kids. And the house."

She hesitated a second, then said, "Look, Danno, take my car, take it home with you again tonight, keep it the weekend at least. I'm into a cooking trip and I'm gonna just stay home alone and get depressed listening to my biological clock going *tick tick tick*. Only kidding. But do it really, go back to reassure yourself. Just stay out of the clutches of the wicked witch when you get back to Montague. Okay?"

"Montclair."

"Whatever. I don't want anyone making you miserable unless it's me."

"You?"

"Forget it. My neck still hurts. Give me one of your famous rubs? I can't even bend my head to eat soup. And their hot and sour is outstanding."

I reached across the table and gave her a neck massage, which had become a specialty of mine. She had convinced me I had a knack for it.

"Nice," she said, opening her green eyes wide. "Just don't stop."

"It's my pianist's touch," I said.

Later, driving home in Elaine's car, it came over me again: The haunted tree had toppled over in the ice storm and Melissa and the children had been seriously hurt. Perhaps something even more horrible had happened. That was why no one had come looking for me.

The ice storm. It was obvious.

— 12 —

As soon as I hit the highway the red Camaro cut me off—
casual, like he was swatting a flea. I floored Elaine's Toyota to
catch up, until I strained beside him. The air between us whis-
tled and shook. Our side mirrors dipped, lifted, hung even at
last. His music swelled out his window and swooshed in my
face, Bam bam *wup!* B-bam bam *wup!*

It was essential to not make eye contact, as we rose on the
same two bumps, up, down, up, down, the highway pounding harder, harder against our hoods. I was risking my life—
to say nothing of Elaine's car—to beat a stranger in some stupid duel, but I had to stay on top of him. My palms were sticky,
my head was throbbing, I could taste blood, hot and sweet as
lust, and it came to me, blood lust, the violent urge to kill. I felt
mighty enough to rip the steering wheel off with my bare
hands.

Somehow, though, he sneaked ahead. His windshield
threatened, then thrust past mine. I grabbed to shift down, but
Elaine had an automatic. I tried with everything I had to sum-
mon more staying power. He eased off, charity, and we fell
even, rocking delicately side by side. We were doing eighty-
five.

I felt him tire of my tease; I could feel everything he was feeling. He knew his muscle car could overpower my puny Toyota at will. He jerked sideways, into me, testing. I refused to yield. This got him mad. He rammed his way in front, inch by inch, taking his time, enjoying it. When he had his rear on me he whipped his car around, kind of shoved its ass in my face, and braked. I was in such a blind rage I nearly barreled into his trunk, on purpose, I really almost did. But instead I gritted my teeth, slowed, and let him have his fun. I honked, a pipsqueak squeak in a giant wind.

As he thundered ahead a hand burst out, middle finger up. I returned the compliment, but it was far better from his end, that was for sure.

I slowed to a crawl, sixty-five. My shirt was soaking.

I didn't get to Montclair till dark, gusting through hours of driving rain. Bob Dylan had turned fifty that day, and a New York station was playing an interview. Dylan was in his trash-the-interviewer mode, strumming his guitar and giving dopey answers. Somewhere on Route 3, the rain stopped.

I got off at Valley Road, passed the college, and took a left on Alexander. As my car plunged down the hill I was over-whelmed by greenery, maddeningly ripe and full, millions of leaves and flowers nuzzling each other and fighting for space. Being away made me notice how beautiful Montclair is in May. It actually frightened me.

I soothed myself cruising down Park Street, with its dis-creet, laid-back splendor, and cut around Sunset Park to Nor-wood. I needed to feel Norwood undulating beneath me, to hug the curves of a Montclair street with my tires. I ran a quick reconnaissance mission on the house. The Volvo was dozing in the driveway, Melissa-style, its nose near the street, and two other cars were at the curb. I recognized the Reiners' Isuzu Trooper by a bumper sticker that said "Package Mine In Paper" and a new one that said "Love Your Mother" next to a drawing of the earth (replacing "Stop the Dolphin Slaughter"). One window was partly open, and I deduced Melissa had been a passenger. I no longer felt crazed; the hours on the road had melted down my anguish into merely a consuming curiosity.

I parked a block away and climbed out into the sweet Montclair air, honey-thick with pollen and flowers. I didn't know I was passing the Gleasons, who of course were outside, plucking weeds on their knees.

"Hello there Daniel," Mrs. Gleason said, a weed dangling in her fingers like a cat with a mouse it caught. "Long time no see."

She always said things like that. It meant nothing.

"Don't you love May in Montclair," she said, referring to the town spring festival everyone goes bonkers over. "This year's *luscious*."

"I was noticing," I said. "The air? Why you're out this late, I'm sure."

"It's the nicest time, Daniel. To weed after a rain? So, how *are* my two cuties?"

"Doing just great."

"You're a lucky son-of-a-gun, Daniel. You know that?" Mr. Gleason said. "A lucky son-of-a-gun."

"Thank you. I know."

We made small talk, which was far more pleasant than I recalled. They were genuinely nice people. It was too bad they were so obnoxious about it.

Finally, with reluctance, I said good-bye.

"Give a kiss," Mrs. Gleason called. "To those cute cutie cuties."

I took off at full tilt, down the uneven bluestone, a man strolling down his street. When I got to my house, I skipped across the ivy and the surprisingly healthy lawn and raced around the porch to the backyard. At the leaded-glass window I was etched in yellow light, then coated by shadow. Through the big window I could see the entire kitchen. The rest of the house was dark except the living room, where every panel of leaded glass was not just full but bloated with light. Gleeful voices cracked the yard. My wife was having a party.

Without warning Melissa sauntered in. It was like seeing a celebrity. She posed at the kitchen window in a new outfit, dark though not black, with swirly gray stockings. She did something at the table with willowy arms that shined in the naked fluorescence. This beautiful woman was mine—I owned her, after all we'd been through. I sat in a plastic swing and watched.

"*What are you doing here?*"

"*Get rid of your guests, Melissa.*"

"*I can't.*"

"*You heard me.*"

"*Give me a minute. I'll think of something.*"

The outfit fit annoyingly well. It made me dizzy, her lacy legs and her wavy arms and their twisty ballet on the table. The air around me was heavy, a forest after a downpour.

I couldn't believe the woman I was watching was "Melissa."

Then she did something ghastly: She smiled, an easy, open smile. Someone had made a joke. She cocked her head, strikingly pretty.

Ed and Joanne Reiner waltzed in, turning in their fingers the stems of our fancy wine glasses, and stood them in the sink. Someone was lurking in the background, a guy with a beard I instantly loathed. Every mouth was working, and there was an inordinate amount of chuckling. This couldn't be my life, I used to stand out here and say, back then, when it was.

The children.

They'd be sleeping already. I had lost any sense of the kind of schedule where sleep begins at eight. In the warmth of their night lights I saw Zach with his conductor's cap heaving, Ramona with at least fifty dolls in orderly rows, embracing her latest favorite, so fickle with her love. Her hair fanned out over the pillow. I'd scale the tree next to the house and peek, maybe climb in the window next to their bedrooms. I could do it quietly.

Then I saw that the haunted tree was gone.

Even the stump had been pulverized. It was established beyond a doubt by the fresh logs on my wood pile. I studied the house and found no damage; it had been eliminated cleanly. Even with all I had done, it was *sneaky* to cut it down while my back was turned.

In the house Melissa was now alone in the kitchen with the bearded creep. I decided, no, I knew, that the creep was Barry Alter. It was exactly how the scuzzball would look. The turquoise numbers on the microwave burned through his beard. It read 10:21, then 10:2 as he stooped into the light, blotting out a number with his beard. There was a chance he brushed her waist with his hand. She turned to face him. I could tell even from the back that she was flirting. (*"It was so romantic in the woods, Barry. I knew I was flirting, but I did it anyway because I wanted to." "I saw you looking at my body and I loved it, Barry."*) I thought they might be crude enough to kiss right in front of me; his beard gave him a nervy, on-the-make look. (*"That kiss was the biggest mistake of my life."*) He slid close, beard thrust out, a very cool customer. I could tell he saw himself as some kind of major-league stud, even though he was nothing more than a failed pianist who had sold out big time. They made that eye contact that lovers do. The jerk was out for what he could get, that was obvious. They were definitely going to do something. She was asking for it and the slimeball knew it.

He was helping her with what was on the table, it turned out, and they soon walked out, with enough space between them to not really look like a couple. They left the light on, turning the kitchen bright yet blank, like a television screen that has no picture.

The clock read 10:22, then 10:23. The plastic swing was scrunching up my thighs. Everything was damp, and my jeans were saturated.

Joanne came rushing into the kitchen and stared through the window. I was caught! I stood to run, despite myself, sinking in mud.

All she did, however, was bend over the table. Then I heard it, over my galloping heart, the piercing whine of a baby. It was why Joanne had come running. She scooped up an infant in pink. That's what they'd been fussing over—she'd had her baby. I wasn't thinking.

A group thronged my table, watching Joanne pull a bottle from a blue Channel Thirteen bag and feed a silently bawling infant. A woman appeared who kept touching the baby's ears and shaking her head. The woman might be the wife or girlfriend of the guy on the make. Joanne said something that made everyone laugh as she fit the baby's head inside her blouse to nurse it, while holding up the bottle in a way that made everyone go completely hysterical. The crying stopped, and Melissa pointed; she had loved nursing. After some yakking Joanne put the baby on the table in her dramatic way, as if teaching a class, and changed its diaper (no plastic disposables for the Reiners) while they all chuckled like it was the funniest thing they'd ever seen. They wouldn't stop nodding and shaking and speaking. She handed the baby to Melissa, who cuddled it. It cut me to ribbons, seeing that. The bearded sleaze raised his arm and was about to snake it around Melissa. He wouldn't stop smirking in his slimy beard. Then he pinched the baby, a pink part that stuck up from Melissa's lap. He moved very lazily, as if the beard weighed him down.

Melissa squeezed the baby, and the guy caressed either her wrist or the baby's stomach. I lost it when I saw that. I don't know why but it was the last straw. I jumped off the swing and stomped through mud to the porch. I stood at the door deciding whether to knock or ring the bell. From there the party felt smothered in flannel, but for the rip of a Reiner "Hah!"

I opened the screen door. I was steaming. Yet I opened it quietly, which tipped me off that I wasn't really going to do anything. As if I didn't already know. I stood there, pretending to get ready to knock, to fool myself, when I knew I would do no such thing. I trick myself like this all the time.

Through the curtain I saw my hallway floor, brilliant patterns of orange on twisting grains of wood, its slick surface shining.

"Melissa, it's me. I'm here."

"Who's there?"

"I think Daniel's back!"

"Daniel's what?"

"Who's what?"

"You're kidding?"

"He's back? Hah!"

"Not Daniel? Daniel!"

"Hello Ed. Barry Alter, I presume?"

I thought it was a squirrel on the roof. Scratching, creaking, then the door fell away before me. It was starting to open, half open, opening, *now!*

I shot down the porch, to hide in the part that bends around the house. Lawn furniture blocked me, and I had to dive over the rail. My legs launched me into the sky. I stayed in the air at least a minute, and came down grazing bushes, steel wool across my cheeks. Mud splashed my palms and splattered on my neck. I spun over, clobbering my shoulder. My heels, both at once, slapped hard wet grass.

I stayed on my back as the door kicked open. The earth shook from it.

"No he isn't."

"Yes he is. He is."

"The rain stopped, Mr. Weatherman."

"Hah!"

"No he isn't. Ed never gets nervous about anything."

"Who needs a weatherman to know which way the wind blows?"

"He does."

"Who's got whose act together?"

"She's sleeping, but she'll be up."

"You don't know what early is."

Melissa's voice sang out. "Believe me, I know what early is."

"Hah!"

"Major bum—"

"Why Ramona used to—"

"Ha—"

The door slammed shut. The porch reverberated.

I felt for blood on my face but it was just mud. I rolled to my feet. My left side ached. When I stood I thought I was fainting, I was so dizzy. Just my luck I'd have my heart attack right here on my lawn.

I stumbled back to Elaine's car. Did I actually believe I, of all people, would make a theatrical entrance, with a romantic speech for Melissa and a punch in the jaw for Barry Alter? Why was I so shocked to see her cavorting around, flirting with men, partying?

I got out of the car to shake the dirt off. I limped toward my house. I had to stop pretending things were different than they were.

"Tell your boyfriend to head home. We have to talk."

"He's not my boyfriend."

"I saw how you were looking at each other."

"You were watching?"

"And I saw those letters, too, Melissa my sweet."

"You saw them? Just a minute, Barry."

"You blew it, Babe. You threw away everything we had."

"You're the one who blew it, Daniel. You don't know what those letters were! You don't know anything!"

"Can we at least talk about it?"

"Daniel, the truth of the matter is you have an imagination that runs away with you. What gets me is you never asked! Are you that afraid?"

The guests were leaving, and I had to walk fast on the other side. And I could tell it was the Reiners. All New Jersey could tell when they heard Ed's merry hoot, his cannon blast into the peaceful Montclair sky.

"Hah!"

"We are having fun," the laugh shrieked to the world.

I twisted to check if the bearded slime was leaving, but I couldn't make anyone out, and had to keep my head down.

As I turned the corner I heard another "Hah!"

I was half a block away. That's how loud this guy's laugh is.

When I got to the fringes of my new city I found the radio station from the college town, and they were talking about Dylan turning fifty. When Dylan turned thirty there was a protest on MacDougal Street off Bleecker in the Village. I'm not sure what we were protesting, but that was back when you couldn't trust anyone over thirty (now you can't trust anyone under thirty!). There was a place called the Hip Bagel on the corner, but the Village was already out of it. And years later, when I walked those streets with Melissa, I reminisced about days in the Village I had never experienced. (Perhaps no one experienced those days; if you remember the sixties you weren't there— another snappy line I like to quote as my own.)

I got so involved reminiscing about reminiscing about something that never happened that I missed my exit. I got lost, the way I always get lost. I actually could feel my grasp of the familiar slide from my grip. A corner teasingly familiar (grocery store with green plastic awning, HANK'S DELI, HEROS, mailbox squatting near a fractured curb), maybe I wasn't lost at all. But the street extended into deeper mysteries, the right train trestle in the wrong place, enigmas of intersections, the terror of being lost forever.

Of course I would not ask for directions. Melissa used to say this was a male ego thing, but the truth is very different. I don't ask because of the pleasure I get in solving a problem on my own, of conquering the unknown even in a trivial way such as digging a highway entrance out of a jumbled mess of streets. I'm not proving anything to anybody except myself. For me, getting lost has a juicy panicky flavor: the world no longer familiar, a maze I'm sucked into even as I seek the way out. It's a chance to find my way in the world again. Why ask for help when I can struggle out on my own? These days I almost never get the chance.

But my new city isn't all that big or complex, and soon I blundered on the wide avenue with timed lights that leads into my neighborhood.

I trudged up my outdoor staircase. The air smelled relentlessly of roses. I went in, sat at my Formica kitchen table, and turned on my tacky radio. It screeched alive with the deejay on the college station reminiscing about May 1966 (which he surely did not experience), when Dylan released *Blonde on Blonde*, twenty-five years ago this month. *Rubber Soul* was five months before, and for me time has been out of whack since, as if the trauma of the sixties broke a gear that kept it from ever running smoothly again.

The deejay named the top five songs on this day twenty-five years ago, and even though some were obscure I could hum every one: "Good Lovin'" (the Rascals), "19th Nervous Breakdown" (Rolling Stones), "Secret Agent Man" (Johnny Rivers), "Kicks" (Paul Revere and the Raiders), and "Time Won't Let Me" (The Outsiders).

I hadn't slept in two days. My knee and elbow throbbed, and I was crusted with mud. I knew at once that I had made a terrible mistake, that I had destroyed my life and wrecked what good I lucked into. I drove Melissa to do what she had

done, or jumped to conclusions and was too chicken to confront her. *Are you that afraid?* she shouted, and she was right. I
had tried to run away from myself, but of course you can't do
that, which is why I was sitting in this grubby kitchen, having
an intense conversation with you-know-who.

There was no way around it. I was the worst emotional
terrorist of them all, a self-absorbed, self-indulgent, self-
destructive maniac blinded by rage. I looked out at the mountain and wanted to run back to Melissa, to the children I had
been trying not to think about, to bang down their door, get
on my knees, and beg them all to forgive me.

— 13 —

Dearest Melissa,

I can't believe the monstrous thing I did. I know it's unforgivable, but I've done a lot of thinking the past few months and hope we can somehow try to work things out.

I miss Monie and Zach more than you will ever know. I love you. I need you.
Please take me back.

Love,
Daniel

When I handed Elaine her car keys I squeezed her palm and gave her a peck on the cheek. I felt carefree, debonair.

"Thanks for the wheels, Babe. You look just great, by the way."

"I do? Okay. So, everything's copacetic on the home front?"

They were expressions that might have bothered me before.

"Perfect, my sweet. Perfect."

"Ooh, you have this *huge* scratch on your cheek. There. It hurts?"

"It's better with your magic touch, Babe. Boy, your hands can *heal*."

"Thanks a lot. I mean, like, thanks a lot."

"Really, I'm fine. Love your touch, Babe."

"Those kids of yours got a ton of mud on my seat. What did they have, some kind of mud fight?"

We exchanged flirtatious screentops at work. When we had breakfast at the Lincoln Diner she laughed so hard at my Gregory Gregory story that she nearly went into cardiac arrest. I had her drop me off to check my mail, even though it was impossible to get an answer this early.

The period when a letter arriving was a long shot passed into the heady time when it was likely any day. I took brisk walks on streets that strayed near Lincoln; I was undaunted even at the prospect of running into Vicki. I weaved through the breathless tranquillity of late morning on a suburban street and acted out reunion conversations with Melissa. Sometimes she called the second she got my letter. Other times I'd see the Volvo outside my apartment and look up to find her waiting at the top of the stairs. She'd be staring at the mountain and wouldn't see me right away.

By the ninth day—five full days of likely response time—I was hearing my children's voices outside my window. I gave up on a phone call.

Elaine cooked a terrific dinner that night. We talked until we had to leave for work. The next afternoon we baked bread and I cooked her a terrific dinner. She loved it. It was the first time she acknowledged my culinary skills.

I came home to an empty mailbox, again. I gave up on a phone call, again. It spun into the nerve-racking period when a letter had to arrive any day. To make it worse, I was now getting mail to baffling permutations of my name, like Dr. Wally Vine and Walther Danton Wild.

Elaine and I were in her kitchen, and I was narrating a seminal episode in the Chronicle of Daniel the Younger, which I had lately renewed interest in telling. To illustrate how romantic Young Daniel had been I pinned her up against the refrigerator. The situation led, inexorably, to a kiss. Magnets that looked exactly like hot buttered rolls popped off the refrigerator and bounced on linoleum. Elaine said we should go out. Melissa's lessons informed me that Elaine wanted to be courted ("wooed" was the word she used), and we went to our Chinese restaurant. Our tastes had melded. We spooned hot and sour soup, nibbled dumplings, and talked about how delicious the food was, how sensitive Young Daniel had been, how complicated our relationship had become.

"I don't know where this is leading, but I need you now," I said.

"I should probably have the old noggin examined, Daniel, I mean, really."

She treated me to a shamelessly vivid orgasmic face as she sipped soup.

"I know it's tough, Danno. What she's putting you through. I feel so bad about it, in all honesty. For you. For those two terrific kids. I *hate* her for it. For what she's doing to you, to us, frankly. That. Just. I mean, *she!*"

Elaine could spit out the word "she" and in one snarling syllable turn Melissa into a bloodthirsty she-wolf who swallowed men whole.

"She wasn't that horrible. I did my share."

"You're so *nice*, Danno. You know, my neck is stiff again, I think."

"Anyway, I did my share to ruin things."

I reached over. She bent to give me better leverage.

"I'm glad you joined civilization and finally got an answering machine. I can call you now and leave heavy breathing, joke joke. Oh, you are *so* fabulous."

She leaned to give me more room, eyes closed in another orgasmic display. "You'll give me a real elaborate one later, right? Maybe, pretty please?"

"I'll give you one like you never had before, Babe. Your body will sing, like Melissa's did. We'll end up in bed under the rain forest for sure."

"You will, won't you?" the real Elaine said. "I hate you when you don't answer. My neck's killing me from staring at that dumb screen. You're the only one who knows how to make it feel better, with that magic touch of yours."

She raised her head. Her eyes were drowsy. I could always massage her into the throes of sexual bliss. She closed her eyes (I felt strangely alone when she did) and moaned. Later, for sure.

"The best part about the machine is I can call and check messages from anywhere. It's a really great feature. Not that I get any calls."

After dinner we strolled Lincoln—deserted, of course, but it was such a cotton-soft night. Spring comes late up here, and only now were trees heavy with leaves. Elaine's heels clattered as I divulged a fresh episode on the early sorrows of Young Daniel. She stared into space, mesmerized by the epic scene I was laying out as we passed that window at Sears where two lawnmowers are stretched out in a backyard in what looks like a relaxing conversation.

We told each other the stories couples reveal just before they sleep together. She described how her marriage broke up: her husband woke her in the middle of the night and said, "I can't do this. I don't feel like *me*, here with you." The divorce was simple—"no-fault" she called it—since they had no kids. "No-fault," she said. "In your dreams! All there is is fault—and blame."

After the marriage (the word gave me flashbacks of Melissa in white on our wedding day) she had to leave Philadelphia. The final insult was an assault in broad daylight, three boys about fifteen surrounding her and putting their hands all over her. "Stay here, Sweetie, we like you," they said. She had to stand there while they pawed at her. She was afraid even to make a face.

"I'm still nervous about going out. You don't know what it's like."

She took my arm.

"What it's like alone, I mean. You can't walk down Lincoln yourself like this. Stores are okay, the daytime's okay, but the street itself's pretty iffy. Never ever at night."

I walked Lincoln Avenue at all hours and felt perfectly safe.

"They ran when they saw a guy across the street. A *guy*, that's all. One kid stops, and I think he's pulling a knife. But what he does is way, way worse. He grins, and says, 'Nice tits you got, Sugar, they're *real* nice.'"

She shivered, wobbling on her heels, and kissed my shoulder on top of my shirt. "It was horrible. But I decided I was lucky."

"How in the world were you lucky?"

"Because I could have been raped, that's why."

It got late and we had to go straight to work. At the end of our shift I slipped out and walked home. I gave myself a good talking to.

Here's my problem.

I've always wanted to be a cad, but unlike other men I can never pull it off. I had glimpsed Elaine's private torment, and that's dangerous with a woman you want to take advantage of. I knew how hurt she'd be when it dawned on her that I had been using her while waiting to resolve things with Melissa. I hurt her once already with the broccoli fiasco. This, of course, is precisely the sort of thing a true cad wouldn't give a second thought to. I, on the other hand, couldn't get it out of my mind.

Two more likely mail days. I developed tricks, looking in the mailbox sideways, covering my eyes until I was directly in front. Nothing worked.

One morning the red light on my machine blinked feverishly. I first had to lie rigidly on my couch and shut my eyes (I created new rituals every day) to hear a computerized message about a spectacular deal on aluminum siding.

It became that period when if a letter did come it would be bad. I knew it in my bones, as I had known that the haunted tree was down.

———————————

Elaine and I went to an expensive Thai restaurant. Melissa's lessons again advised me to announce I was treating. I don't know why it mattered, but Elaine was thrilled. We polished off a carafe of wine.

"I can't wait to get home," she said. "I really think I'm drunk."

"Don't worry. I won't take advantage of you."

She gave me a mysterious look, and said, "You owe me a backrub, by the way. Don't think for one second you're getting off the hook."

I sneaked away to call for messages, hoping against hope. Whenever I fantasize about something with exact details I always come up dry.

I told Elaine how sexy she looked when I got back. She was in a gold sweater with thick cabling, which hung to the end of a noodle-length skirt. As we stood to leave her spike heels lifted her body upward to me, in readiness.

We walked arm in arm down Lincoln. As soon as we got inside her apartment she said, "You're not getting out of that backrub, mister."

She sashayed to the bed, shot me another mysterious glance, and tipped out of her heels and onto her stomach.

"One backrub please," she said. "That's an order."

I dug into the gold cabling so hard the sweater hopped up to expose bare skin. Her back was moist on my fingertips.

"Yes, a thousand times yes," she said. "Please patent your touch, promise me you will."

I jabbed my thumbs around her bra strap and kneaded her shoulders, then slid my hands out from under the sweater and along her thighs, where the brief buoyancy of the skirt dissolved into coarse stockings. I fondled her knees, in front and behind; one of my tricks as a lover is to pay attention to obscure parts of a woman's body. She made babbling noises of approval and delight.

I was way over the line of an honest backrub.

My hands crawled under her skirt. The stockings turned silky on the surface, plump within, a delicious heft that I clenched in both hands. The very violation of it drove us wild. She spun around. Her breath blew hot on my neck. I pushed her sweater up as her legs wrapped around me and she dragged me down on top of her.

Her voice, a far-off murmur. "No."

The voice got closer. She was trying half-heartedly to stop me. I forced her legs apart, shocked by pleasure as her body split under me. I was just strong enough to squeeze in between her knees.

"I want you too much to stop."

"I'm telling you stop. It's too mixed up, Daniel, I don't want—"

"I *know* what you want. I want to explore you. Every nook and cranny."

"Stop! Daniel *please*. Just no! No! *No!* I'm sorry."

She tried to push me off, but against my rippling muscles she was nothing. She had not made it absolutely clear.

"Daniel. I don't want to. I'm sorry. I really am sorry."

"I want you. To explore you, make *love* to you. Don't you understand?"

"I do. I really do. But no. Daniel. *Daniel! Please just stop!*"

She definitely wasn't fighting with all her might. In my mouth was a salty taste, blood lust, the urge to take whether she wanted to be taken or not. I hadn't felt this good in months.

"Stop. You have to Daniel. Daniel I'm so sorry, *please*."

I held her arms down and looked her in the eye. "I'd stop if you truly wanted me to, Elaine. Truly. Confess! You've been teasing me all night. You're too sexy not to be grabbed and made love to."

"Daniel, you've gone crazy. Plumb loco. You *are* crazy!"

I nibbled her neck. Her elbow got loose and poked my eye. My back was being punched. She was really fighting now. She almost got her knees back together so I brought my weight down like a sledgehammer. With a shiver, her legs spread apart once more. This time even her thighs gave in. As her body went flat under me I felt a panic so sweet I could ram through what was left of her clothes, break her open, make her mine.

"Can we just talk for just a lousy second. Hurting me, you're *hurting* me!"

I had to keep forcing her, maybe even hit her. I considered it, I admit it. My own physical power aroused me so much that I ransacked every corner of my brain for the cold, hard, idiot rage I needed. But I came up empty. All I found was mush.

With contempt I let her go.

She sprang up, as if her body had been compressed. Humid heat escaped between us. She was a mess, skirt at the waist, underpants at her knees. The gold sweater, skewed off a shoulder, contrived a pathetic décolletage. She was half sexy model in a salacious photo, half dazed victim of a beastly crime. It took a surprising time to realize she was a wreck, and she staggered into the bathroom. A comb scratched through her hair, harsh strokes, a frenzy.

She came out and sat on the bed. "Daniel, Danno. Oh, Danno," she said, taking my hands. "I know how much you hate me."

"I don't hate you, Elaine. It's just that so much is going on in my life."

"I'm sorry, really. Please, it would be emotional suicide for me. Dinner was—I'm this big sucker for romance. I'm sorry. I know you just were, but I just was—"

"Yes, I just. I just almost. Elaine, I can explain. It was crazy."

"The craziness is my fault. This relationship, where it's at, I mean."

"I couldn't stop because I wanted you so much."

"It was my fault *totally*. Please let's just start from scratch, okay?"

"Don't give me that look with those beautiful green eyes. I'm helpless against it. Any man would be."

For some reason this depressed her.

"Don't deny that you hate me," she said. "Don't deny how much you despise me."

"Elaine, I'm sorry. You have to know how crazy my life is now."

"This whole situ*ation* is my fault, Danno. Don't you understand that?"

I came home to a legal envelope from the county courthouse, addressed to Waldo Daniel Veil. I never rip open mail in the street, but I forced it open on the spot. It was in shreds when I finally dragged the letter out.

It was a summons for jury duty.

Explain this: I lived as Daniel Weil in two states, was a registered voter, paid taxes, owned cars, a house, telephones, and am never called. I come up here, create a totally bogus identity, and I'm snagged in six months.

Elaine and I had dinner again a few days later. We went back to her place and sat on the bed talking, Platonic friends once more. She treated our last night together as another of the social blunders she was convinced she committed constantly with men. I thought I was imagining it when she touched me more than usual. Melissa (who lately never left my head) warned me that a woman never does this accidentally.

"Our relationship's had so many ups and downs, Danno. You're here, you're not here, you *want* a relationship, you *don't* want a relationship, you want to be alone, you want to be with me. She made you crazy, *she* made you afraid. I can't stand Marissa, in all honestly. I can't."

"Mel*i*ssa."

"Whatever. She's not here in this room. I always wanted to ask if she made you quit the *Times*? Sounds like the kind of thing only *she* could pull."

At midnight, I stood at the door to leave. She drew up behind me.

"You don't have to go," she said, and ran a pointy nail down my spine. "Unless you really want to."

So, despite everything, I began what I assumed would be a neat and tidy affair with Elaine. For one weekend she was perfect: smart, sexy, and completely un-needy.

We awoke under the rain forest. "I'm really very happy," she said, and flattened against me with an uninhibited tendering of flesh that brought home the fact that we had just slept together for the first time. "I've learned to take things in stride, a little at a time, starting this second."

Elaine was always learning new behaviors, and was starting one right now.

We sat in bed and talked about our relationship. She'd sit up, as she warmed to her favorite topic, but hold the sheet up to conceal her breasts. Then she'd slide out and stand naked at the window, checking the weather. After a moment she'd wrap herself in a robe of wholesome purple terry cloth. She'd arrange it meticulously, as she did everything she wore, and sit at the mirror to brush her hair with vigorous, two-fisted strokes. She brushed with startling ferocity, that vicious streak that came out when she beat up a slab of dough. I sort of fell in love with her as I watched, a miniature, circumscribed kind of love, like teenagers feel without knowing it.

She took a shower. I called to learn I had no messages.

The next day I got a letter from Melissa, with one more stamp than necessary. It was on a sheet plucked from Ramona's spiral notepad.

Dearest Daniel,

Yes, what you did was monstrous. And your feelings about the children were touching. Unfortunately, actions—even yours!!!—have consequences. The kind of hell you brought on this family is not something any of us will ever forgive, not now, not tomorrow, not ever.

And so my sweet, love of my life, the first (and perhaps the only) man I will ever love, everything you had here is gone, you killed it you bastard!

Please trust me that you will never see your children again.

.....Count on it, pal.

> Sincerely,
> Melissa

— 14 —

I didn't like Jack the instant I saw him. He said hello by making his hand a gun and shooting me. He wore a pinkie ring. I hate men with pinkie rings. He led me into a conference room lined with fat legal books. One caught my eye: *Separation Agreements and Ante-Nuptial Contracts.*

"So," he said, "what's the scoop?"

People always say things like that to you when you work for a newspaper. They think it's cute. Before I could answer he held up the hand with the ring while Kathleen, his partner, strode through the door.

She was the kind of woman I've always been afraid of. She looked me square in the eye, legs gliding, hips swiveling, as if wading through waist-high water. She had on a skimpy dress, barely businesslike even on a hot June day in a shabby office of a third-rate city. She was tanned, one of those people who break out in blemishes from the sun; the tan showed how harsh life could be, how it wore her down. She slid into a leather chair so old the cushion was pink. The way she sat, legs crossed, hands on a knee, shoulders firm and high, seemed designed to coax me into confessing a crime I didn't commit. Her body could lure me into it. It was worldly and comfortable to deal with. You can talk to me, it said. I've been there. I understand.

I trotted out all the gory details, even my name change. They didn't bat an eye. I showed the letter, which I had photocopied at *The Journal*. I was glad to have something to pull out and shove into Kathleen's eager hands.

"You're in good shape, Daniel," she said, dropping the letter. It sunk deep between her thighs, even though her legs were crossed. "There is no legal tool in the state of New Jersey that can keep you out of that house."

Jack chimed in. "The operative fact's you are still married to her. She may make you out to be the bad guy, but she's still married to you."

"Unless in the interim the lady got a divorce," Kathleen said. With her tough manner I barely realized she had used a term like "lady."

"That's six months, min," Jack said, "but could in a year, max. Separation was, yes." He ticked off months with stubby fingers, starting in January. When he got to June he was at the pinkie ring.

"It's unlikely she started, Jack, the day the guy split."

Neither of them had the slightest moral problem with my behavior.

"So she can't keep you out of the house," Kathleen said. "You still own it. We'll produce a court order if we have to. You are still married. You still own that property. You move back in and she'd have to file a motion to enjoin you from staying, to restrain you from living there based on these said facts. You have property rights. They are not in dispute. You can take things. You *own* them."

She was referring to the house in Montclair, not Melissa's body. But there was a whiff of sexual adventurism in Kathleen's attitude, as if she wanted me to take possession of something more. It was with the ruthlessness women unfailingly show when they give advice on handling another woman.

"You still have a right to get back in," she said.

I looked out a window, across sagging roofs and defenseless chimneys, to the mountain, steamy with heat. I forced myself back to Kathleen's eyes. In the rosy light of the window

I could make out her pupils, flecked with gray—very pretty eyes, actually, with their wise-ass, sexy wisdom.

"I'm not concerned. It's what I said about seeing the children. That's the main issue to me. That she's not letting me."

"Let her," Kathleen said, gazing out the window. Her eyes snapped back, aiming little pinpricks of sunlight. "This the lady cannot do."

She lifted the letter from her lap and stretched to put it on Jack's desk. Her legs were tanned and bare. Jack tapped the letter with a ringed pinkie and said, "They are still your children. You will never lose the right to see them. *Never.*"

"She'd have to prove you unfit," Kathleen said. "And that is one *very* tough burden. We're only talking visitation here, not custody, which is a horse of a different color. A different scenario that will no doubt come later."

They were getting revved up.

"I just hope," I said.

"Daniel," Kathleen said. She hiked her dress and lowered it evenly over her knees. "Your parental rights flow from your being the father of these children. Alleged action or actions on your part have absolutely no bearing."

She smiled, sunlight in her eyes, a hundred indulgent stars.

I was told to wait. Jack photocopied my photocopy of Melissa's letter, not realizing it wasn't an original. Kathleen made me promise not to contact Melissa, "under any circumstances, for any reason." At first I didn't understand, but as I stepped into the brick-oven heat of Lincoln Avenue all I could think of was forcing Melissa down on a bed and ripping off her clothes. I wanted her to struggle as I overpowered her, to struggle desperately hard.

"Remember the ice storm?" Elaine asked. "First time we touched?"

"How could I forget."

She sat up in bed, sheet stretched up over her breasts. It bugged me, how she was modest in the oddest ways. "You remember how you held me as I walked up your staircase? And when the storm melted you finally admitted that we *had* a relationship. You talked about how scary it was to you. It was so sensitive. I was so moved."

"I remember. Yes, at the diner, and walking in the street."

"And you told me a theory about beauty? How you feel terror at something that's really beautiful? That everybody does? That's my problem, I think. Everything's so good between us right now, Danno, it's scary."

"I'm not a good risk now, Elaine. I should really say that."

"I'm learning to accept what is. Starting now. Haven't I been good?"

"I don't want to complicate your life."

"That's what Sandy said Peter said. He stayed over anyway."

"You told me. I want to warn you."

She hesitated a second. "I'll take my chances, Love."

She tossed off the sheet, stepped into her slippers, and walked naked to the window to check the weather. She stood there, squinting at the sunlight and fluffing her hair.

---

ridin into the sunset? (VEIL)

yup. with me? (PETER)

count on it, pal (VEIL)

I had to tell Elaine before I lost my nerve. I found her in the lunchroom, reading notices on the bulletin board. I stood behind her and said I was going home with Peter.

"This women's network thing is really interesting," she said. "Sandy says Brian doesn't want her to go to the Woman-Talk meeting because it threatens him. Peter didn't care. If she did."

"So, I'm going home with Peter?"

She hesitated. "It's fine with me. Of course it's fine with me."

Her hesitations were getting on my nerves. She was obviously peeved.

I had to say something.

"So, looks like she still can't find a roommate," I said, about an ad from a woman named Audrey, who worked in advertising, and was pitifully nice and also pitifully homely. Her ad had been up for weeks without one phone number tab being plucked.

"Who wants to live with *her?*" Elaine said, with that viciousness she could show. "Have fun with Peter."

I should have just left the room (I didn't have to stay at her place every goddamn night) but instead pulled one of those hideous gaffes I specialize in.

"Don't worry," I said. "I still love you."

"Why the fuck is it," I said, as soon as I got in Peter's car, "that every fucking women's group has a fucking name with no fucking space between it. Like WomanSongs, one word, or WomanPoems, one word, or WomanTalk."

"I saw it," he said. "With *no* fucking space. That women's group. *Women's* group. Sandy chewed my ear off half the night about it."

This was as close as he would come to confiding he was spending time with Sandy. It was funny. I knew about his relationship with Sandy from Elaine and he knew about my relationship with Elaine from Sandy.

He was warming up. This kind of subject always animated him. He tapped the wheel and said, "So why no space? You must have a theory, of course."

"My theory is it's a reaction to penis envy. You celebrate female anatomy by dropping a space. The beauty of something missing."

"God, I love that something missing."

Sleeping with Sandy was having an influence; usually it took longer to bring him around.

"So, tell me what the bitch pulled this time?"

He gunned the engine on the empty highway. My exit skidded by.

"She might remarry. To this sh-shit-for-brains scumbag l-lawyer."

"She's probably just yanking your chain."

"P-p-probably. It's not the first time she said it."

"See. You have evidence. She has a history of pulling crap like this."

"I want her out of my fucking hair, with this jerk. But the k-kids make it hard. Might move. It's complicated, Daniel, complicated, my friend."

He rattled a rat-a-tat on the steering wheel, using all his fingers like a piano. "So, my man, yours? Or shall it be Sweet Elaine's?"

"Mine this time. I hope Jack can fix things."

"No one can *f-fix* it. But Jack and that broad Kathleen— ain't she a piece a work?—can get it back in working condition."

"Yeah," I said. "Still . . ."

"The way it is, my friend."

He slowed to legal speed. He was out of it.

"You know, she got that guy off on a rape charge by convincing the jury it had been, you know, consensual? She's really good. Nice bod, too."

"Yeah," I said. "And you can tell she knows it."

He smiled. It made me happy enough to bring up a subject we avoided.

"Know what I like best about Elaine?" I asked.

"No. What do you like best?"

"Her lack of demands. That she's content to have a casual relationship."

I was truly surprised that it came out as a joke.

We couldn't stop laughing. We had tears in our eyes when he dropped me off.

"We gotta talk," Jack said. "Let's talk. You and me."

I waited about twenty minutes while he calmed down a woman on the phone and made faces to me as he did it. It always throws me when people mistreat others in front of me and assume I'll never connect their betraying a confidence with them and betraying one later with me.

He got off, stared at the phone in disgust, and said, "First off, she got herself a high-powered firm. Kelsey, Spiegel, Smuckler & Lutz. Manhattan, Park Avenue. Three-hundred something. Fifty-third Street, maybe fifty-forth."

Even up here people try to impress you with their feel for Manhattan.

"Then she got a hold of these." He punched his ring into a yellow legal pad. "These here lousy son-of-a-bitch affidavits." His handwriting spiraled down like a Slinky. "I mean, *this* isn't them, but it is them."

"Which say?"

He looked at the door. Kathleen was in court and due any second. He didn't like her not being there. Neither did I, to tell the truth.

"These make you out to be a bad guy."

Neither of us was in a hurry.

"So how's my friend Peter doing?"

"Same old same old. Great guy. A really great guy."

"Yeah," Jack said. "So, anyway."

After as much silence as he could allow he said, "The lady now asserts that the children are having psychological difficulties because of certain acts, allegedly negligent, on your behalf, the going-out-to-get-milk-and-vanishing in particular, that negatively impacted the mental health of said children, who as a result are therefore undergoing counseling of a psychological nature. She has depositions from more than—" he checked his pad "—more than one—" he double-checked "—but less than four—" that settled, he flipped a page, yellow paper flapping— "psychologists, yes, psycho*logists,* who have reason to believe the source of said problems, *alleged* problems is, *alleged,* we're talking, in a manner of speaking, are caused by . . ."

I wanted to cut him off with, "Give it to me straight, Doc. I can take it." Or, "Cut the crap, she ain't got nothin' on me."

But all I could get out was, "Okay, so what's the bottom line?"

He put down the pad and scrutinized the page.

"That these problems are caused by . . ." He became bothered by his pinkie ring and had to adjust it. When he ran out of time, he made his hand into a gun, pointed at me, and said, "By *you,* Danno."

The finger was aimed at my heart.

"And if so called upon they will testify so in court, represent this before a judge. In other words, the bottom line is that the testimony will be that it is injurious to the mental health of said children at this point in time if you had visitation. At this point in time."

"I see."

"*Any* visitation."

"I understand."

"It's not insurmountable, but we'll have to confront it head on."

"Can I see what she said? What she got them to say?"

Kathleen opened the door at last. It was like a balky screw finally turning. She slid into her usual shiny seat. She wore a suit, closer to gray than black in the window's merciless brightness. It was the kind of color that changed as sunlight struck it.

"I don't think you want to see them, Daniel," she said, picking up the thread. "These things are brutal to read. To prevail in court she absolutely must make you out to be a monster. A *total* monster."

She surveyed her nails, which were polished and filed into perfect crescents. It's always intriguing to see that a woman has perfect nails; it says something about her.

"There's also the matter of . . ." Jack said, tilting his head to align it with his handwriting, "Eileen Striker."

"Give me a break please Jack please," Kathleen said. "You know they won't get to first base with that unless he did it in front of the kids!"

"Eileen Striker," I said. "Who in the world's she?"

"Forgot?" Kathleen said. She had a sharper edge to her today. "I'm sure our Ms. Striker'd be offended at that. You'd enrage *two* women."

"Assuming we don't have a fraudulent deposition here," Jack said. "If he never had relations with, Helen? *Ellen?* Selker? *Smelker?*"

Then it hit me: Ellen Smuckler!

A name instantly separated from Melissa's law firm: Smuckler! She was using Ellen's husband's fancy Park Avenue law firm.

I didn't help Jack out, though. I said, quite accurately, "Honestly, I don't know any Eileen Striker, or whatever it is."

I glanced around. The only decoration I could study was a diploma that said *Kathleen Rita deMartino* in type so frantically italicized it made me dizzy.

The phone rang. It was the same woman as before. I could tell by the faces Jack made. My time was up. "We can fight this, Danno," he called, as I stood at the door. "And we can nail her, nail her in court. Nail her, Danno!"

I began to hate being called Danno. Not the name, but the way people start using it whenever they feel like it.

"It's so ugly out," Elaine said. It makes me crazy when someone takes the eerie mystery of an overcast morning and writes it off as "ugly." They actually make me see the ugliness. "Where the heck's my robe?"

Of course it was too damn much to ask Elaine to cross a room without putting something on, even though we'd just spent the night together. Unless of course she was in one of her nude model moods.

"You can use my shirt. It's right here."

"This flannel? I hate stuff like that on me. I feel like a *man*," she said, as if it were the most horrible thing she could feel like. I had half a mind to tell her Melissa wore my shirts all the time, and she didn't look anything like a man.

"Whatever you want," I said.

"What I want to do is to snuggle, Love. Like this. Except I really have to go to the bathroom. Can you go for me? Pretty please with sugar on top?"

Because it was Sunday the place was empty, and I slipped into the lunchroom. Without checking behind me I ripped off three flaps from Audrey's ad. She'd feel better if she got a few nibbles, even if no one ever called.

On the radio the twenty-year-old deejay announced that this weekend had been the twenty-second anniversary of Woodstock. Peter and I winced. The deejay said how exciting Paul Simon's concert in Central Park would be. I ripped into Paul Simon, whom I loathe, in a whimsical, scintillating way. Peter took it all in, nodding. How could I not ride home with him on Sunday?

"To Sweet Elaine's?"

"I guess so."

"You in a hurry?"

"No. I am definitely not."

"That's good."

He studied the dashboard until we were on the wide boulevard with the timed lights. He rolled through a red light and made the usual illegal left turn; we owned that corner.

"Nine nine nine nine four point three," he said, as we sped up the ramp. "We have to do it at exactly sixty miles per."

His car was hitting one hundred thousand miles, a lot of miles for a car three or four years old, and it came from driving every weekend to see his kids. He looped a cloverleaf and came back in the other direction. He was burning miles. White highway ribbons wobbled and waved. He turned again.

"Ninety-nine nine ninety-seven. On the dot. And counting."

The sun had taken over the sky behind us. At dawn I could see the industrial roots of the city, the railroad tracks hugging empty, sooty factories that once produced thousands of jobs, dusty men trudging home to wives and dinner. I felt, at that moment with Peter, the loneliness of the city itself, how much it wanted to work and give if only someone would take what it had. We were in the city's childhood, a world of chugging railroads and throbbing factories, where you finished work bone-tired and returned to a kitchen that smelled of meatloaf. It was so near I was nostalgic, for a life I never knew.

"There she goes," Peter said. "One hundred thousand on the but—but—but—button. Right now. Yesssssss! My friend. Yes."

I watched in awe. I know it sounds silly, but I was profoundly moved. He had taken a circuitous route so I could be with him.

"So I'm d-dropping off the kids? Jackie, right?"

"Yeah. She's wearing what?"

"T-shirt, no bra, very short shorts. Barefoot."

"Fucking barefoot. How bad was it."

"I should just j-jump her and f-fuck her. She's begging me. She's *pleading* with me!"

"Having a man desire them sexually is this very big deal."

"She's not home at first. She always manages to not be home. So I have to wait around with Jen and Josh for fucking maybe t-twenty minutes."

It was the first time he ever spoke his son or daughter's name to me.

"I tell them to try the backyard. Sure as hell she's there, in that outfit, she has to go into the yard where she can't hear when she *knows* I'm gonna fucking ring the f-fucking f-front door. She's gotta hang me up when I have to drive way the f-fuck back. So we can bicker in f-front of the kids for a change. You should see how they look at us fighting! And I didn't mention the sh-shoes!"

He counted off the glowing squares of the odometer, a row of zeros with an eight in the last slot. I wasn't certain Jackie had done it on purpose (despite Melissa's lessons, I was still in the dark about how real women thought) but I knew Peter was so angry it didn't matter; he had to pillory Jackie, prove what a spoiled, thoughtless, selfish little bitch she was. It was his anguish over all he had lost, and it was still red hot. No one understands male rage, what they do to us. All you ever hear about is *them, them, them.*

"What kinda shit she pull with the shoes? I can fucking imagine."

"I send this money, right? And Jen's in ripped s-sneakers. All this dough and my daughter, *Jen!* She's in fucking rags. Jackie claims it's a style! *Jen wants it!* Gimme a break! For f-fucking once gimme a f-fucking break!"

He coasted to the curb in front of Elaine's. Each time he pronounced his daughter's name it was excruciating.

"Oh Daniel, my friend."

The words expanded to fill the car. Peter never called me Danno. I think he's the only person I wouldn't mind it from.

"You know what it's like to visit your children in time slots? To have that part of your life up and running even though a marriage is d-dead as a fucking doornail? You see your wife and r-r-remember the *good* stuff? The good times? I'll tell you. Let me tell you. It's like you're decapitated but still walking. Like your fucking head's chopped off in some f-fucking guillo- tine but you don't know it. You see them, and then you remember your head's c-cut off and you're really dead. But somehow you're still w-walking, walking, walking the fuck around."

I looked out at Elaine's apartment. The light was on and she was waiting up for me.

— 15 —

Elaine unlocked the door because I couldn't find the key she had given me to use. She had her terry cloth robe on with the candy-striped apron lashed over it. As soon as I was in she bolted to the stove to tend to a steaming pot of basmati rice that was about to explode. She fussed with it, candy-striped back to me, tipping the cover to give the rice a gasp of air and a gulp of spice. When Elaine adds ingredients she doesn't sprinkle with her arm but bends at the waist, tilting like a railroad gate, once, twice, three times; I believe it is her way of measuring.

She faced me and said, "I think we should talk. I think we *have* to talk."

"Sure."

"Why don't you sit down," she said. "And stay a while."

"Okay. Can I take off my shirt, at least? It's really hot in here."

I felt the rice choking for breath on the stove. Its aroma was a cheerless replacement for the amiable rubber of Peter's car heat.

"You don't have to put your shirt away," she said. "You don't have to always worry about being so exactomundo-ly neat."

I hate clothing left on chairs. Elaine dumped hers everywhere.

"The chair's fine," I said. "It's no big deal either way."

"With you nothing's a big deal. *Nothing* is."

"Well excuse me for breathing."

"I'm sorry. I'm just always so afraid of saying the wrong thing with you. I'm *always* afraid. Every second I'm afraid."

"I love basmati rice. The smell."

"I completely forgot I was making it, and I probably ruined it."

"So what's up? Boy, that smells good. You know how much I love basmati."

"Why in God's name do you think I'm making it? *You* like it. You know what's on my mind. You must have figured *that* out."

"You said you wanted to talk."

"I know. But I want to be absolutely certain you want to listen."

What was coming, of course, was the dreaded *talk about us*. I reached over and tucked my hand under my shirt collar. The flannel was still warm.

She stripped off her apron and tossed it in a clump on the counter. She took the chair across from the one with my shirt and said, "I know how much pain you're in, Danno."

"You have to know the legal hassles I'm going through."

"Yes, but I feel so very sad about us." She was talking to my shirt. "It's why I ruined the rice. I put in too much cumin for how you like it. I mean, I know you're upset about your children and what *she's* doing to your life. To *our* life! I've been very patient. I honestly believe that I've been very patient."

She took her attention from my shirt and looked in my eyes. The robe was belted tight, high at the neck, as if to hold overwhelming feelings in check. I felt her yearning. She was offering all she had, and I was the boneheaded man who couldn't comprehend the happiness he could have. I felt hopelessly dense, in the way I often felt hopelessly dense in Elaine's eyes.

"But, I mean, you have to think about us. *Our* relationship. That's what I want to talk about. *Our* relationship."

There were suddenly three of us in the room: Elaine, me, and Our Relationship. There's nothing as claustrophobic.

"I'm thirty-seven, Danno, almost," she said, looking at my flannel shirt. "And I'm just drifting. I'm *still* just drifting."

She stopped. The word "drifting" had caused her particular pain.

"We don't even use the word 'love'! I don't want to lose everything we worked so hard to build. I don't want to lose *us*, the *us* we built. I *have* to think about children, children someday, whether I want to or not. Please understand what I'm saying. Please listen."

"I think about my children all the time And I'm dying over it, if you must know. I even miss my wife sometimes."

She bounded over to the stove. She sneaked a look at the rice, blinking at steam. Then, studying her feet, she marched back. She was wearing house slippers with high chunky heels. Even Elaine's slippers had big heels. I had seen this woman completely naked in every imaginable position but never walking barefoot.

"You don't understand how serious I am on the children subject," she said, as she this time took the chair opposite me. "It's a simple statement of fact. Of biological fact, if I may put it that way."

"I understand the child thing," I said. "Completely."

"I'm not sure you understand *anything* completely. I'm almost thirty-seven and I don't want to wait forever. I'm just *drifting*."

She paused to let the painful resonance of "drifting" pass.

"And I can't, wait I mean, even if I wanted to. I'm still waiting to hear some positive response on your part. You're hardly talking. You can be honest with me. I promise you can be honest."

This reminded me of a theory.

"Let me tell you a theory I worked out. I think men are used by women to fulfill this biological imperative, children. The whole shooting match, love, romance, marriage, family, is all set up solely for women to make babies with the healthiest mate they can get. The biggest and strongest to plant his seed."

"No theories please, Danno, I'm just not in the mood."

"But it makes sense, from a kind of Darwinian perspective."

"You're not listening. I swear to God you're not listening."

She unbelted her robe. Elaine had no idea how powerful her sexuality was, that if she opened her robe and put her naked body against me I would agree to everything. Not follow through, of course, but at least agree. All she did, however, was layer the robe tighter. It stayed up at the neck, too.

"I'm sitting here talking a blue streak, pouring my heart out, and you're not hearing a single word I'm saying. *Us*, Daniel, what about *us*?"

"Elaine, you're acting like a wronged mistress."

As soon as it came out I knew it was mistake, but I couldn't stop.

"You get in this rotten mood. You moon around like a zombie—you're in this zombie mood—and you dump on me the second I walk in. First you ignore me, then you dump on me."

"Danno, you are being, I'm afraid, very, very, *very*—" she reached for the big guns—"in*sensitive*."

"I'm sorry I said the mistress thing."

"Actually, Danno it's quite true. I'm afraid it's quite apt."

I was dumfounded.

"No, you're definitely not. You're much more."

"No, I'm not much more to you. In all honesty."

She was being the calm one, and it lent an aura of authenticity to her statement.

"You don't know how rough it's been for me lately. I'm so, so alone."

I was making an effort not to whine.

Out of nowhere, she said, "You know, Peter's with Sandy again. *His* place this time, which was a mess. They talked about his children for hours."

"Peter?"

"Yes, Peter. He's *miserable*, too. His ex is worse than Marissa."

"Me*lissa*. What ever happened to our friend Brian?"

"He—" She hesitated, then said, "He doesn't seem to be in the picture anymore."

She tugged the robe tight. It accentuated her breasts, and at once she was teeming with femaleness, in the manner of Melissa. Elaine, misreading my reaction, made my agony worse by maneuvering behind me to give my back a hug, then pulled away to shut off the rice. As her body lifted off I felt the depth of her needs in the weight of her flesh. The shape it left took the form of a simple insight: I had to have Melissa.

"So let me ask you straight out," she said, loosening the robe in front. "I know what you've been through. I know how you feel about those wonderful kids. But I have to know something." She hesitated, then added, "I have to know one thing, okay? What about *us?* I know you hate me for asking."

"No, but Elaine, I have to be honest. There's no way I can live without Melissa. I like you. I really like you. But without Melissa, without my children in my everyday life, it just doesn't seem *real.*"

I couldn't believe I had said it. Neither could she.

"I thought you hated her."

"In a way I do. But I'm not ready for this. With you."

"I knew you'd say that. I still had to ask. I owed it to the rel*ationship.* Such as it is. You should probably go right now."

"Now? Elaine, I *need* you. I couldn't be happy with my ex!"

"I don't want you to stay. Please go."

"Can't we talk more about the relationship?"

"I think we've talked quite enough for one night, thank you. If not for one lifetime. Leave. Go. Now."

"There must be something—"

"What part of the word 'go' don't you understand?"

"Please, Elaine, I can't be alone tonight. I really need you."

"Don't start touching me like that or I'll break down and say, okey dokey, *stay.* I'm looking out for numero uno for a change. Say goodnight, Gracie."

Enough was enough. I threw on my flannel shirt and walked out. The wooden staircase reverberated under me. Before I hit the ground all her lights went out.

I came to Kathleen's office early as usual, to relax in her waiting room.

"You didn't have to come in today."

"I was in the area."

"Nothing's new again. I know you miss the kids. I see how depressed you are. I like when you stop by to talk. I'm here for you, whenever you want."

I was in love with Kathleen, briefly, intensely. It passed.

"Yes. The kids. I think of good times with my wife, what we had."

"This is all part of it. I explained that to you. Are you all right?"

"I'm fine. I really am."

"And with the holiday, everything's slowing down. It's Thursday this year so the whole week's gone. You can hang in there?"

"Sure I can. I'm fine."

"Not freaking out on me?"

"No. I'm fine."

July Fourth hit hard. In Montclair there's a parade, a community event that every group in existence takes part in. Even the recycling committee has a float. You should have seen my kids last year. The air was diamond-sharp, like when you're indoors all day and step outside. Zach marched down Midland Avenue in his conductor's cap, skipping every few steps for no reason but sheer exuberance. Ramona rode high on the float. Her eyes found mine in the crowd, and she smiled.

On the real July Fourth I was in the Lincoln Tavern regaling Peter with a ferocious assault on Jim Morrison and the Doors. That morning in Paris there had been a disturbance at Morrison's grave because it was twenty years to the day that he died. I don't know why it ticked me off. I had started out miffed; halfway through I was apoplectic with rage. Two women at another table asked what I was screaming about when I got to the Oliver Stone movie on the Doors. I hadn't seen it, but that didn't stop me from reviling it as the cheap, glitzy, dishonest, disingenuous, self-indulgent piece of slop I knew it to be. They thought it was weird to rant and rave about a movie I'd never seen. Soon the four of us were embroiled in a kind of cute-tease argument. They were both pretty obnoxious, but it was one of those times I would find myself flirting with someone who got on my nerves, and do it anyway, hammering away like my life depended on it.

We decided to go to my place to see the fireworks. They held a quick summit about taking their car, which I could tell was code, as to whether we were worth it. They agreed to give us a chance because there wasn't much else happening that night. (Peter said nothing, of course; I was still on a tear about Jim Morrison.) They followed us in their car, giggling and chatting. At the bar, or as we hiked my staircase, we barely got three words out of their mouths.

Their names were Mona and Sheila, and they got even creepier inside.

"Your place is *enormously* airy," Mona said, eyeing the living room.

"I love old furniture," Sheila said. "I love your terrace, too."

As soon as they sat Mona made a face and said, "Ya know, your couch *stinks*. I think it's mildew."

"No, it's yukkier than mildew," Sheila said, sniffing. "I bet something spoiled spilled. Like a smell with an aftertaste."

"Yeah," Mona said, "Puky. Somebody toss their cookies here?"

She slammed the cushion with a transparent heart-shaped purse. The shaft of lamplight on the couch instantly clogged with swirling dust.

"Don't spread it, you silly!" Sheila shouted. "Don't!"

"The rug stinks too," Mona said. "*Diapers!* That's what it is!"

We went out on my "terrace" to watch the fireworks. Mona squeezed my hand. When they ended Peter took off with Sheila, after a fervent exchange of code. I'm embarrassed to say it wasn't the first time I was desperate to keep a woman from leaving even though she made my skin crawl. I tried Saddam Hussein, Dan Quayle, Jim Morrison dying in a bathtub, anything to keep her there. She hummed "Pinball Wizard," which of course is by the Who, whom I also hate, maybe more than I hate Jim Morrison.

"You sure hate a lot of things," Mona said. "Hate's not good for you."

I sang a few lines from "Pinball Wizard."

"You can't sing," she said. "Which is too bad since you know an awful lot of songs."

"That's my problem," I said.

I pulled out of her that she had been married, and it broke up because her husband "got nasty whenever he felt it." Her last boyfriend also "got rough just once too many." When her shoulder was dislocated the third time she gave him the boot. She was nobody's doormat, she said.

I trotted out the Chronicle of Daniel the Younger: On His Own, the Middle Years. She really listened. When a woman really listens I fall in love with her, at least while she's listening. I could have skipped my romantic embrace on the terrace and the rest of my routine. "I don't want to go to bed with you," I said, caressing her amid the acrid scent of exhausted fireworks. "I want to make *love* to you. Since I saw you in the bar. I want to explore every nook and cranny of your flesh, of your body, of your soul."

"Heights get me dizzy, very. I feel like I'm gonna fall. Or *hurl*, maybe."

In bed she was surprisingly lovely; it was just her personality that gave me the creeps. Through it all she murmured, "Stop, you *have* to stop," without making an effort to stop me. At a crucial moment she whispered "No," vaguely trying to push me off. It was unbearably exciting.

The next day she told me how nice I was, how gentle.

"You're a guy who never gets angry, I can tell. I feel so safe with you. I always get these guys with crazy tempers. I mean *crazy!*"

When she left Sunday we exchanged phone numbers. We had arranged a dozen dates. The one I looked forward to most was a trip to Manhattan, where she had never been.

"You're so gentle, you're such a gentleman," she said, clutching her see-through purse and beaming from my stairs like she'd never been so happy. "I can't wait to be shown around the Big Apple by an expert."

I never saw her again. She never called me, and I never called her.

"It's all just so strange, Kathleen, how she's acting."

"Yes. Your case gets more and more interesting every day."

That's one thing I never like to hear from a doctor or a lawyer, that my case gets more and more interesting every day.

"Just try to relax, Daniel."

I did try to relax. I was, after all, totally free, to take long walks, to stay out days, to approach any woman and start anything. I had other far more depressing romantic encounters. At *The Journal's* annual barbecue I tried to get something going with Judy Simon, at least for a night. She gave me the brush-off. I'm fairly sure I made a fool of myself.

It got harder to meet Peter for drinks because he was with Sandy. I went alone to the Lincoln Tavern. I got through evenings watching games on a bar TV with men I didn't like about sports I didn't follow. It was easy to hook up with women. Afterward I'd have to walk hours to shake it.

My children were everywhere.

Elaine and I were cordial at work. On nights off I'd walk past her house. I could smell what she was cooking; it was summer and her windows were always wide open.

I roamed about, like I roamed when I met Melissa in Washington Square. I'd wander into Woolworths, not looking for Vicki but willing to run into her. I spied her once in cosmetics, unscrewing a lipstick and raising it to the light. I hid behind a back-to-school display until she left. On the store Muzak I recognized the Beatles' "Blackbird," with a flute playing lead. It didn't sound that bad. The flute, in particular, was very pretty.

I watched more and more talk shows and erupted in bitter tirades, out loud, in my empty apartment.

My rituals got me through.

I'd sit on my stump in the empty lot every morning after work and watch the sun come up. A raucous flock of fat-bellied blackbirds gathered at dawn to jostle in the trees, flutter their wings, and shriek at the sky. One would strut a branch above me, legs twitching, head bobbing, and caw, caw, caw.

— 16 —

"I don't like seeing you like this, Daniel."

"I'm fine. I'm really fine. So?"

"There's still confusion coming from their end. She does-n't seem to have a lawyer these days. It just gets curiouser and curiouser. I don't even know who to call with these papers."

"Is that good or is that bad?"

"I'm afraid it's anybody's guess."

———

I was lying on my couch, knees stiff, hands over my eyes, my latest listening-to-messages ritual, when Melissa's voice some-how emerged from the clutter of clicks and clattery clacks.

"Oh, figured Daniel, you're not home. I don't know if I'm talking to you or if you're talking to me, but we should talk, no lawyers okay? Now's a good time. Kids are at the camp with these friends. We need to talk. I? We've both been dam-aged so much, and I just want to say I'm willing to at least *hear* you out. I was so out of it, after your letter, not the I'm-leaving-but-I'm-okay letter, the let's-talk-about-getting-back-together letter, you don't know how people glommed on me after you, you, did it. I have so much to say, we have so much to say to each other. I understand so much more about myself, about *you*, as a matter of fact. What you did was horrendous. You know that. You must, the children, I mean mainly. I know you know the children part. I could tell from what my lawyer, my *former* lawyer, said your lawyer—who is that woman? she knows so much about us!—said you said. Am I making any sense? Anyway, I mean I finally tonight got the nerve, or stupidity is it?, to pick up the phone. I stopped hating you, I think, and I stopped hating myself too, I think. I also stopped hating something you don't know anything about that happened, that just *happened*. I shouldn't be going into all this. Talking to you makes me lose it a little, I mean actually talking to you, sort of talking to you. I hope you're not listening to this with someone! My God! I'll assume you're not. Anyway, Daniel, rotten stuff happened to me, really *shitty* stuff, I mean before all this. I mean, that's why we should talk. I have to tell you something and you can do what you want. I mean I, just because you did something horrible doesn't mean you're a horrible person! But, you weren't *there*. I needed you and you weren't *there*. Oh, Daniel, we can't let us lose everything. What I'm saying is I just hope—"

A malicious beep wiped her out. The startled machine recovered with a vigorous program of strenuous clacks.

"Me again. Stupid machines. What I'm saying is I *need* you. And you need me, even though you don't realize it. Ha ha. Anyway, we have to talk about what happened to me. I guess to you? Call. It's truly very important. That we talk. Ummmmmm. Kids are okay. *Great*, really, I mean, considering. Call. Please call really. We'll do lunch. Ha ha. Bye."

"Peter, I need a favor."

"Name it."

"Your car."

"My car? Why don't you take my ex? I'll throw in the c-car."

I could tell Sandy was at his place. He became so jovial his stammer changed, as if he were doing it on purpose, as a joke. I heard her guffawing.

"I don't know when I'll be back."

I almost jerked the wire out of the wall. I couldn't stop pacing.

"Hey, my kids are with the bitch half the summer. I have another c-c-car I can use. Someone too cheap to fix her air conditioning!"

This caused a near nuclear explosion of laughter in the background.

"I only have half a tank of gas."

"That's no problem. I owe you one, Peter."

"Hey."

"Peter. My friend."

"Hey, ya b-bastard."

I lowered into the squeeze of a plastic swing. The backyard, pitch-dark, smelled of rotting wood. A light went off, three went on. The house, restless with light, at last grew still. I heard a flute sing a scale, hovering high, turning, somersaulting, ripping itself apart. The house, meanwhile, just sat there.

The back door opened and a woman who looked like Melissa floated out in a white gown. She reached toward the sky and danced, flailing her arms, flinging out smoke, and sucking it back. The gown swirled around her.

"*Melissa!*"

I stepped off the swing. It stuck to my thighs, sideways, lifting with me.

"It's me! *Me!*"

I finally made it to the light.

"*You!* I got so *scared!*"

She clutched a cloth to her chest, like a woman caught without clothes.

"I decided to come. Not to call. I needed to see the kids. You."

"I didn't know who you were. In the dark. Who knew my name."

"I'm sorry. I just miss the kids so much."

She dropped her arms and gaped at me.

"I'm shaking. I can't catch my breath. The way you jumped out."

The lights of the house ringed her hair, a fringe of white static.

"I'm really sorry. I should have called. I wanted to catch them still up."

"You know you can't see them now."

The light snapped as she shook her head.

"I know I'm not supposed to. I just miss them. And you. I miss you. You look so beautiful. I forgot how beautiful you are."

"They're at camp. You got the messages? Both?"

"Camp! Of course. I forgot. I'm really losing my mind. The pine forest? When we went for a walk to look for deer. Among other things."

"Yes," she said. "I remember."

The white gown, up close, was an oversize T-shirt. She held a dress of Ramona's, white, frilly, bigger than a girl's but too small to be a woman's. Light clung to the dress as it fell into a basket that materialized at her feet. A beautiful woman's mysterious incantation to the night turned out be a mother yanking her daughter's dress off a clothesline. I tried to kiss her; exacting on degrees of physical affection, she granted only a forehead-to-shoulder nuzzle.

"You're all sweaty."

"I had to drive all night."

This inspired her to press fully against me. Her body felt huge, naked, distant, a statue bathed in spotlights.

"I was waiting all night. I *knew* you'd come."

She picked up the dress and shook it. Whiteness flared through her like lightning. It caught the clothesline and flashed over my head. I glimpsed the outline of her breasts.

"I thought you'd shoot me if I showed my face."

"I almost did, the way you scared me, coming out of the dark."

"You're always so afraid."

"I'm still furious about what you did. The *way* you did it. I may never forgive you. Children were involved, forgetting me, of course. I shouldn't even be talking to you. You did a sick, horrible thing."

"I know. Believe me, I know."

The air was heavy around us. She slept in a big T-shirt like this, but usually only in the cold of winter. There were never enough covers for her.

"You look good," she said. "Single life agrees with you."

"You won't believe what I thought was going on. I freaked. I couldn't accept getting older, still planning my life, still *dreaming*. I thought crazy things. You, Barry Alter! I don't know why I'm blurting this out but being here with you—it's too much. You have to let me explain. Melissa, *please*."

"I want you to. You just scared me, all of a sudden just *appearing*."

The house was too powerfully illuminated to enter. We retreated through layers of darkness to the swings and sat. The house towered above us, shocking, gigantic, as if in flames.

"I see you got rid of the tree," I said.

"I had to. I never liked being alone in the house."

"Or anywhere, Melissa. Melissa?"

"I understand. Daniel, everything's okay, everything's okay. It is."

"I hope so."

"It is."

"I can't get over how beautiful you look. Your hair's different."

"It's longer. You can't even *see* me. Are we allowed to be doing this?"

"Our lawyers'll kill us. But I had to see you. After your call."

In profile she was striking, sharp features on the night, more blue now than black. Through a sliver of transparency was a slash of hair, her mouth moving, starting to speak, saying, "So, you went to this place."

"Yes. And I did really well on this job. I know it's insane to mention it, but I've been fantasizing telling you. I was even promoted."

"Oh Daniel, why did you *do* it!"

"It *was* horrible. But I can explain. Wasn't I crazy with Barry Alter?"

"A lot happened that we have to talk about."

"You don't know how crazy it was. You don't know what's *out* there."

"I know what's out there."

"Those lawyers were murder."

She pushed back on the swing, legs extended. She was barefoot.

"I'll say," she said, sweeping past, toes bent, T-shirt billowing around her. "They made a huge deal out of you supposedly sleeping with Ellen Smuckler. Ellen Smuckler! And I went along with it. By the way, they split again. Turns out she was screwing some bra salesman from Boston. I'm serious. She even saw me once up there and was afraid I saw *her*."

"I want to tell you everything I did, Melissa, everything I've done."

"So do I. I'll start. I'm starting now."

She swung again, swooping low, legs way ahead of her body.

"I did have sex with Barry Alter."

"What?"

Her ankles breezed back, swished forward. Air rushed onto my face.

"I said, I did have sex with Barry Alter."

Her toes grabbed wet grass. They skidded, then squeaked.

"But it was not my choice. I didn't *choose* to do it."

Her legs, very long, very bare, clamped the grass and held her still.

"I don't blame you for after I left."

"It wasn't after you left."

Her fingers found an imaginary flute. Her posture showed how well-trained she was, crouching, her neck bent.

"So. Barry Alter wasn't after I left."

"No."

"He wasn't."

"No, he wasn't. It's suddenly very hard to talk about. Even though I told you a hundred times in my head already. Even when you were still here."

She played again. It was complicated, and she had to work at it. After she got it right she said, "I have to bring that dress in. I finally caught up on laundry, and Monie'll kill me if it's wrinkled. It's been hard enough on her already. When I come back I'll tell you the whole thing. It."

"It? What? What whole thing?"

She pried herself up on the swing. "It," she said. "I'll tell you it."

She fled to the house, light streaking through her T-shirt. As she mounted the back porch I felt it *feel* the weight of her. From the glare of the house she called, "And I have to put something on. Come in if you want."

The rooms were all stunned by light, and a forgotten rich-ness, orange-toned wood, acres of chairs and lamps and tables, posters and wall hangings, flowers and flowerpots, books, a thousand books, sheet music, rugs, shoes, jackets, pencils, piles of envelopes everywhere, a modern kitchen, a mansion com-pared to where I had been. How did I acquire all these pos-sessions? In the living room the bedroom rocker balanced on an Indian rug. Next to it the bedroom music stand was splayed out, a flute where music should rest, which Melissa insisted you should never do. The bathroom offered new towels, thick and baby blue.

Melissa came down in shorts, still barefoot, wearing the same T-shirt. I read "Tanglewood is my Ode to Joy" out of the eighth notes that squirmed from Beethoven's mouth and across Melissa's breasts. She tasted from a mug ("It's Better in the Woods!") and dumped cold coffee in the sink.

We couldn't face each other without blinking.

"I want to show you the sitting area I set up," she said. "With really pretty white wicker. I'm very proud of myself that I managed it during, you know . . ."

I followed her white T-shirt bouncing across the porch. After all the fluorescence I couldn't find the ground. The grass dropped under my feet, as if I was falling into a pit. The sit-ting area was on white gravel where the haunted tree had been. I took a white wicker love seat. She took a white wicker chair. There was a mug with old coffee on a white wicker table. She put the mug on the gravel, where it sunk with a crunch that echoed into the trees.

"They wanted to leave just mulch, but I decided on white gravel," she said.

"You always liked wicker."

"Yes. I sit out here and play."

The area was so white and shiny I felt we were on stage with lights trained on us. No neighbor had a light on.

"So?"

I heard the refrigerator tremble as it started up.

"You know, I'm mostly worried this is going to hurt you. I'm okay about it, I think. It was in Tanglewood. *Near* Tanglewood."

"We're talking before I left?"

"A month, I think. Less. Remember the program that led up to the dinner concert? He was gone by then, but this was when it started."

She watched her toe dig into gravel, bury itself, then burst out.

"It started in the woods. It was warm for then, Indian summer, even though it was almost winter. Did I mention the dress? You know we had this long flirtation. From last summer? I told you about it, right?"

"Yes."

"Did I say I was wearing the mauve dress? That thin thing, very pretty. It's big in my mind, what I was wearing. We were able to take off our coats. We were high from how well the campaign was going, and I was dancing around. I felt like a nymph in a fairy tale. You won't understand but it's a certain way a dress you like fits. I felt so good in it. He had that straw basket, wine, fluted glasses, elegant sandwiches on tiny little French bread, cheese that smelled so disgusting I knew it *had* to be super super chichi. White zinfandel. He *remembered!* And one long-stemmed rose. He tries to put the rose in me *here.* I slide away and twirl around a tree, playful, romantic. He catches me and kisses me. I let him. A real kiss, Daniel, a *kiss* kiss. That was my first mistake. I'm sorry. I shouldn't have done it, but I felt so *beautiful.* So *light,* so *free.* I didn't *weigh* anything. I was somehow weightless. And *beautiful.*"

She stopped. Her own words had astonished her.

"That was the really big mistake, letting that happen. Then he tells me I'm the most beautiful woman he's ever seen. The *most.* He's said that before. He says, he says, 'Let's run away together, you're *so* beautiful.' And I say, 'I can't. I have children.' That was stupid, *much* too flirtatious. And yet it felt good. I buy it and don't buy it at the same time. I do that; I think all women do that."

"Men do it too."

"He puts his arm around me. That was mistake number two. I let it stay on my shoulder as we drank the wine, all of it, mistake number three. And his arm's on my shoulder, right here, the whole time."

She pointed to her shoulder blade, an inch below her neck.

"I didn't move it or push it away and laugh. Mistake number four."

The refrigerator trembled off. It made the whole house shake.

"Finally we get to the hotel and I invite him into my room, I *invited* him, Daniel. I have to say that upfront. We were having so much fun, I felt—and this is the sick part—I felt *flattered!* I don't feel un*safe* with him at this point. Do you understand? Mistake number five. And in the room he kisses me again. I try to keep it from being a *real* kiss, the woods, that's one thing, but my room? There's a *huge* difference. But I was complimented into it, if you know what I mean."

She was leaning forward, as if about to dive off a cliff.

"Mistake number whatever I was at."

"Forget the mistakes. And?"

"You don't know how many times I told you this in my head. When you were here, even, I was telling you in my head."

"Melissa, I—"

"Now I'm having trouble."

She had been holding her own against the silence, but now it closed in and swallowed her up.

Across the yard I heard a faucet stutter on.

Melissa said, "And now he's all over me. I try to push him off, but his hands are on my belt, my waist, *here*. I'm sort of against a wall where there's one of those mini-bars? I feel him pressing *there*. And this really scares me, even though I know I started it. I know how stupid and immature this sounds, I'm ashamed of it, but it's true. I still don't feel in any kind of you-can't-get-out-of-it danger. I've *always* been a flirt. I know that. The danger is part of it. It goes way back, two therapists even. Like I want on some level to be abused. Melissa abuse, Daniel abuse, *again* abuse. I blame myself. For so *needing* to have a man want me. Every woman does, but not as much as me."

The way she spoke sounded like she was crying—a kind of quiver in her voice—but actually Melissa was very calm and using flat, businesslike tones, as if making a presentation to a group of executives for whom English was not a native language.

"And then?"

"Okay, enough's enough, I think. I'm thinking I can talk my way out of this even as he's pushing me down on the bed. I push him away but he's not letting me. He keeps saying he wants me, as if that justifies what he's doing. As if that makes it okay. He *needs* to do it. He wants me. I'm beautiful. *He* wants me."

"My God, Melissa."

"I'm flat on my back now. The bed's hard, brown, very, very stiff, you know, ho*tel* hard. And I'm really fighting. He shoves up the dress—it's short, there's not much to shove, wearing it was my biggest mistake—and it suddenly occurs to me—it, like, *dawns* on me—he's going to force me. That he *can* force me! I can't believe it. 'Barry don't,' I say, 'Please don't.' I try to push him off. He's *amazingly* strong. He weighs a *ton!* Then he stops, I think I convinced him, and he gets on his knees over me on the bed and *puts on a condom!* He turns away, *modest!* That was one of the times I could have run. I *still* think I could have run. Mistake number I have to stop. I could have kicked him in the balls like you're supposed to. Screamed? I never knew I could be so scared. And then he does it, pretending it's loving. I didn't really fight. I admit it. I'm thinking, maybe he doesn't *know* I want him to stop? The horrible thing was the harder I fought the stronger he got, I swear. I was speechless when he put on that *thing*."

She stroked her knees, staring at the white gravel.

"And feeling him *inside* me! It's such a private feeling. I don't know for a man, but for a woman it's a kind of *secret* feeling."

She was rubbing her knees so hard the wicker creaked. Her big toe knocked over the mug, an oval of gravel instantly brown, then black.

"He finally leaves. He *kisses* me! I don't tell him what he did."

"Melissa, I . . ."

"Didn't you see I was a wreck? You knew *something* happened."

"Yes."

"You saw me acting weird. You couldn't put two and two together? All you notice is that I'm different in bed. *That* you notice! I start writing letters to him. To myself. Hundreds! On planes, taxis, once in Atlanta when I'm telling a bunch of rich old men why music is so important to them they should put my orchestra in their will. I finally confront him and he disappears to Europe. Anything legal is very complicated to do. It's worse because I waited so long. I know. I checked."

"I saw the bruise on your neck."

"What's funny is I don't remember how it happened. In all honesty. I think he hit me. I tried to fight him off, didn't I?"

"Melissa, you were physically overpowered. Of course you were."

"It was that male rage, Daniel, that crazy insane male rage women are so, so terrified of. And we're right! Men *are*, they *get*, so *angry!*"

"I wish—"

"He became this *monster!*"

"And I wasn't there to help you."

"No, you weren't. And I didn't tell you right away because I thought I was asking for it. Can you believe that? I was petrified. And I thought I *made* you run away. I learned a lot since. What's scary is every single woman I talk to has *some* story like this. Sometimes something a lot worse."

"I know."

"It attacks the very core of you."

"Yes."

"The things you love best about who you are. As a woman."

"Yes."

"It's more your heart than your heart. Do you understand that?"

"I think so."

"The whole basic man-woman equation goes haywire. Like the first time I was crazy. You want so much to be attractive, it's the end-all and be-all of your life. Then you're ashamed! *Ashamed!* I never even knew what that word meant before!"

"Melissa, we have to work this out."

"And finally when I get my act together to tell you, you vanish, you go out for milk and never come back. That first night was hell, Daniel, absolute living hell. For that I may never forgive you. With the *children?*"

"I'll never forgive myself for it, believe me."

"I hope you understand that if not for Monie and Zach I wouldn't be here. I mean, *you* wouldn't be here. I wouldn't give you a chance to explain. You wouldn't *deserve* a chance. I'm thinking of the kids, honestly I am."

"I know."

"Carol Bloom got me through. We talked about the Barry Alter thing. About Gideon. One night I had Lissie Meadows over and her boyfriend—this oboist with a beard who thinks he so cool, but they're the worst—and the Reiners—they had Jessica, she's so cute—what was I talking about?"

She was bringing me up to date on friends, despite herself.

"Yes, and everyone leaves and I break down. You're gone, maybe never coming back, but I feel you in the house, in the yard. Monie woke up—she's been doing that—she felt it too. She and I hugged in the dark without saying anything. I know I wasn't a perfect wife."

"Oh, stop. I wish you had told me. I've done so much wrong."

"Zach said you just needed a vacation. He did the best, on the outside."

"You don't know how I feel, Melissa."

"You knew I wanted you to come tonight."

"Yes, I thought you'd kill me. I thought you hated me."

"I do, in a way. In a way I always will."

"Melissa, I don't know what to say. I want to help you heal, make it up to you. Pay you back, somehow."

"Don't sweat that, my friend. You'll pay. You can count on it, pal."

She got up and squeezed in next to me. She let me put my arm around her. Despite all I dreamed, planned, started, got ready to start, pretended I started, screwed up after I started, the one certainty of my life was that it had revolved around one woman, and she was right next to me.

"You left and never came back," she said.

"I am back. I'm here."

She shifted into her oracular mode.

"When a man leaves like you he comes back a different person. To a different woman."

Her oracular mode. I made her into so many *things*.

"And when a woman has that happen she's different. Men are different. My body is different. In the mirror even. I see Monie differently. The pressures she'll face. The conflicts, contradictions, the crazy confusions."

"I think I understand."

"I felt so alone, Daniel. Even when you were here you weren't here. Then all of a sudden you're *not* here. I couldn't breathe. I had no *air*. My whole life had no air. Do you understand what I'm saying? I'm talking before you left. I didn't even know till I realized I couldn't breathe."

"Can we work this out, Melissa? Can we pull it together?"

"I honestly don't know."

"I want to try to explain."

"In the morning. You can tell me everything in the morning."

"Melissa, you were hurt and I did nothing. I didn't know. I didn't *see*."

"I know. I want to hear what happened to you. Your stories, I'm sure. You probably have some new theories."

"Some of it's pretty funny. If you ever feel like hearing."

"I do. But not now."

I took a breath. "You know, it smells like a forest out here."

"It always did," she said.

She turned so her back nestled into me. "I'm exhausted," she said.

So was I. I had never been so weary. My hands slid over her back to the usual spots, our old sleep position, on her shoulder, over a breast. It made her shiver, and she burrowed deeper into my chest.

"You're safe now, Melissa. Safe."

"I hope so."

Melissa had been hurt in a vicious, insidious way, and I didn't try to protect her. I didn't try to help her. I didn't even notice. How could I have become such a monster, me of all people?

My eyes wouldn't stay open. Hers were already shut. I kissed the back of her neck, the tucked-away spot beneath her hair. She shivered again; this time I absorbed it in my arms. Perhaps I could explain, perhaps I could help her heal, perhaps we could rebuild, perhaps she could forgive me. But for now I hugged her, scared out of my wits, and making plans like mad, as we were carried off to sleep, holding on.

Martin Golan lives in New Jersey with his wife and two children. A journalist, he has published poetry in literary magazines. **My Wife's Last Lover** is his first published novel.